Praise for
USA TODAY bestselling author
Jordan Dane

"Jordan Dane is a fresh new voice
in young adult paranormal fiction."
—P.C. Cast, *New York Times* bestselling author
of the House of Night series

"In her first YA novel, adult thriller writer Dane pens a macabre
slow-burner.... Thoroughly eerie, the plot includes flashbacks
and nightmares involving crossing over into the spirit world,
while Dane's well-developed characters provide an authentic
exploration of guilt, loyalty and belonging."
—*Publishers Weekly* on *In the Arms of Stone Angels*

"Deliciously dark! Gritty and suspenseful,
In the Arms of Stone Angels is a new take on the
paranormal. One of the most compelling and honest voices
in young adult fiction!"
—Sophie Jordan, *New York Times* bestselling author of *Firelight*

"*On a Dark Wing* is a gripping paranormal thriller
with all the emotion of budding teenage romance,
and Abbey brings plenty of attitude to the story. Intelligent,
emotive storytelling offering a very different side to death."
—*The Cairns Post, Entertainment News*

"Dane's YA is a great new tale about death, love and starting
over.... Paranormal fans will love this. A compelling page turner."
—*RT Book Reviews* on *On a Dark Wing*

Books by Jordan Dane

from Harlequin TEEN

In the Arms of Stone Angels
On a Dark Wing

INDIGO

AWAKENING

Jordan Dane

HARLEQUIN®

entertain, enrich, inspire™

Recycling programs
for this product may
not exist in your area.

ISBN-13: 978-0-373-21076-3

INDIGO AWAKENING

In loving memory of Michael Marolt

The Harley is for you, Mike.

 { 1 }

Sunset Boulevard—Los Angeles, California
Summer—After Dark

Lucas Darby stumbled through heaving waves of neon signs and drifting shadows, straining to make sense of the muffled whispers he heard. Drugs had forced him to endure a never-ending silence, where even the music in his head had died. But now the voices had emerged and quenched a killer thirst in his soul. Even though he couldn't make out what they told him, simply hearing them brought light to his shadows.

Unable to focus his eyes, he ignored the blur to concentrate on what he heard in his mind. Most of the words were too garbled. The few messages that came from deeper inside him, those words felt like his thoughts, but they were in voices he didn't recognize.

I hear you now. Don't stop.

Even when he let his thoughts reach out, he had no idea who *"the others"* were or if they heard him. Without drugs to cloud his brain, the voices had returned, and with fresh eyes, he saw the colors, too. Beautiful prisms of fluid light radiated off ghosts without faces. Bodies drifted in front of him in colors that wavered like heat shimmers off hot asphalt.

"Watch where you're walkin', kid."

Lucas got shoved. An old man's face leached from the darkness before it got swallowed by glistening ooze that bled down his world.

Sorry.

He didn't know if he said the word aloud. Even at fifteen years old, speaking didn't come naturally to him. His mother told him that as a baby he hummed a strange melody before he ever spoke. One day, the music stopped and he felt as if he'd lost an arm.

He missed the music. Nothing felt right without it.

Over the years, drugs had invaded his body like poison, but as the meds drained, new sensations finally came. Strong perfumes mixed with body odor and the smell of alcohol, fryer grease and hot dogs wafted on the night air. Images spiraled in front of him. Shapes of people emerged from a rush of colors and made shadowy obstacles as he kept his feet moving on a sidewalk that didn't end.

Don't stop. Stop and the Believers find you.

Lucas didn't know if those thoughts were his. He only knew he had to obey.

The Copperhead Club—West Hollywood

Rayne Darby kicked back at the bar drinking alone, nibbling on stuffed olives and nursing a watered-down pineapple juice with extra cherries and an orange slice. She scrounged for food wherever she found it. Not because she had to. Three squares and the food pyramid had never been her thing, but her lame excuse for dinner had triggered thoughts of her mom. Her parents would hate how she lived, especially if they knew she had her seventeen-year-old butt in a bar.

But with both of them dead—killed in a private-jet crash five years ago—they never knew how she turned out. Some kids might envy that she didn't have anyone waiting up for her and no one argued about the choices she made. Living on her own for the past six months, she did whatever she wanted, whenever. Sometimes she liked how freedom tasted.

Now just wasn't one of those times.

Liquor bottles on mirrored shelves were awash in green spotlights with two bartenders eclipsing the eerie glow as they worked. Rayne had moved her bar stool into the shadows near a stockroom. Avoiding the light made her feel invisible. Hunched over her drink with her head down, she wore what she had on earlier that day, not bothering to change— faded jeans, her favorite black Led Zeppelin T-shirt and an old brown leather jacket that was too big for her. Something she'd inherited from her father.

Everything about her said, *Don't mess with me.*

She'd come to hang with the band, but when a sudden rush of dark wrapped around her mood, she didn't feel like playing nice. She found the nearest shadow and morphed into it. With school out, forgettable jobs by day made the Copperhead something to look forward to...*most nights.*

Raising a finger, she got the attention of Sam, her favorite bartender, and fished cash from the pocket of her jacket. Sam had given her that squinty *you're full of shit* look until he carded her last year. She had the cred. Her ID looked totally legit. At first she thought he'd turn out to be a real tool and boot her ass anyway. But after he saw that she didn't abuse the privilege by ordering alcohol, he let it go.

Besides, beer tasted like horse piss. Not that she had firsthand knowledge of that. She only knew she didn't like beer. One night of puking into a nasty public toilet in another bar had cured her of wanting a repeat. After she visited the capital city of *Spewcanistan* on a not-so-temporary barf visa, she decided to lay off the booze bullet to the brain and make a change in scenery. Here, she felt at home, especially with Sam watching over her like a big brother. The guy turned out to be seriously cool.

"With all the fruit juice you're downing, I'd say you're fully immune to scurvy. That could come in handy if you were a pirate." Sam shot her his signature deadpan expression.

"I'll keep that in mind if I see Johnny Depp."

"You ready to switch up to OJ, live on the edge?" the young bartender asked as he wiped the counter and gave her a fresh napkin.

"Think I'll have the main course. Dose me with spicy tomato juice, straight up."

"At the risk of sounding like I'm stalking you, you want extra celery?" Sam crooked his lip into a smile.

"Good one. LMAO," she said with her serious face. "Yeah, whack me with extra vegan sticks. Thanks."

"Coming right up, moneybags."

Sam tolerated her and never questioned why she racked up frequent-flyer miles at the Copperhead. Even during the school year, she came to hang. The truth was that she hated being alone in her apartment. She needed the noise, but tonight she had more of a reason to show. She knew the band.

Archimedes, Watch Out was a pop-punk band with solid gang vocals, on tour out of Texas. She followed them on MySpace and Twitter and had seen them before at the bar. Austin, the keyboard guy, had a fierce stare online that gave him edge, but in person he had soft marshmallow for a heart. The front man, Dalton, had an amazing voice that would take them far, and Tommy played sweet riffs on guitar that matched his eye-candy good looks. All the guys were totally hot looking. That worked for her. She needed the distraction of being in a crowd with a drool-worthy boy buffet on stage, guys who knew how to dish out a heaping side of decibels.

With a fresh tomato juice in front of her—and practically a

whole thing of celery—Rayne tossed a bill onto the counter for tip money, then noticed her cell phone light up and felt the vibration on her fingertips. She recognized the number. Her jaw tightened as she debated answering. Against her better judgment, she nudged her head to Sam and gestured to let him know she'd be in the storeroom, the only quiet place to take the call. Being a regular had its privileges.

After she got behind closed doors, the music dulled to a belly thump as she said, "What's up?"

Her older sister didn't waste any time pissing her off. "What's that noise, Rayne? Where are you?"

"It's my stereo. I've got it cranked to brain bleed." Rayne didn't have a stereo. "Why are you calling, Mia?"

"Where's Lucas? Is he with you?" Mia got her attention by going full-on parental. If Rayne ever felt the need for drama from another mother, her only sister knew how to pile it on.

"What are you talking about? Why would he be with me? You've got him under lock and key, sister dearest." When she heard only a deep sigh on the other end of the line, she dialed back the smart-ass and asked, "What's going on, Mia?"

"Haven Hills called. He's not on the grounds. They can't find him."

"What?" Rayne slumped against a metal utility shelf. "That's not possible."

"Well, apparently, it is." Mia's voice carried a razor's edge. *Typical.* "He can't do this. I'm responsible. If you're hiding him, I swear I'll find out."

"Damn it, Mia. Why do you always…?"

She didn't see the point in arguing. Her sister was as flexible as concrete. Rayne had learned that the hard way. Haven Hills Treatment Facility on Sunset had been the home for their younger brother, Lucas, for the past three years—a real suck fest for Luke—but Mia got off on being in charge after their parents died. The private mental hospital had ties to Mia's employer—the Church of Spiritual Freedom.

I never should have let her take you, Luke.

Losing her baby brother to guys in white coats had broken something in Rayne. Even though Lucas needed serious help, Mia's rushed decision to commit him had shattered what remained of their family, and Rayne had never seen her sister's betrayal coming. She felt stupid. And worse, she'd let her brother down in a way she could never make up for, not when Mia had restricted her visits to him. In his condition, she never could explain, either.

That had been the last straw before she'd moved out. Rayne couldn't fake being okay with her sister using Lucas as a pawn between them. He became the main reason Rayne had put everything on hold. How could she get on with her life when his was in the crapper? Luke didn't have anyone else who really cared about him. He couldn't even look after himself.

She was the only one who loved him the way he turned out.

"Will you call me when they find him?" Rayne grimaced, hardly believing she actually had to ask. Instead of answering her question, Mia had one of her own.

"Will you let me know if he contacts *you?*" When Rayne didn't say anything, her sister sighed. "Yeah, didn't think so."

She tightened her jaw when the silence between them got too loud.

"Mia, he's my brother, too. Please."

This time, her sister had something to say.

"If you get arrested for drinking, don't call me to bail you out."

After the line went dead, Rayne resisted the urge to hit something. *Nice, real nice.* No chance in hell her only call from the gray-bar hotel would be to Sister Buzzkill. Even though Mia knew how to flip her switch, anger wouldn't help Luke.

She stashed her cell in her jacket pocket and headed out the storeroom door. She had to go home in case he called, but if he didn't, then what?

Oh, God. Would he even know how to reach me? Did he keep my number?

Imagining Lucas on the streets of L.A., messed up and alone, made her sick. In her mind he was still a kid—and in serious trouble. With everything piled against him, she had no idea how he'd left Haven Hills in his condition, but a worse question screwed with her head.

Where the hell would he go?

Sunset Boulevard

When Lucas saw his reflection in a restaurant window, the face of a stranger stared back. Hunger had drawn him to the smell of hamburgers and fries, but once he got a look in the glass, he stopped dead. With bruised smudges under his gray eyes and his tangled hair, he didn't recognize his own face, but he saw something more in his reflection. He'd soon be drug-free for the first time in years, and the electric blue shimmer that radiated off his body had returned—fortified by something new.

Something more powerful.

You're the one, aren't you? A girl's voice came from nowhere.

The sound of her jacked with the hair on his neck and sent a slither of cold down his arms. The way she whispered—from inside his ear—made him look around, expecting to see her. Her whisper lingered like soft breath on his skin—something intimate and pure—but no one stood next to him.

The one? What are you talking about?

He concentrated hard, listening for her, but nothing came. Hearing her, he felt even stronger, connected to something bigger. The muffled voices reminded him of an orchestra tuning its instruments, but her voice rose stronger above the din like a haunting violin solo. He sensed her in his head. In his body. In every strand of his hair.

Why can't you hear me? With his mind reaching out to her, he pleaded for an answer, but when *all* the voices stopped, he felt sure that she'd punished him.

Don't stop. I'm listening. You can talk to me, he told her.

The comforting murmurs returned, but the girl stayed silent, even though he still felt her with him. Lucas turned back toward the glass window. He didn't need to see his own reflection to know what had happened.

He felt it.

Brilliant spears of white shot through cobalt-blue and magnified the energy inside him. In blinding glimmers of pearl, the pulsing light made him want to smile, but he didn't. The colors that grew stronger were nothing more than a ticking time bomb that had been masked by the drugs he'd been given to control him.

A countdown had started—and the girl had sensed it, too.

Because of what you are, the Believers will hunt you down.

"What am I...exactly?" He said the words aloud, not to her this time.

It wouldn't take the Believers long to realize he was missing. Once they found out, they'd track him. If they caught him, they'd never let him get away a second time. What he'd done to escape them felt like a stupid accident. Hours earlier, he opened his eyes to see he'd hidden in a delivery truck leaving the hospital. Because of the drugs, he didn't remember actually doing it. He'd left the facility without much of a plan, dressed only in slippers and hospital-issued stuff. When the truck stopped at a streetlight, he got out and never looked back.

After his head cleared enough for him to figure things out, he knew he had to find something different to wear. When a drunk, homeless guy took his eyes off his stash, Lucas stole spare clothes and grabbed a handful of coins the man had panhandled and kept in a lidded cup. Now everything Lucas wore stank. He hated it, but he fit the part of the invisibles that haunted the streets of L.A.

Lucas knew his escape had been nothing more than dumb luck, or a cosmic shift of the planets, or some other freak anomaly. To stay free wouldn't be easy. The Believers had money. Lots of it.

Don't trust anyone. No cops. The girl's voice mirrored what he'd been thinking, except for one thing.

Lucas needed to find a phone.

Outside a 7-Eleven, he found what he'd been looking for. He fumbled through his pockets for spare change and the crumpled piece of paper that he'd brought with him from Haven Hills—the one his sister Rayne had given him with her phone number on it. When he heard the ring, he shut his eyes to picture her face. He wanted to imagine her happy, but that was too hard.

Come on, Rayne. Pick up.

As the phone rang, he tried to remember if the number she gave him had been her cell or where she lived. Soon it would kick into voice mail. *A message.* He'd have to talk for real and say something. With things screwed up, what the hell would he tell her? *Damn.*

Don't trust anyone. The girl's voice replayed in his head, but he had to make the call. Even though Rayne would have his return phone number, Lucas knew he couldn't hang out and wait for her to call back. The Believers had too many ways to track him. Instinct urged him to keep moving. He didn't want to put Rayne in danger, but he wouldn't cut her out of his life without saying goodbye.

Goodbye. What was good about it? How would he say good-bye to the only person he wanted to see?

Disappointment punched him in the gut, especially after he heard her outgoing message. He didn't know how much hearing his sister's voice would affect him until he felt a tear slip down his cheek as he listened to her recording. When the beep sounded, he wiped his face with the back of his hand and took a deep breath.

"Rayne, it's me. I'm sorry. I couldn't stay there anymore. That place… Something's not right and I can't trust Mia. She was gonna let them transfer me to Ward 8. I couldn't let them do that. You're the only one who ever—" He stopped and gripped the phone tighter, trying not to sound pathetic. "I want to see you, but that's too dangerous."

He knocked his forehead on the pay phone. Ward 8. Why did he say *that?* He couldn't explain his instincts about it, not over the phone. His message sounded lame, and with a clock ticking in his head, he felt exposed, especially after he spotted the store's security camera pointed at him.

"I gotta go, but—" he swallowed, hard "—you can't look for me. Promise me you won't. It's not safe. You'd only make things worse for both of us and—"

When her message system beeped and cut him off, he shut his eyes and took a deep breath to force the drug fog from his brain before he called her again. This time he had to talk faster and say what he really meant.

"Hey, it's me again. What I called to say is…I love you, Rayne. I'll always love you."

When he hung up the phone, he felt like crap. He'd sounded like a drugged-out loser—a paranoid one. If Mia had convinced Rayne that he was mentally unstable, his message to her had sealed the deal. Although he wouldn't blame Rayne for how things turned out, he felt a weight in the pit of his belly.

Because he loved her, he'd severed ties with the one person he could count on. Whatever came next, he'd be alone to face it.

But Lucas didn't have time to make things right. A ripple of energy surged through him like a psychic shove.

They're coming.

An urgent vibration made his insides twist, and the sensation turned into painful needle pricks. A danger sign. He didn't have to hear footsteps like normal people. The Believers were coming for him. He felt it. *No. Too soon. I'm not... strong enough.* He edged into the shadows of an alley to focus his mind and body. When he felt the push of energy again, he didn't have to see them to know they were closing in. This time he didn't worry about drawing attention.

Lucas ran.

West Hollywood
Thirty Minutes Later

After opening her front door, Rayne saw the blinking light that she had voice mail and rushed to her phone. She prayed that the call had come from Lucas, but after hearing his message, she was even more worried. She flipped on a light and slumped onto a bar stool near her kitchen to listen to her brother's messages for a second and third time.

"I couldn't stay there anymore. That place... Something's not right..."

His voice had been shaky. She barely recognized him, especially with the traffic noise in the background. Still, he had called her. That was something, wasn't it? But what had scared him enough to ditch Haven Hills in his condition?

"...I can't trust Mia."

Those words chilled her. Rayne didn't trust Mia, either, but, even drugged, Luke had sensed that their older sister had an agenda. Something in his voice made her believe he was actually afraid of her.

And what was Ward 8?

What's got you spooked about Mia and that hospital, Lucas?

Rayne dialed the number he had called from and listened as the phone rang off the hook. She dialed the number again. Once more. Twice. On the third time, someone answered.

"Hello?" An older woman's voice.

"I got a call from this number. Can you tell me if you see a tall kid waiting around? He's my brother. I need to talk to him."

"No one's standing here, honey. I came to get beer and heard the phone ringing. Figured I'd answer it."

Rayne shut her eyes. She'd missed him.

"Okay, well, can you please tell me where you are? I need to find him."

"Yeah." After the woman gave her the closest intersection, she said, "Hope you find your brother, sweetie. And just so you know, I drink responsibly."

"Uh, yeah. Thanks, ma'am. For everything."

Rayne knew the area where Lucas had made the call. She hung up the phone and shrugged out of her jacket before she replayed the message again. When she imagined him alone on the streets of L.A., her eyes stung with tears. He'd lived most of his life with someone caring for him and under medical supervision. Without his meds, what would happen?

"Damn it, Mia. What did you do to him?"

Lucas had to be desperate to break free of Mia's control and escape the hospital and whatever Ward 8 was. Rayne felt sure her sister knew exactly why—but she'd never admit it, not to her. After the legal mess of guardianship and trust funds had been settled, Mia grew distant and relied on attorneys for answers. She quit talking to Rayne about Lucas, about everything. The distance between them grew worse—and so did the arguments—but everything turned really ugly when Mia used visits to see Lucas as a way to control them both.

That was when Rayne knew she'd lost everything. She had no control. No power to change the way things were. Now she'd lost Lucas, too.

"I want to see you, but that's too dangerous…. You can't look for me. It's not safe. You'd only make things worse for both of us…"

Rayne didn't know what to think. Seeing Lucas—how could that be dangerous? And how could she make things worse by wanting to take care of him? He sounded freaked and totally paranoid. What if Mia had been right about his condition…that he really *did* need a hospital? She wanted to do what was best for him, but—

"What would that be, Luke?" She wiped her eyes.

If Mia had struggled with the same doubts about what was best for him—but hadn't clued her in because she'd been a kid—would Rayne finally accept the tough calls her sister had made for their brother's own good? Could she help Mia find him now because it would be the only thing to do?

By escaping the mental hospital, Lucas had forced her into doing *something.* He'd called to say he loved her, but she couldn't sit back and let things ride. Maybe this would be her only chance to get it right—to do what she was too young to do the last time.

Things are seriously jacked up. She wanted her sister to be wrong about Luke—*needed* her to be.

Whenever Rayne got nervous or scared, her mind went to weird places. Most of the time, those feelings had to do with her sister. Sometimes it did her good to picture Miss Perfect Mia with a ripe zit—ready to harvest—in the middle of her forehead.

But if she'd been wrong about her sister, that would mean Luke was really sick,

Rayne needed him to be the sweet, shy kid she remembered—a gentle boy who had always been different—but what if he wasn't? What if the voices in his head had turned nasty—something Mia had tried to protect her from? Taking Luke's side wouldn't be easy either way. Backing him up—against Mia's money and doctors and her weird employer, the Church of Spiritual Freedom—it would be the two of them against the hospital, the courts and God. The law and God would be on Mia's side. *No pressure.* They'd never win a battle like that, not without getting their asses smoked by lightning.

Before she hit Replay—to hear his voice again—a harsh knock at her door made her jump. When she looked out the peephole, her stomach tightened and she felt sick. Her sister glared back as if she had X-ray vision and saw through the door.

Worse, she had a cop in uniform with her.

"Damn, Mia. What now?"

When Rayne opened the front door to her apartment, her sister didn't bother saying hello. She barged in with the cop behind her. The guy in uniform didn't show his badge. He only did what Mia told him to do.

"Go ahead. Search the place," Mia said with a wave of her manicured nails. "You've got my permission."

"Lucas isn't here, Mia. Just look around. Hell, you can see every inch of this place from the front door."

Nice. Princess Mia had stomped all over her privacy, with a cop no less.

"Hello, I'm emancipated. You need a dictionary to look that up?" Apparently being an emancipated minor meant nothing. When the cop didn't look at her and kept rummaging through her junk, Rayne crossed her arms and glared at her sister.

"When is my life ever going to be mine, Mia?" When her sister didn't answer, she turned to the cop. "For the record, I don't give you permission to search, *5-0,* if that means anything."

It didn't.

Typical. Dressed in a fancy pants suit, Mia had on nosebleed heels and looked like America's Next Top Model. Her idea of casual Friday. Taking an inventory of the room with her eyes, she didn't have to say anything. Whatever Mia thought about the way she lived, it wouldn't be good.

Rayne's unmade bed and beat-up sofa patched with duct tape would make easy targets. Cinder block and wood planks held her secondhand TV, and she had cereal bowls in the sink and a load of dirty laundry piled in a corner. She expected Mia to hurl a snark attack on her target-rich environment, but when she didn't say a word and walked over to the only well kept part of her existence—the one new thing she had spent money on—Rayne braced for snark 2.0.

"Oh, my Lord. What is that?" Mia peered into a tall cage, lit with UVB and heat bulbs on a timer, which dominated a corner of her small apartment. Her sister's face scrunched into a tight ball of disgust as she glared into the scaly face of her pet iguana.

"That's my roommate, Floyd Zilla. Don't get too close. He hasn't eaten."

To make her point, the iguana lashed out its tongue and lunged toward Mia, making her jump. Rayne snorted a laugh.

"That thing probably carries diseases," her sister said.

"So do you, but hey, for what it's worth—" Rayne forced a grin and lied "—I think he likes you."

Mia narrowed her eyes and didn't say anything more about Floyd, but when she headed to the kitchen, Rayne rolled her eyes and slumped onto a bar stool, watching her sister look through her fridge and pantry. After Mia held up a box of Scooby-Doo Mac & Cheese—with a raised eyebrow—she looked as if she expected an explanation.

Rut roh. Busted.

"That's for Floyd," Rayne lied. "He's on a high-carb kick."

Mia rolled her eyes and said, "Well, at least you've got fresh fruit, but what's with the parsnip?"

"Uh, the fruit and parsnip are Floyd's stash, too. He's hardcore vegan. I make him a special salad and fruit mush since he's got no teeth. Wanna try some?"

"That figures. The lizard eats better than you do." Mia sighed and shook her head at the rest of her food. "Hot Pockets, ramen noodles, Ben & Jerry's. Are these your idea of groceries?"

"That's only my breakfast junk."

Mia grabbed her jumbo bag of Skittles and hung them in front of her nose. "Breakfast?"

"They go in my cereal. Gawd." Rayne took back her Skittles. "Besides, I get my major food groups at Mickey D's like most of America. My way of pitching in to save the economy, one Big Mac at a time."

"You think that's funny, but I don't see the humor. You're almost eighteen. I expect…more."

"Who are you to expect *anything* from me? I moved out. Why I did isn't a secret, not between us, so you've got no right getting your Spanx in a bunch over how I live."

Mia shot a sideways glance at uniform boy and tightened her jaw. Rayne knew what that meant. Her sister had a thing for arguing about private stuff with other ears around. She had no problem dishing out her typical one-way spew, but whenever Rayne pushed back, Mia freaked out over not being in control. Rayne could've stoked the fires in front of the cop to watch her sister squirm, but she chose not to. Someone had to be the adult—and if she had any chance of getting Mia to tell her about Ward 8, her long-shot odds would improve if they were alone.

It didn't take long for the uniform to finish his pillaging. He didn't say much. He only shook his head when he was done. *Like, duh, no Lucas? Seriously? Huh.*

"Wait for me in the car," Mia said. "I need to speak to my sister."

After the guy shut the front door and they were alone, Rayne didn't wait for her sister to pick the lecture du jour. She had plenty to say.

"So was that official business? Did you even file a police report…or an Amber Alert? Or is that cop on the payroll of your precious church?" When Mia didn't answer right away, she said, "Yeah, thought so."

"Look, Rayne, the bottom line is that we're family."

Yeah, I feel the love.

"When were you going to invite me over to see your new place?" Mia said, pretending to be hurt. "It's been six months since you moved out."

Her sister zinged that one out of left field. Rayne almost got whiplash. *Yeah, right. Try NEVER or when bacon grows wings.*

"Your invite to my housewarming party must've gotten lost in the mail."

"I know Lucas called you." Mia leaned her elbows onto her kitchen counter and kept her voice low, as if they were two BFFs talking. "You don't know what's going on, Rayne."

"Then gimme the deets. That shouldn't be a big deal. He's my brother, too. I only want to help."

"You can't. Whatever Lucas needs, I've got it covered. I just can't have you getting in the way."

Getting in the way? What Mia said hurt—*bad*—but Rayne didn't let it show.

"Only the hospital can help him. Lucas may look normal on the outside, but he's really sick, Rayne. A new doctor took an interest in his case after I pushed for it."

Great, a new doctor. What did this new doc have to do with Luke's transfer? Mia had faith in that crazy church and their "system." She believed whatever the doctors told her. Rayne didn't have a good feeling about what her sister said. She'd had her fill of doctor theories, but she kept her mouth shut and listened.

"Dr. Fiona Haugstad. She's head of psychiatry at Haven Hills. She was in the process of reevaluating him but never got a chance to finish. She said that if he got off his meds, though, he could be a danger to—"

"Wait a minute," Rayne interrupted. "Back it up. You said you knew that Lucas called me. How? Are you *spying* on me?"

"You don't understand. You never have." Mia didn't look her in the eye and she didn't answer her, either.

"That's because you don't let me in. You always treat me like a stupid kid."

"You're not stupid, but you *are* still a kid. What's wrong with me being the adult?" Her sister shrugged. "Look, none of us got much of a childhood. That sucks. Lucas got the worst of it, but all I want to do is shield you both from worse stuff."

"Hard to believe there's worse stuff than dead parents and ending up in a mental hospital for life. But hey, if you say there's a bigger, badass boogeyman out there, maybe Lucas will believe your spin on his crap-tastic life. He's drooling 24/7, thanks to you."

Rayne didn't buy the protective-older-sister routine. After their parents died, Mia got off on being in charge and making all the decisions. At first, that had been a comfort, until men in suits and official documents took over their lives. Rayne hated lawyers, and judges were no better. Suits only cared about paperwork and everyone agreeing to whatever, signing stuff about sibling guardianship and court petitions.

Eighteen years old at the time they lost their parents, Mia had convinced Rayne that she should trust her. Rayne didn't know any better and she wanted to believe her sister could take care of them. Because Mia asked her to, she signed on a line saying she agreed with her sister about what would happen to them.

After that, stuff happened fast, and a judge made it all legal. Mia set up trust funds and took control of everything, including Lucas's care and his share of the inheritance. Back then, Rayne believed Mia and thought that staying together would be the right thing to do. They'd all be under one roof, so they could deal with losing their parents together and still be a family.

But when Lucas needed more than a roof over his head, Mia had him committed almost overnight, as if she was ashamed of him. She locked him away at Haven Hills, like nothing more than damaged goods.

"Like I said, you've never understood." Mia finally looked her in the eye. "Did you actually talk to him or did he only leave a message?"

Mia's big show of concern could be boiled down to one thing. She was prying, hoping she'd get to hear Lucas's message. *Well, too bad.*

"You haven't earned the right to an answer, Mia. Sorry."

Her sister looked sad, for real. A part of her wished things had turned out differently between them, but an even bigger chunk made Rayne hold back. Her sister, as always, didn't trust her enough to confide in her, not even about Lucas. They both had a heaping pile of disappointment on their plates, and it didn't look likely that either of them would get dessert for playing nice.

"So what's Ward 8? You were having Lucas transferred there. Was this new *miracle* doctor doing the transfer or saving him from it?"

Rayne didn't see any clever way of bringing up the transfer. Her brother never explained why he was afraid of Ward 8, but if Mia had any question about whether she had actually talked to Luke, now she'd know he never did more than leave her a message—and questions without answers.

"How did you—?" Mia gritted her teeth. "Please…stay out of this. For once, do what I'm begging you to do. For Lucas's sake."

Rayne stared at her sister in disbelief.

"Sure. Don't I always, sister dearest?"

From the look on Mia's face, she knew what Rayne meant. "Sure" meant "So Not Gonna Happen." The mounting mistrust between them had started with the shock of losing their parents, and anything left had gone swirling down the toilet ever since.

Mia left without another word. Rayne really hadn't expected her sister to suddenly confide in her about Lucas, Ward 8 and his questionable medical care. But if Rayne had any doubts about what she would do, she'd made up her mind after "talking" to her sister. With cops on the church payroll, it made no sense for Rayne to report Lucas missing on her own. That would be a total waste of time. Mia would see to that.

Rayne filled Floyd's food bowl with salad mush she had in the fridge and replenished his water dispenser—enough to last him for a while. With Floyd satisfied, she searched her cell phone for a recent photo of Luke to take with her, one taken on a better day at Haven Hills when he almost recognized her.

His sweet face had a crook in his lip for a half smile and his beautiful gray eyes looked sleepy, as if he'd awakened from a long nap. It was one of her favorite pictures of him because she could see the little boy he used to be. She grabbed her leather jacket again, the keys to her motorcycle, and locked up her apartment, heading out to search for Lucas. She'd start at the convenience store where he had called her.

Unlike Mia, her brother didn't have the law in his pocket

or a church with money to fall back on. Luke had no one—
except her—but Rayne felt sure about one thing.

Mia had been hiding something about Lucas. *Definitely.*

Minutes Later

Before Mia got to her car, where Officer Preston waited
for her, she placed a call. She wasn't looking forward to reporting that Lucas hadn't gone to Rayne. How did everything get so screwed up? It bothered her that her sister had
found out about Ward 8. How did Luke know about it? With
all the medication he'd been under, how could he be aware
of such a secret part of the hospital that linked directly to the
church and their beliefs? Not even Mia knew what went on
there. All she knew was that Ward 8 was the unconventional
last stop where the church took over—the last hope for patients who resisted more traditional care regimens. She had
hoped that Dr. Haugstad could have intervened with better
news on Lucas's behalf, but now she might never know. She
didn't have time to dwell on that now. On the second ring, a
husky voice answered her call.

"It's me. He wasn't there."

"He's your brother, Mia. Where would he go?"

She only knew the man by one name—O'Dell. His low,
guttural voice made her skin crawl—like he stood too close
and whispered in her ear—but she needed him to have faith in
her. The Church of Spiritual Freedom had assigned the man
to search for Lucas discreetly, making sure anyone of authority
outside the control of the church's many resources would not
get involved. She had no choice but to cooperate. The church
had insisted and needed to control what might turn into ugly
public exposure if things weren't contained. O'Dell would be
the key to everything. If she failed in his eyes, she'd never become part of the inner trust circle, and that wasn't an option.

"I'm taking Officer Preston to our old house. The last place we were a family. He might go there."

In truth, Mia had no idea where Lucas would go. Their old house wouldn't be likely with him being on foot, but it would buy her time to think of a next step. She had to find Luke, and that meant relying on a man like O'Dell to help her. Everything depended on it.

"Call me after you check it out," O'Dell said. He ended the call without waiting for her to say anything. Not a good sign. Where would Luke go?

Running had taken everything out of Lucas. His chest heaved as he tried to fill his lungs; his legs burned and he felt sick. In the shadows of a dark alley, he bent over with dry heaves. On an empty stomach, he had nothing to throw up. Being confined to a mental hospital and on medications, he'd been robbed of everything. He felt weak and didn't know who he was anymore.

He'd gotten ahead of his pursuers, even though he still felt them. He slid down a brick wall in the darkest corner of the alley, panting, and closed his eyes. He needed rest. It would be easy to fall asleep and let fate take over. The drugs that still lingered in his system left him confused. He ran from Haven Hills to escape what he felt sure would come. The nightmares had escalated and driven him to run, but even outside the hospital, he couldn't stop them.

He flashed back to the dark dreams that he had about Ward 8.

Whether he had his eyes closed or not, his exhaustion and the shadows in the alley made the memory of his recurring nightmare come in blinding bursts of sounds and images that made his heart pound. He had so many night sweats over it, he couldn't tell what could be actual memory caused by the drugs or only paranoia over what could happen if he got sent there. Over the years, drugs had controlled his body and made it a virtual prison—a cage he couldn't escape, even now. He didn't know what was real. He only wanted to leave it all behind him and make it stop.

Only one thing felt solid and kept him from giving in to the fear and letting the Believers find him.

The girl's voice in his head.

You have no idea how powerful you are.

Her voice made him open his eyes. He struggled to his feet and used the brick wall to stand.

Come to me. I can help you.

The girl's voice helped him make that first step and the next. He had to find her, but she'd given him an even bigger gift.

She made him care what happened to him.

Burbank

In a dimly lit room of his bunker command center located in Burbank, O'Dell walked through murky shadows as he felt the surge of energy he got off the supplement drink he'd downed. The power drink, his concoction, increased the anabolic effects after his usual workout. He felt pumped as he squeezed a rubber ball to strengthen his hand and forearm muscles. He called his ball routine "flexing the snake." Most women shot him a raised eyebrow whenever they heard that, but O'Dell had the tattoo of a snake wrapped around both his forearms. Whenever he gripped the rubber ball and squeezed, his muscles flexed the snakes and made them move.

His twin snakes got him noticed and earned him respect. O'Dell liked traveling outside the herd. He didn't punch a clock. Day jobs were for suckers. In this place, he was in charge. Flashes of color from the bank of computer screens swept over the faces of his people. The darkness made it easier to focus on their surveillance. Each station monitored a different street grid for L.A.

O'Dell and his people had hacked the city's traffic cameras—looking for Lucas Darby and others like him, using a facial-recognition program they called the Tracker.

They had eyes everywhere.

O'Dell went to his office, located on a raised platform behind the bank of computer operators. A huge window kept him connected to everything that happened below. He sat behind his desk to replay the footage of the Darby kid at the pay phone. Even in low light, he saw the kid crying and wiping his eyes, and he had a pretty good idea why. When the boy looked up at the surveillance camera, it was as if he knew he was being watched. That made O'Dell smile.

Damned freak!

He remembered the file he'd gotten on Darby. It had been thin. The bare essentials with no other explanation. O'Dell got assignments in the form of a digital file he received online. Dossiers of targets included surveillance photos to scan and load into the Tracker with details to help facilitate the abduction, discreetly. He had a search grid and faces to hunt down. Whenever he scored a hit and acquired his target, he'd put them in a holding cell located in his bunker until he could arrange for a secured pickup via an online status-tracking site.

The guys that picked up those kids were dressed in white and came in an ambulance. They always drugged the kids they transported, too. Although the medical attire and setup could have been only for show, he didn't know where the kids went and didn't care. Whenever his crew got orders to dispose of spent bodies, they were given a secure rendezvous point and strict orders not to look into the black body bags, but O'Dell broke the rules once and peeked. He recognized one of the dead kids, a boy he'd hunted, and he never looked again, especially after he saw the condition of the body. These kids only meant a paycheck and bonus money to him and his team.

He didn't know how or why the targets were selected. The covert organization he worked for had a compartmentalized structure. He figured they had satellite operations all over the globe, but that was only a guess. If kids like this existed in L.A., they had to be other places, too. O'Dell took care of his assignments, even though he didn't know much about the organization above his head. Not knowing who was higher up the food chain might bother some people, but he liked that no one knew about his operation, either. Everything was on a need-to-know basis. If anyone got caught by authorities, they knew nothing that would put the group at risk, and online security could be shut down fast.

O'Dell liked how things were, and he got off on the thrill of tracking down these brainiacs. Supposedly Indigo kids had high IQs and were the next evolution of mankind with their *special* gifts. *Yeah, right.* If they were so evolved, how could a drama major make them look as dumb as a mountain of pea gravel?

He shook his head with a smirk. The idea of using the kid's sisters really turned him on. The hot sister, Mia, would have to track and turn in her own brother to prove her loyalty to the church. That girl had to be plenty greedy. She could make real money with the right attitude. But for her to get on board the money train, she'd have to betray her brother and work against the younger sister—the one that kid had called and cried over. His gut told him baby sis would be the one to watch.

O'Dell caught the eye of one of his men below and called him up to his office.

"I want someone at that pay phone where the kid made the call," he told the man. "He could come back. And put a surveillance team on his other sister, Rayne. Use those gang kids if you have to, that MS-13 crew, but don't tell them anything."

The Mara Salvatrucha 13 gang had originated in Los Angeles with a violent reach that had spread across the United States, Canada, Mexico and even into Central America. O'Dell found them useful, and since they were on his turf, it paid to have gang members on his side.

"What if she becomes a problem?"

"If she gets in the way, have them convince her that'd be a mistake. Do whatever it takes to put the fear of God into her."

"I'm on it."

O'Dell grinned. *Let the freak show begin.*

Rayne had started her search for Lucas at the public phone he'd used to call her. The convenience store wasn't that far from the hospital. It made sense he would head there to call, but where would he go next? She hung out and watched people before she questioned the clerk on duty and everyone who stepped foot into the store. To jog memories, she showed Lucas's picture on her cell, but no one had seen him.

Now, three hours later, Rayne felt exhaustion creeping into her muscles as she rode her father's Harley low rider, searching old haunts and new ones. Her bike carried good memories and she needed the positive karma as she tripped into a past she had shared with her brother. The vintage Harley reminded her of those days. As kids, she and Lucas had watched their dad work on the motorcycle to restore it, and when their mother didn't know, he took them on short trips. It was their thing and the reason she'd inherited his low rider when Lucas got hospitalized. Her father had used strict language in his will on how the bike would be handled. No one, not even Mia, could intervene and overturn his last wishes. Rayne had scored the keys from a disapproving Mia after she was old enough to get her license and needed wheels.

Riding her father's bike made her feel as if she hadn't gone alone. Her dad's spirit rode with her. She sensed his quiet strength and remembered how it felt to have his arms around her, holding her tight and keeping her safe like he did when she was little. Memories of her father gave Rayne a connection to channel Lucas, but it was hard to fight the hopelessness of looking for Luke, the needle in a haystack the size of L.A.

In a few hours it would be dawn. She had no luck spotting him, but as the night wore on, Rayne got a strange feeling. Luke's paranoia had rubbed off. Ever since she'd left her first stop—the pay phone where her brother had called her—the hairs on the back of her neck had tingled. Something felt off, like eyes were on her, but when she looked in her rearview mirror, she didn't see anything suspicious. No car sped up when she hit the accelerator, and no one tailed her when she made a turn.

Still, she felt *something*.

When her paranoia jacked with her adrenaline and forced her into making her search longer by taking extra maneuvers, she figured it was time to call it a night. Her last stop would be a place not far from West Hollywood—the old Griffith Park Zoo, off Ventura Freeway near Glendale.

Lucas had his own reasons for trekking through the old L.A. zoo grounds, even though he'd been too young to ever see it in operation after it closed in the sixties. He'd been to a boy's camp not far from the abandoned zoo. Lucas loved to hike the trails. The underground tunnels and old cages and pits, tagged with graffiti and street art, had lured him as a kid—a choice slice of nature in the heart of the concrete and asphalt of L.A.

Rayne turned onto Crystal Springs Drive and drove the curving, narrow road that led to the main entrance. Memories

eased through her mind as she rode, but at night the moonlight played tricks on her eyes. Trees shape-shifted into lurking beasts with eyes, and the trailheads could've been good
places to film Hollywood slasher flicks. Yeah, mega creep factor, but she had one good thing going.

If someone had tailed her into the old park, they'd be easy
to spot now.

Rayne parked her motorcycle near the entrance, took off
her helmet and breathed in the night air as she listened for
sounds. She peered through the darkness for any signs that
she'd been followed. The constant thrum of freeway traffic
got muffled by the hills and dense trees of the park, but she
saw nothing out of the ordinary. No headlights behind her.
No sound of tires on gravel. The only light came from the
city skyline in the distance.

Satisfied that she was alone, Rayne grabbed a flashlight she
kept stowed on the Harley for roadside emergencies and secured her bike. She entered the park and followed the asphalt
trails through decrepit animal pens covered in overgrown
vines and walked in silence, at first. Given the size of the zoo,
she decided to yell Lucas's name. If he was there, making noise
might draw him out.

"Lucas, it's me, Rayne."

When she got farther into the park, closer to the larger
bear and lion habitats, she took a deep breath and prepared for
the worst—the underground tunnels. If Lucas wanted shelter
and a solid place to hide, unfortunately for her he would've
headed for the belowground maze. His favorite part. It was
the last place she wanted to be at night, but for Lucas, she had
to risk it. It was what he would've done. The way he was,
Lucas didn't see demons in the zoo tunnels, like most people
would have. He chose to see adventure and possibility—and
the beauty in nature reclaiming the grounds.

Guided only by the narrow beam of her flashlight, she found the yawning mouth of the tunnels and headed down. Every step she took, her boots crunched on decayed leaves that littered the stone stairway. Spiny fingers of dead vines marred the walls and covered the street art of painted skulls and gang signs. In daylight, the art was impressive—almost like a church—but at night the images looked like hell, literally.

For Lucas…I'm here because of Luke.

Rayne repeated that in her head, trying not to jump at every shadow, but she felt like a damned chicken. Her skin itched like it crawled with bugs, and the muggy stench of mold and animal poop hit her hard. If she didn't have her flashlight, she would have been in total darkness. Only dim light from the moon leached through rusted metal bars in flickers and spiraled down tunnel openings as she crept by. Her night vision sucked from the glare off her flashlight, but that couldn't be helped.

"Lucas!" She called his name as she felt her way through the dark with a hand running across a rock wall to steady her steps. The deeper she got into the bowels of the deserted zoo, the more her voice echoed and sent chills skittering down her spine.

"Luke!" she called out again.

With her throat feeling like sandpaper, his name came out sounding raspy. She cleared her throat to yell again, but when something moved up ahead, Rayne gasped and stopped dead.

The moon? A shadow?

Instinct made her turn off the flashlight and shut her eyes tight for a second to get her night vision back. Had she only imagined it? She held her breath and searched the dark for anything that moved. She prayed that whatever she'd seen had only been a branch blowing in the wind up top or some other harmless thing. Normally her luck was *for shit,* but if she hadn't stopped cold, she never would've heard it.

A footstep…and another.

Someone had followed her into the tunnels. Rayne wasn't alone.

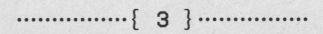

{ 3 }

Griffith Park Zoo

Rayne's heart pulsed in her ears, overshadowed by the hard thump it made against her ribs. Someone had followed her. She couldn't catch her breath. After she shut down her flashlight, her night vision took time to kick in, making her nearly blind. From what she saw, she'd made it to a larger part of the tunnels, some sort of workroom. One shadowy corridor stretched behind her, where she had heard the footsteps. Another way out was dead ahead.

She hoped the footsteps had been Lucas's, but when he didn't call to her, Rayne shrank into the shadows and shut her eyes to listen. Luke never came. Instead, she heard a slow, melodic whistle. It echoed and bounced off the stone walls. The search for her brother had turned into a living, breathing Wes Craven flick.

"Come out, sweet thing." A guy's voice. "We know you're in here."

We? Rayne wanted to puke. The jerk spoke in a creepy singsong voice, like a psycho killer. He pretended to play around, making everything a big joke. She thought about running, but after her stalker broke the silence, more whistles came.

More voices.

"We saw you, little girl."

"Yeah. Come play with us."

Sounds echoed from every direction, making it hard to figure out how many there were, but Rayne knew one thing for sure. They had her surrounded. Belowground, even if she screamed, no one would hear her. How did these losers find her? She hadn't seen any headlights tailing her into the park. Where had they come from? Questions came at her, but she sure as hell didn't intend to find out what they wanted.

Rayne had only precious seconds to call 911. She reached into her jacket pocket and pulled out her cell. Underground, she had no bars. *Damn!* Her fingers flew over her Droid touch screen, but nothing worked, and while she'd spent the night looking for Lucas, her battery had hit the red zone. Rayne stuffed the phone into her pocket and looked for plan B.

Desperate for a place to hide, she felt along the stone wall as her eyes adjusted to the blackout. Eventually she caught a faint light, a glimmer of moon shining through a metal grate above her head. Without hesitating, she wedged her boot onto a foothold and scrambled up the wall like a rock climber, clawing her fingers into breaks in the stone. It didn't take long until she found where the moonlight came from.

A narrow ledge near a ventilation shaft blew a faint breeze onto her face. They'd have to look up to find her, and she'd have a fighting chance to kick them in the face if they did. But when Rayne hoisted her leg onto the ledge to pull her body up the rest of the way, she heard something smash and looked down to see a dim glow fade to black. Her cell phone had fallen from her pocket and shattered on the rocks.

It was toast and so was she.

"What was that?" one of the guys yelled.

"Think it came from over here."

Rayne had run out of time. She had to move. *Now!*

Getting a closer look at the vent shaft, she had wiggle room to squeeze into it. She could crawl to the end and jostle loose the grate that led outside. After all her lousy luck, she let herself hope that she had found a way out, until she wedged into the cramped space and the stone walls closed in on her like a coffin. The stale, dank air made it hard to breathe, and sweat dripped off her scalp as she inched toward the moonlight on her belly.

When she grasped the bars of the grate and shoved, it didn't budge. The vent felt rock solid and she didn't have enough room to maneuver to kick it out. *Oh, man. Don't do it. Don't cry.* With her face against the drain, Rayne took a deep breath to fight back tears. She had to stay strong and not act like a victim. She'd be outnumbered and alone, but if they came after her, she wanted blood.

Their blood.

As the whistles got louder, she looked over her shoulder to see lights strafing the stone walls below her hiding spot. The voices and whistles intensified. Rayne wiped her slick palms down her jeans and clutched her flashlight tighter, the only weapon she had. Once they found her smashed cell phone, these jerks would have her. She'd be trapped, but she wouldn't go down without a fight. Rayne gritted her teeth and sat motionless in the dark—until the moon did a funny thing.

The shaft where she hid got brighter.

A pale blue light filled the dark corners around her. At first, she thought they'd found her and one of them had shone a light down the vent, but when she turned to catch where the glow came from, Rayne saw something move in the dark outside.

A guy. Edged by the moon, he looked more like a ghost.

Like Lucas, he was tall, but that was where the similarities ended. Wearing a hoodie, he looked fierce with his face covered in shadow, like the scary knight dude in *Assassin's Creed*. Rayne almost called for help, but didn't. He could've been with the others, but something else stopped her. His body tensed and shook. He looked consumed by a blinding rage. When his mouth opened in a scream, no sound came out. He stretched out his arms and lifted his chin toward the moon, shaking as if he hurt.

She couldn't take her eyes off him, and a sudden chill gripped her hard.

Her body tingled with a rush of static electricity. Even the hairs on her forearms stood on end. Stranger still, Rayne felt a sudden and overwhelming rush of emotion flood her mind and heart—memory flashes of her father and mother when they were alive. Their love felt tangible and real, and it filled the hole in her life where her parents and family had been.

She pictured Lucas's grinning face and imagined Mia's familiar soft giggle when she was a kid and they shared a bedroom. In that moment, it felt as if she had her family back, the living *and* the dead. The phantom touch of her father's arms made her feel safe, and the faint scent of her mother's favorite perfume lingered. Rayne couldn't help it. Tears came for real this time. One by one, the memories sucked up her fear like a sponge.

She didn't feel alone, but how the hell could that be? Rayne wanted to believe that the power of her mind had reached out to calm her, but she'd never felt anything as strong before. Was that what people meant when they talked about a near-death experience…memories that flooded them like a merciful anesthetic before they kicked off?

Or maybe another explanation stood in front of her eyes.

Rayne watched the strange boy with the outstretched arms. How could a boy so filled with rage be the cause of the love she felt now? He had to be part of it. Everything she felt had triggered after he showed, but when something else moved behind him, her fear threatened to rush back.

He wasn't alone.

A large lurking shadow crept forward. *Oh, my God!* She peered through the dark to make out the shape. A massive dog stepped out from behind him and stood at his side—the biggest dog she'd ever seen. It had an electric shimmer that radiated off its body. An eerie glow stabbed through its eyes as if the light had escaped from inside its belly.

The damned thing moved and drifted like a ghost. Rayne could've sworn it never touched the ground. She blinked twice, but the phantom dog didn't go away, and that boy never looked down. Frozen in that moment with him, Rayne felt strangely calm and watched as he kept his face lifted toward the night sky. She thought things couldn't get any weirder, but when that ghost dog brushed against him—

The boy caught fire.

Blue fire.

"She couldn't just disappear. Find her," a guy yelled. "We're not leaving until we do."

His voice clenched Rayne's stomach into an aching knot. Despite the freaky stuff happening outside with hoodie boy and his ghost dog, Rayne couldn't ignore the threat coming from beneath her. If the jerks found her smashed cell phone and looked up, they'd spot the only place she could be and it would all be over.

"Hey, found something. Check it," a voice called out. "It's gotta be hers."

They must've found her cell. Rayne held her breath, not making a sound.

"Yeah, looks like. What's that up there?"

A beam of light blinded her. She squinted and covered her eyes with a hand.

"I see a boot," another one said. "Little girl found a fraidy hole."

Rayne pulled her legs in tight and grabbed the metal bars near her head to make it harder for them to pull her out. But as she tensed her body for a fight, a ghostly sound echoed through the tunnels. It started low and menacing, but as it got louder, she cringed. The growl magnified into the distinctive yowl of a fierce panther or lion. Rayne crooked her head to listen, not believing her ears.

"What the hell is that?"

One guy must've heard it, too, because he sounded scared. He wasn't the only one.

"This better not be a joke."

None of them had time to talk. More noises swept through the maze. A shrieking elephant. Howling dogs. It got so loud that Rayne winced. It hurt her ears, but she had to look. When she scrunched toward the shaft opening, she nearly choked.

"No, this can't..." She gasped.

"*¡Ay Dios mio!*" one of the guys yelled and made the sign of the cross. "It's the devil."

An inferno in cobalt-blue raged through the tunnels and inched up the stone walls, but instead of heat, she felt icy cold. Even her breath turned to vapor. She should have burrowed deeper into the hole, but she couldn't turn away. Ghost animals spiraled out of the flames. The hellish menagerie looked more like a hallucination. She wouldn't have believed her eyes, but the guys who had come looking for her saw and heard everything, too. In the chaos, they yelled and scrambled for cover in total panic. If she hadn't been so scared, she might've laughed at the sight of them running like barnyard chickens.

But she wasn't safe, either.

She heard something that made her skin prickle—on instinct—even before she saw a dark cloud spiraling through the shadows, caught in flickers of light. A flapping noise swelled into something really loud. A swarm of bats filled the cavern. They weren't ghosts. They were real and *alive*. Their bodies pummeled the guys, who dived for cover and swatted at them. When that didn't work, they ran, covering their heads.

Rayne screamed when the bats came for her. She felt the weight of them slap her legs. Repulsed by their hairless, freakish bodies, she kicked and pushed them off until a shrill scream erupted and drowned out their grotesque screeches. The shriek had come from her. She cowered in the shaft with her eyes shut, making her body into a tight ball. Her heart raced like a rapid-fire drill, and every inch of her shook.

Make it stop! Please!

Rayne braced for whatever came next. Cringing in the dark, she'd be alone to face it.

Minutes Later

As shocking and sudden as everything happened—the blaring shriek of stampeding phantom elephants, the gross swarm of bats, the fierce lion and the whole freaky circus, live and dead—*everything* shut down to such a deathlike stillness that Rayne thought she had died.

No glow from blue fire. No icy chill. All of that vanished when the tunnels turned pitch-black. Rayne lay in the dark with her ears popping from the abrupt, sucking vacuum. She couldn't see anything, and the trauma of her own screams made any noise muffle in the startling calm. When her shaky breath and the frantic pounding of her heart came back to her, she dared to lift her head and look over her shoulder, but a solitary voice stopped her dead.

"You can go now. They're gone," a boy said.

His soft voice took her off guard as it echoed off stone and filled her with a peculiar warmth. He calmed her and made her believe he told the truth. Still, she didn't move. She couldn't. After an agonizing debate in her head, Rayne dared to speak, even though she couldn't look.

"Lucas?" She called her brother's name and waited for an answer, willing the next voice she heard to be his.

"Who's Lucas?"

She shut her eyes and let out the breath she'd been holding.

Rayne inched toward the shaft opening. Every muscle in her body squeezed tight with dread until she looked down. Her eyes grew wide and her jaw dropped with a soft gasp. The entire cavern dazzled in flickers of light that floated on wings.

"Oh. My. God," she whispered.

Fireflies were everywhere. Their yellow glow blinked and trailed light like tiny fairies. The terror she felt over the bats had been replaced by magic she hadn't seen in L.A. Rarely were fireflies witnessed west of the Rockies. Up north, yeah, but not in L.A. How had he done it? Rayne didn't question that the boy had summoned them.

She just knew.

Standing below her, by the dim glow of a flashlight that one of the guys had dropped, the boy pulled down his sweatshirt hood and let her see him. When he did, fireflies swept toward him en masse on silent wings. They spiraled and flickered around him, casting him in a warm glow. After a few landed on his body, more came and did the same, unafraid of him. Their small bodies pulsed in pale yellow glimmers as they clung to his clothes and down his arms. They made the boy smile until in a slow, gentle sweep, he lifted his arms and they flew into the air to fill the darkness with their light. They had come in numbers at his beckoned call and now they vanished at his whim, as if he'd conjured them from nowhere.

"How did you do that?" she muttered as she watched the fireflies streak through the shadows, down the corridors and into the night.

When they were gone, he said, "Do what?"

He'd said it so softly that she almost didn't hear him. She couldn't get a clear notion of who this boy was. He scared her badly one minute, yet warmed her heart in the next with fireflies and his gentleness with them. When he denied what he'd done, his words felt like her doubts creeping back in.

What had she seen…really? Rayne still felt under the influence of her hyped adrenaline, and getting saved had made her plenty grateful, but one thought took root when she looked at him again. He looked…beautiful. Seeing him in the shadows, looking up at her, did a number on her heart—a reaction she fought against. Stuff like that only happened in the movies.

With the fireflies gone—vanishing as magically as they had appeared—Rayne got hit with a major reality check. She suddenly felt stupid and she probably looked like hell. Hoodie boy didn't. If she looked up *chill* on the *Urban Dictionary,* his face would stare back.

He definitely had seen a gym once or twice, too. Tall and muscular, he had broad shoulders and narrow hips. He looked rock solid in his jeans and sweatshirt. He had dark hair that looked like he'd just gotten up from bed. Yet what sucked her in were his eyes. Rayne wanted a closer look, but she had to have answers.

"What happened?" she asked. "For real."

"Don't know. Just got here." He shrugged and picked up the flashlight on the ground. "Thought you could tell me. Looks like you had a bird's-eye view."

"Oh, hell, no." Rayne shook her head and pointed at him. "I saw you."

"Saw me what…exactly?" His face flinched for a second, into a strange, dark smile.

She hadn't heard it before, but the guy had a faint British accent. She'd almost missed it.

"Those fireflies, for one. But you were outside and you had that monster dog. He was a ghost or something. I could see straight through him." When his smile turned into a grin that brought a rush of heat to her face, Rayne couldn't shut down her stammering. "You caught fire…and th-the flames… they were b-blue."

"Blue flames…and a ghost dog, you say?" Now his face turned into a full-on smirk. "That's freakin' awesome…or more than a little crazy. Which is it?"

Without thinking, Rayne blurted out, "Crazy runs in my family. Guess I gotta go with that."

Hoodie boy lowered his head to hide a grin. "Then we have something in common. I'm a tinfoil hat away from scoring a padded room at the *bizarro* academy. My name's Gabe Stewart."

"Gabe as in Gabriel…like the angel?"

"Not even close." He grinned, giving her something else to like.

"I'm Rayne…Darby."

"Rain…as in a spring shower?"

"Close, but no." She spelled her name for him. "When I think of rain, I flash on mud puddles, wet socks and my best Hello Kitty Vans all squishy."

"Thanks for the spell-check, and bonus points for the visual," he said. "But don't knock the rain. I'm a big fan. It's nature's music. You ever dance in it?"

She scrunched her face and said, "In the rain…on purpose? No."

"When you hear nature's music and give in to whatever you're feeling, wet socks and shoes and mud puddles don't matter much. It becomes more about the heart, I'd say." He lowered his chin but kept his eyes on her. "You planning on moving in, or are you coming down anytime soon?"

Rayne didn't answer right away. She chewed her lower lip and stared at the guy who had saved her nearly smoked bacon. She didn't know anything about him, except that he had a thing for rain, knew how to lie, could spontaneously combust and was a real party animal. If she weren't worried over finding Lucas, she would've totally hung out and waterboarded him to get at his real story, but whatever.

"What if they come back?"

"Not likely. You smell that?" he asked. When Rayne shook her head, the guy named for an angel hit her with a slow smile, another weapon in his arsenal. *Totally not fair.* "One of those ass hats peed in his pants. Trust me. They won't be back."

"Then, kudos. You really know how to clear a room."

"Yeah, and you're still delusional. Take a pill and get over it." Gabriel wouldn't give an inch on telling her the truth, but he didn't rush her to come down, either. His rather charming accent camouflaged an all-American smart-ass-itude.

"You never answered my question from before," he said. "Who's Lucas?"

"He's my brother. You see anyone else here? I'm looking for him."

"Nope. Only those losers…and you." He shrugged. "Strange place for a family reunion."

"Not if you're a bat, apparently."

He flashed that maddening smile again, the semi-shy one that said he knew more than he would ever say, but he never rose to the bait, either. It didn't appear likely that Gabriel would admit to anything. *Ever.*

"I'm coming down," she said.

When Rayne had climbed the stone wall, she'd been motivated by a gang of guys chasing her—that made it easy.

Now, as she stared down to the rocks beneath her, everything looked ridiculously high and dangerous. Her stomach lurched at the sight and she got dizzy. If she slid out nose first, Rayne pictured a major face-plant and an urgent need for "web redemption" on *Tosh.0*.

When she hesitated, Gabriel stepped closer.

"You need any…"

"No," she answered way too fast.

"…help?"

Now or never, she flipped onto her belly and backed her way out of the vent shaft. She hoped she looked like a beautiful butterfly emerging from its cocoon, but more than likely, she resembled raw bratwurst being squished into a sausage. *Gross!* Gabriel would get a full-moon butt shot, but at least she wouldn't see his face while she did it. As she shimmied out, Rayne regretted every gym class she'd ever skipped. She clung to the edge with her boots clambering for a foothold in the stone.

Going up the wall, she'd been careful. Hanging with her butt out now, careful didn't enter her mind. All she wanted were her boots on the ground, pronto. The first toehold she found, Rayne placed all her weight on it, desperate to get down and look graceful doing it.

That was not what happened.

Big Mo and Mr. Gravity took over. Everything shifted into slow motion as Rayne felt her momentum give in to the pull of gravity. She fell backward, with arms flailing, and cringed as she waited for the pain that would only half eclipse her embarrassment, but something broke her fall.

When Rayne landed in Gabriel's arms, breathing became optional.

Eighteen-year-old Gabriel Stewart should have walked away and not let the girl see him at all. He'd done what he came to do—got rid of the intruders. She'd be the last one. The jerks who had stalked her, he made sure they'd think twice before they ever came back to the old L.A. zoo again. *My turf.* But when Gabe spotted her looking out the drain shaft—frightened and alone—something made him want to do more.

Stupid! Everything he had done tonight had been stupid and too risky, but now, as he held her in his arms, he forgot...*why exactly.* Her eyes triggered something in him—*a need.* The years of him running, hiding, not trusting anyone—they had come at a price that she made him feel.

"Uh, sorry." After he realized he held her too long, he swallowed and heard his own gulp. *What a tool!*

"No, really, totally me. I should've..." She finished with a sigh.

He put her boots to the ground, but his hands couldn't let her go. He loved the way she felt soft and warm against his arms and chest. He missed touching. Holding worked, too. She made him feel all those things in a rush, as if he'd opened his eyes and breathed for the first time.

"I'm a klutz. Sorry." She smiled, and even though she had a hard time looking at him, he saw that her eyes were pale. Not blue exactly. They were gray and unforgettable.

"So...what do we do now?" she asked as she pushed away from him.

Gabe crooked his lip into a smile and stuffed his hands into his jeans. "If we're smart, absolutely nothing."

She narrowed her eyes at him and said, "I don't think we're talking about the same thing."

"Probably not. Too bad."

The girl stared up at him with an intensity that made him uncomfortable. He kept his face unreadable, but inside, his belly tightened. He could see she had more questions, things he had no intention of telling her. He wanted to ask about her brother, too. She had come to the abandoned zoo at night for a reason, but Gabe didn't give in to the growing tension between them.

He couldn't risk letting her in.

"Come on. Let me walk you to your sweet Harley."

"If you know about my bike, you must've seen me ride in. I mean, why were you even here in the first place?"

Yeah, good question.

"Just lucky, I guess." He shrugged and led her out, back the way she'd come. If she knew anything about him, the girl would thank him for letting her walk away.

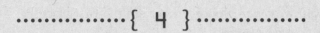
{ 4 }

West Hollywood

Lucas kept his feet moving and stuck to shadows, still fighting the meds that made him groggy and slow. He had to stay ahead of the men who tracked him. Although he hadn't lost them, he felt pretty good about gaining ground, except for one nagging doubt that kept him wandering without direction—*waiting.*

The girl in his head had stopped talking. Without her, he felt lost. The other voices kept him connected and sane, but they weren't the same. Her voice had become his anchor. He heard it when he needed her most. Now he felt adrift in a strong current, floating aimlessly without sight of land.

He had to do something. Be somewhere he felt safe. Once he got a good look around, he found a sign to Griffith Park and it reminded him of something he should know. That sign brought his feet to a dead stop.

The old zoo. He used to hike there, near a boy's summer camp his parents had sent him. There were plenty of hiding places and he knew the grounds well enough to get totally lost without traffic cams. With any luck, he could make it there before the sun came up, but as he headed toward Glendale, the girl's soft voice whispered in his ear.

Find me. You have to find me.

Where are you? He reached out to her with his mind, but she didn't hear him.

She kept talking. *Wherever you are, you're too far. I barely feel you.*

Lucas stopped, not knowing what to do. He'd felt her essence in his mind strongest back the way he'd come—back where the men hunted him.

But it's not safe for me there, he told her.

When she interrupted him, he knew she couldn't hear him.

Use your gift to find me, she said. *It's the only way. Trust me… please. You have to trust me.*

The only way. Her one-way messages were making an odd sense. She'd connected with him and done her part. Now it would be up to him to do the rest. He'd have to find her on his own and use a "gift" that the Believers had suppressed with their drugs, but Lucas felt the pull of his instinct, too.

His brain told him that the old zoo would be familiar ground and would make a solid place to rest, at least for a while. Yet the girl and the voices had awakened something in him. He couldn't explain the powerful connection—her hold over him—but she had become his future, something he couldn't lose. Even though he knew that going back the way he came wouldn't be safe, what would his freedom mean if he wasn't whole?

Lucas took a deep breath and turned around—fighting his strong urge to keep running. When he did, he focused on nothing but her.

I'm coming. I'll find you.

Griffith Park Zoo
Twenty Minutes Later

"Well, that sucks all week," Gabriel said. "Must have been a parting gift from the bastards who followed you into the tunnels."

Rayne stood in the shadows of the parking lot where she'd left her Harley. The tires had been slashed, totally shredded. She'd need new ones. Her roadside repair kit wouldn't cover the damage. She wasn't going anywhere.

"Do you have a cell I could borrow?" she asked. "Mine got trashed." She'd picked up the pieces of her busted cell phone, but they wouldn't do her any good.

"Sorry, no," he said. "Fresh out."

Fresh out? Rayne pulled a double take at Low-tech No-tech boy and dragged a hand through her hair. She had to take a deep breath to calm down. She didn't expect him to be Verizon, but come on. He looked normal—*sort of*—if she didn't count his Pied Piper bat entourage and the fact that she could roast marshmallows on him. *What normal guy doesn't have a cell phone?* Rayne still felt shaky over her ordeal and, at this hour, add exhausted, too. With her bum luck, she had no intention of hoofing it out of the old zoo in the dark, but she had run out of options.

"Who doesn't have a phone?" Her words sounded harsher— and high-maintenance whinier—than she meant them to be.

"Me." He shrugged. "Guess I'm the one guy in L.A. who doesn't text like an idiot. I'm not exactly big on the friends-and-family plan."

"Do you have a car? I could use a lift to get these tires fixed."

He scrunched his face. "Not really. I'm working on the engine, but I could…" When Rayne let out a deep sigh, he stopped and said, "Sorry."

She fought to control the tears welling in her eyes, not doing a very good job of it. When she turned to wipe her face, her fingers trembled. Rayne knew adrenaline had worked a number on her, but she couldn't help it. She felt like such a…

girl. She needed to find Lucas, but without her ride, she'd be useless to him.

"Look…" Gabriel began. Low and soft, his voice brought a second rush of tears that she couldn't hide. "I know you're tired. You probably want to get home to your folks."

Yeah, my folks. Rayne clenched her jaw but didn't say anything. The only one who would miss her had a scaly green body and enough salad mush to last awhile.

Luke was another story.

"I got a place we can go. It's not much, but you could rest while I work on my truck. It won't take long. When I'm done, we'll load your bike and I'll take you anywhere you need to go." He smiled and reached out his hand to wipe a tear off her cheek. "I promise. You'll be safe…with me."

Gabriel touching her face felt like the most natural thing. Rayne had a connection to him that she couldn't explain. Her head told her to be wary. Trust had to be earned. Being on her own, if she ever invited a guy over to her place or dated someone, she had to be more careful. She'd be alone if the guy turned out to be a perv.

She didn't know why she'd made the sudden leap to thinking about Gabriel as a boy she'd want to see again. It was hard not to think of him that way, especially after he saved her. Rayne felt a strange bond with him and he intrigued her. She definitely wanted to know more about him, but someone like Gabriel looked too perfect for a girl like her. People she knew would think she'd won him in a raffle. She couldn't trust her heart, not with a guy who looked and acted like *him.*

But something else had taken over. A feeling, gut instinct, *whatever.* At that moment under the magic of the moon, Rayne believed Gabriel and followed him.

Minutes Later

"You live here?" Rayne asked, trying not to channel Mia.
"One of the places, yeah."

"Oh, like this is your summer place. Yeah, I get it."

Gabriel Stewart lived at the zoo. He'd found a corner of an old maintenance shed and made it home. Something about that suited him, though Rayne couldn't help but feel a pull of loneliness. Being on her own, she knew what it meant to fly solo, without a family, but this wasn't normal, not even close. His choice of isolation felt deliberate.

Gabriel had run away from something.

"Cozy," she said.

He had a sleeping bag on cement as his bed, and a rusted blue truck had been pulled inside the shed's garage bay and had its hood up. He had a small camp stove, a bag for his trash, and a stack of his clothes were folded and stashed on a low row of cinder blocks, to keep them off the dusty concrete floor.

Folded…really? Rayne heaved a sigh.

All things considered, Gabriel turned out to be a neat freak, a flaw she decided not to hold against him, especially after something far more interesting caught her eye. The guy had strange wood carvings lined up near his makeshift bedroll.

"You make these?" She picked up a carving of a dog. The wood felt smooth in her hand and she ran a finger over the amazing detail of the knife work.

"Yeah. When I can't sleep."

Rayne put down the wooden dog and gazed at the countless carvings of animals that filled his space in the shed. From the looks of it, Gabriel didn't sleep much.

"Well, I gotta work," he said. "So you can get home."

Gabriel lit candles near his truck, something it looked as if he'd done many times before, and did as he promised. He got to work.

"If you get cold, I got an extra blanket. You see it?"

"Yeah. Thanks."

Rayne grabbed the blanket and burrowed into his sleeping bag. That should've felt weird, but it didn't. With heavy eyelids, she watched him work. In good light, she noticed his eyes were the color of amber, and right now, they had an intense focus that made her jealous of the truck. A few times she caught him stealing glances at her when he thought she wasn't looking. That made her smile inside.

Before she drifted off to sleep, she noticed the corner of a paper tablet sticking out from under a backpack. The notebook looked familiar, something she'd seen in art class. After she pulled it out and flipped it open, her eyes grew wide. Vivid images of sketched faces filled the pages, drawn in pencil or charcoal. Some were scary and all were incredibly detailed.

Kids mostly, kids her age.

"Are you an artist?" she asked.

"Not really," Gabriel answered without looking up. "I just like whittling."

"No, I'm talking about these sketches. Did you do these?"

When he saw what she had in her hands, his expression changed. "That's my sketchbook. It's private."

His reaction brought a rush of heat to her face.

"Sorry. I didn't mean to—"

Gabe had the strangest look on his face. Not what she expected. It was as if she'd caught *him* doing something bad, not the other way around. She hadn't meant to intrude on his personal stuff, but his reaction surprised her.

He looked afraid.

He stopped working on his truck, wiped his hands and came to her. He knelt by the bed and reached out, asking for his sketchbook. After she handed it over, he set it under his stack of clothes and didn't hide it. That made her feel worse than if he'd flipped out.

"It's okay," he said. "Just…don't do it again, okay?"

"Yeah, sure."

After Gabriel went back to work, Rayne kept an eye on him…and his sketch pad.

West Hollywood

Lucas had crossed over a dangerous threshold and he knew it. He felt the intense presence of the men who hunted him. Everywhere he looked, he spotted a traffic or security camera pointed in his direction. He didn't care anymore. He'd lost his objectivity, and with each step, his gift sent a punishing shock across his skin. He'd grown numb to the pain, and his craving need to be with the girl had blinded him. His instinct to run had gotten jumbled up with the bad stuff he sensed, and only one reason made the risk worth it.

He had to find her—the girl in his head—and finish what he'd started. She had become his compass, his North Star. L.A.'s skyline had turned steel-gray. The sun would be up soon. His feet hurt, his stomach rumbled from hunger, and his body craved sleep, but all of that meant nothing.

He was close—*to her.*

Talk to me. Keep me awake, okay? He willed her to listen as he kept his feet moving on never-ending pavement.

She never answered him. The girl only kept talking. *You're getting stronger. I can feel you.* Her voice gave him the only comfort he needed.

Up ahead, Lucas saw a strip mall lit in neon. Not a big deal until he noticed a difference in the light. The neon glowed brighter and radiated rings of dazzling color in a subtle pulse. He stopped and marveled at the difference as if he were a kid seeing his first Christmas.

Near the stores, an intersection grabbed his attention. He let his mind wander and he went with it. The streets were an X that marked the spot, and the visual image of a bull's-eye hit him and drew his eyes across the street. His next mind link went to an old parking garage that stood several stories high. Surrounded by a cyclone fence posted with signs that the property had been condemned, it looked empty and forsaken.

However his mind had pieced together the puzzle, he knew the girl would be there, in a garage targeted for demolition. A strange, unremarkable place to start his new life, but there it stood in its mediocrity. He didn't question how he knew; he just did. Lucas crossed the street, picking up his pace as he got closer. Flashes of a girl teased his mind in precious fragments. She carried the face of his future, every shade and color of her.

The girl in his head came to him in prisms of crystal. Her essence was reflected in countless images caught in the refraction of bouncing light. He imprinted every glimpse of her into his memory. Her skin, a soft curve of a lip, the incredible way her mind held him without a touch. He didn't have to see her to know everything he sensed about her would be real.

She had blinded him to everything—even the van driving slowly behind him.

Griffith Park Zoo

Gabe didn't realize how tired he'd been until he lowered the hood to his old truck and blew out the candles he'd worked by—except for one. Cupping a hand near the flame so it wouldn't blow out, he carried the monster candle to where the girl slept.

Rayne. Her name reminded him of springtime and music and a life when he could dance in the rain—the last time he felt safe…and loved.

Under the flickering light of a candle, he stood over her now, gazing down as she slept on her stomach. Hearing the rhythm of her breathing relaxed him, and with her eyes closed, he could stare at her all he wanted. He could've stayed there, watching her sleep, but that would only be torture over a life he could never have. He knelt and pulled the blanket over her shoulder.

With his truck ready to run, Gabe knew she'd soon wake up and leave. She had a brother to find, and despite how much he wanted to help her, he couldn't. He didn't have a choice. Even if she asked for his help, he'd have to say no. Yeah, he'd come off looking like a major jerk wad and he'd totally deserve the tag.

It would be better for her to get pissed at him for refusing to help than to drag her into his screwed-up existence. Gabriel backed away from where she slept and crawled into the flatbed of his truck to shut his eyes for a while. Before he blew out the candle, he looked at the girl's face. Maybe for one night she'd keep the nightmares away.

Maybe.

West Hollywood

Before he spotted a way through the fence of the condemned parking garage, Lucas saw a dark van hit the gas as he crossed the street. The headlights were blinding as the vehicle barreled for him. It swerved at the last second and screeched to the curb. Shadows moved behind the windshield. When a door slid open, an interior light came on and Lucas saw two men jump out. He didn't stick around to see what they wanted.

Lucas didn't yell for help. He didn't have to. He let his mind reach out—to her.

I got company.

Yeah, we see. What she said almost stopped him cold. *We?* This time, she'd heard him, too. Lucas didn't know what to think, but he had no choice now. These men were Believers. Every instinct in his body told him so.

Around back. Look for a hole in the fence, she told him. *Head for the garage roof. That's where we'll be. Stall them.*

Stall them? Lucas knew he couldn't stall these guys for long. They were too fast and in better shape. Whatever came next, he would lead them to her—*to them*. None of it felt right, but he did as she said. As he rounded the corner to a long city block, he spotted a section of cyclone fence that had been cut and bent. He hunched a shoulder and shoved his way through the opening without slowing down. His skin stung where the metal raked and slashed his back and an arm, but Lucas didn't stop.

He ran up an entrance ramp and got swallowed by shadows, feeling his way to her. Every step he took, he heard the men closing in on him, but he didn't look over his shoulder. He focused only on her, even with his legs burning and his lungs heaving for air.

Lucas took every shortcut. He ducked and hid when he could and changed directions in the dark to stall, but he couldn't shake them. When he got to the garage rooftop, he had nothing left—and worse, he didn't see the girl. She wasn't on the roof. With nowhere else to go, he turned to face the three men who had chased him most of the night. His body covered in sweat, he gasped for air and could hardly stand from the stitch in his side.

"Hold it…r-right there," Lucas yelled and held up a hand. "You're surrounded."

"You little sh-shit." The tall guy spat.

The three men looked like cops or ex-military with their buzz cuts, G.I. Joe muscles, right down to the Dockers and polo shirts they wore like uniforms. The tall one looked in charge and apparently had no sense of humor. When he waved a hand, the other two grabbed Lucas by the arms. He shoved his weight and kicked, but the men were too strong.

"Call my s-sister Mia," he panted. "Tell her…I can't go b-back to that hospital."

"Well, you're right about not goin' back there, but I think we need to get somethin' straight." G.I. Joe glared and clenched his jaw. "I bet you think this is a big misunderstanding."

Lucas stopped struggling. The guy stared at him and never blinked. Not once.

"But you need perspective on how things are gonna be," the man said. "And I know just where to start."

When the guy stepped closer, Lucas flinched and shoved back. Still, the man never blinked.

G.I. Joe grabbed him by the throat and said, "First, you're gonna pay for making us run."

Lucas felt the pain of the first punch and saw stars. The rest made him numb, as if the assault were happening to someone else. An agonizing slow motion he couldn't stop. City lights and faceless shadows made a hellish merry-go-round until everything came to a sudden stop.

When Lucas saw shadows appear on the parapet wall, he turned to look as the guy threw a punch. On impact, he lost his balance and stumbled backward when the men holding him had let go. Lucas fell to the ground and hit his head on the cement, hard. The shock sent stars shooting across his eyes, and a blinding headache drove shards of pain down his neck. He escaped by letting his mind drift away. He felt weightless and free of his failing body.

"Why did you let go of him, assholes?" G.I. Joe yelled.

"Because of them," one guy said, raising his arm.

Lucas heard the muffled exchange between the men and saw a blur of movement as G.I. Joe looked over his shoulder to where his man pointed. He didn't have to see straight to know who had joined the party. Lucas sensed the girl strongest now, in the twilight between hurting and merciful oblivion. Fighting the blackness, he had to see her. He raised his head and looked. Even with the men standing over him, he found her shadowy silhouette that seemed to come out of nowhere.

She wasn't alone.

Standing on top of the garage parapet wall, she stood shoulder to shoulder with the others—the voices Lucas had heard. Every one of them had brilliant blue auras. They were like him. The white noise of their whispers got louder and sounded like the buzz of a beehive until the words became clearer as he connected to them. One word stood out and stayed with him—*home*—a word he hadn't felt in a long time. When he gazed into the faces of the others, none of them looked afraid. They glared at G.I. Joe and his men as if they were intruders, trespassing on their turf.

"Back off," the man said. "This is none of your business."

"It is, actually. He's very much my business." The girl crossed her arms and narrowed her eyes. "He's mine."

"You have no idea who you're dealing with," the man threatened and pulled a gun from the waistband of his pants.

"I could say the same." The girl didn't flinch at the sight of his weapon.

When a slow smile spread across her face, she jumped off the parapet wall and moved closer. The others followed and tightened their circle around the men, who were outnumbered, but the gun kept G.I. Joe in charge until the girl stepped in front of the others.

"There's no need for violence," she said with her voice low and disturbingly calm. "You don't want to harm this boy...or us. Nobody has to get hurt."

The man had a smirk on his face that faded fast. He stared at the girl until his breathing became shallow and strained.

"What are you...?" When the man stopped, the gun in his hand shook. The tremor inched up his arm as if it crawled under his skin, a living, breathing thing. "Stop doing wh-whatever you're doing…or I'll sh-shoot."

"I can't let you do that." She cocked her head, an innocent gesture, and time froze.

Lucas sensed the struggle between the girl and the man. He half expected to hear the blast of the gun, but that didn't happen. In a shocking move, when G.I. Joe couldn't control his tremors, he dropped his weapon. He held his hand as if it hurt, and with eyes wide, he backed off in a sudden panic.

Two blond-haired boys stepped in front of the girl and confronted the men. The boys were little and skinny and they looked exactly alike. Lucas thought he saw double. The moon captured the color of their hair and reflected it, giving the twins an odd glow. Their faces made them look like angels, but their eyes and their defiance told a different story.

The boys were…*peculiar.*

Lucas couldn't hold his head up anymore. With his headache getting worse, he collapsed and stared into a steel-gray sky dotted with fading stars until he closed his eyes and gave in to the dark.

Not even the sound of the three men yelling kept him awake.

Griffith Park Zoo

Something woke Rayne. Whatever it had been, it lingered on the fringes of her mind, a memento of her restless sleep. She opened her eyes and stared at a corrugated metal ceiling. The pale glow of morning filled the shed and had replaced the shadows that she remembered from last night. It took her a moment to realize where she was. Gabriel must have finished working on his truck. The candles were out and the hood down. She would've stayed under the warm blanket, but when she didn't see him, Rayne sat up.

That was when she heard it, the vague noise that must've stirred her awake. A moan. A gasp. Something jarred the truck. When she heard a miserable cry, she threw back the covers and ran toward the back of the vehicle. The tailgate was down. Gabriel had fallen asleep in the bed of his truck.

The nightmare had been his.

Rayne crawled onto the flatbed, but as he thrashed and cried out, she wasn't sure what to do. She'd read that waking someone in the middle of a nightmare might be traumatic, but letting him suffer didn't seem right, either.

"Gabriel. It's me, Rayne. You're having a bad dream."

"Hellboy. Come," he mumbled. "What is it, boy?"

She touched his arm to wake him, but when she did, he grabbed her with a tortured expression on his face. He looked trapped in a nightmare. Staring into his haunted eyes, Rayne knew he'd be beyond her reach, but when a whine and the faint click of a dog's paws on the concrete floor outside the truck made her jump, her fear shifted into overdrive. She heard Gabe's ghost dog and felt its presence as if she could reach out and touch it, except that she couldn't. Her eyes followed the sounds, but she saw nothing.

Nothing!

"I'm warning you. If you get near me, I'm gonna mark your territory. Back off, Casper."

Rayne felt like an idiot, talking to nothing and telling nothing to back off. She didn't know what to do, but Gabriel took that decision away from her. He got up and leaped off the truck as if he were on a mission. Rayne kept her distance, but she followed him.

She had a bad feeling.

Gabriel headed for his sleeping bag with his eyes wide open, as if he were fully awake. He grabbed his sketch pad and a charcoal pencil and sat cross-legged on his bedroll. Out of breath, he panted and stared at nothing, seeing past her and everything else. He rocked back and forth, still in the throes of his misery with his hand racing across his sketchbook.

He drew what he saw in his mind—*without looking down.*

"Gabriel. Are you…awake?"

In unfaltering strokes, he filled the blank page. Sweat trickled from his temple and he winced as if the effort of drawing pained him. Rayne inched closer. With shaking fingers, she brushed back a strand of his dark hair and trailed a finger down his flushed cheek. Nothing woke him.

"That's my sketchbook. It's private."

Gabriel's words repeated in her head as she watched him draw. He looked possessed by a vision only he could see. Stopping him now would be out of the question. Rayne fixed her gaze on the page, eager to see what had been so important to him. A terrified face of a scared boy with long dark hair and pale eyes took shape on the paper. She dropped to her knees to look over his shoulder. With his drawing almost finished, she'd seen enough. Rayne gasped as she realized what Gabriel had done.

The face of her missing brother stared back and a huge hand had him by the throat. Lucas looked scared. *Terrified.*

 { **5** }

Griffith Park Zoo

"Gabriel. Listen to me." On her knees, Rayne held his face in her hands. She stared into his glazed eyes as he sat on his sleeping bag with his sketchbook in his lap.

"What did you see? Tell me." She gave him a gentle shake, hoping he'd wake up.

"What…h-happened?" Gabriel finally fixed on her, but he looked dazed. He slumped in exhaustion and leaned into her arms. Rayne held him, totally confused by what she'd witnessed, but she needed answers. For Lucas.

"I need you to talk to me." She hugged him tighter and whispered in his ear, "Please, no lies this time."

"What are you talking about?" he mumbled as he pulled away from her. "Omission isn't lying…exactly."

Rayne grabbed the sketch pad and held up the drawing of Lucas.

"Tell me about him. What did you see?" She jabbed a finger at the page. "It looked like you had a vision."

"No, that's…nothing. I have dreams, not visions. I draw. No big deal."

Gabe turned away, unable to look her in the eye. He had a wall of secrets, and she had a feeling his sketchbook visions were only part of the things he wanted to keep from her. Somehow she had to find a way to reach him. Gabriel was definitely a puzzle she wanted to piece together, but after seeing what he'd drawn, Lucas needed her more.

"Gabe, you don't understand. That boy you drew, that's my brother, Lucas. He's missing."

"What?" He grabbed the notepad and stared at what he'd drawn. "Are you sure? Maybe I just suck."

"That drawing, it's practically a photo. You're a damned Michelangelo. You don't suck."

"But I don't know your brother. How can I draw him?"

"You tell me, van Gogh."

"You shouldn't do that."

"Do what?"

"Van Gogh was a Dutch Postimpressionist, totally different from an Italian Renaissance painter like Michelangelo."

"Art history? Really?" She stared at him in total disbelief. "Don't go Rain Man on me. Please…I need you to focus."

Rayne tossed the art book down and held his face again. She forced him to look into her eyes. "Right now. Close your eyes and remember what you saw. Don't leave anything out."

After a long moment of strained silence, Gabriel did as she asked. He shut his eyes and talked. Some of what he told her didn't make sense. He talked about Christmas lights and pirate treasure where X marked the spot. By the time he ran out of things to say, his vague recollections weren't much help, except to make her more worried. Lucas had been scared. That showed in the drawing. Gabe didn't know why Luke had a beefy hand at his throat, and he tried to downplay that part, to make her feel better, but it didn't.

"That's it," he said. "That's all I remember. Whatever I saw, it wasn't like a video. I only get impressions. I could be way off base."

Rayne wiped her eyes with the back of her hand.

"These visions of yours…the dreams? Are they…?" She held back, not wanting to say what was on her mind, but she had to. "Are your visions what's already happened…or are they something in the future, things that can be changed?"

Gabriel heaved a sigh and raked a hand through his hair.

"I have no idea. Before you, I didn't even know any of these kids were real. Now I don't…" He didn't finish. Gabe picked up his sketchbook and flipped through the faces, stopping on the scariest ones as if he were reliving what he'd seen. Rayne wanted to hug him, but he looked rapt in misery that no one else could fix.

He shut his eyes and sighed. "Why didn't I know they were…real?"

"I don't know, Gabriel." She touched his cheek, fighting a lump in her throat. "But I gotta find my brother. Will you help me? You're the only one who's *seen* him."

Gabe did a double take and stared at her way too long. When he didn't volunteer to search for her brother, heat rushed to her face and she narrowed her eyes.

"Luke's in trouble. You saw that and I believe that you did. I need you, Gabriel."

"I'm the last one you need. Trust me." He shook his head. "What about your family? Why haven't they gone to the police? Can't the cops help? They got guns and uniforms and stuff."

She thought about telling him her complicated story and sharing that Luke had escaped Haven Hills, but she didn't know how Gabriel would take it. A kid on the loose from a mental hospital would give him plenty of reason for not getting involved and saying no.

"I can't go to them. It's a long story." Rayne flashed back to her sister's face. Mia had cops on her church's payroll and an agenda when it came to Lucas. Calling the police would be a waste of time and only draw attention to what she really needed to do—find Lucas and talk to him without Mia.

"I don't know what you expect me to do," Gabe said. "Sleep until I create another masterpiece? I can't control this stuff. And I'm…not exactly doin' it on my own."

"What are you talking about? I saw you draw Lucas. You were *sleep-drawing*." Before he detoured into another lie, she remembered something else about his nightmare. "Who's Hellboy?"

"What?" Gabriel glared at her as if she'd slapped him for no reason. "Where did that come from? Hellboy's a comic book hero."

"Yeah, for normal people, but that's the name of your ghost dog, too," she argued. "Where did you find him? Scooby-Doo-gatory?"

Gabe didn't answer. He needed convincing.

"When he torched you, he yanked you into *X-Files* territory, didn't he?" She touched his arm. "I saw Hellboy at the tunnels. And while you were dreaming, you called his name and he came running like a good boy. I heard him whine, Gabe. He scared the hell out of me, but I know what I heard and didn't see."

Okay, that sounded weird even to her, but from the look in his eyes, Gabe had grown tired. Dodging questions had turned into an Olympic-caliber event for him. She didn't have any proof and her accusations were totally absurd. All she had left were her instincts about him. Something about Gabe made her think he came from money. The way he spoke, his quiet confidence, the art stuff he pulled from nowhere, even his weird humor and how he stacked his clothes—something clicked that he wasn't a typical runaway. Everything in her bones told her he was a good guy with one helluva story.

Besides, she had no one else.

"Will you help me, Gabriel?"

When he looked her in the eye and clenched his jaw, Rayne stared at his lips, willing them to say what she wanted, but that didn't happen.

"I...can't," he said.

When Gabe got up and headed for his truck, Rayne felt gut punched.

The girl had ripped him up inside. Gabe couldn't look into Rayne's smoky eyes, glistening with worry and hope, and let her believe that he'd be the answer to her problems. He was no one's answer—*to anything*. He got up and pretended to mess with his truck.

Jerk! Finding out that the faces in his sketchbook were real had heaped the icing on his stupid pity cake. *What a loser!*

All this time he thought his nightmares were a punishment he deserved—a parting gift from a father who only saw him as a freak and his personal failure—something to be fixed. It hadn't even occurred to Gabe that the kids in his dreams were real, because hiding out had become his life. Now that he knew those faces weren't conjured from his own demons, he'd have a choice to make—risk everything to get involved or turn into a guy who only cared about his own ass.

Some choice.

Rayne's brother, Lucas, had definitely stepped into something nasty. Gabe had held back what he'd seen, for her sake. Lucas had been terrified, not just a little scared. And the guy with a meaty hand at her brother's throat might've taken out his anger on him. Right before Rayne woke him, Gabe felt pain before his connection zapped out.

But something even more disturbing hit him—something he hadn't told Rayne.

During the dream, some of the faces that he'd already drawn flashed in his mind. He hadn't remembered that until he flipped through his sketchbook again. Maybe those kids were trying to tell him something. What if Lucas wasn't the only one in danger? *What a screwed-up mess!* Given his situation, cops were out. Even if he got involved, without Rayne knowing, he could make things worse.

Time and effort. That was what it had taken for him to find a quiet existence, living off the grid where he wasn't on the run. What he had wasn't much, but he lived with his choices because they affected only him. Now that he knew about Lucas and these other kids, sitting on the sidelines felt wrong. But if he got involved, his troubles could bring on a new level of hurt to kids who already had it bad.

Gabe didn't know what to do. Only one thing seemed clear. He had to let Rayne go, even if he looked like a jerk for not helping her.

"I could use a lift for me and my bike," she said, low and soft. "Are you still offering?"

Gabe didn't see her come up behind him. He couldn't turn around. When he heard her voice, his guilt barometer hit the red zone. Smacking him upside the head with a baseball bat would've hurt less.

"Yeah." He shut the tailgate to his truck. "Look, I know this won't mean much, but—" he looked over his shoulder "—I'm sorry. I hope you find him."

Rayne didn't say anything. She didn't have to. Nothing she could've said or done would make him feel any worse.

Downtown L.A.
An Hour Later

Cut into the side of a hill covered in vines and weeds and scraggly trees, a shadowy tunnel entrance gaped its dark mouth to swallow an old railroad track that led into it. This section of downtown L.A. had been a busy warehouse district.

Now not much went on. That was why they used it.

"I'll catch up. You take Benny," Rafe Santana told Kendra Walker as they unloaded the stolen van. "I gotta ditch the wheels."

Rafe had more in mind than getting rid of evidence. With the new kid still unconscious, that meant the others had to carry him the rest of the way and they'd be distracted. He wanted to make sure they weren't followed.

"Be careful," she said as she touched his chest with her hand.

As she rounded up the others and hauled the hurt kid to where they could take care of him, Rafe looked down to see Benny hadn't left.

"But I wanna stay with you," the kid argued, tugging at his shirt with his face scrunched tight.

Rafe knelt in front of Benny.

"I know you do, but I need you to take care of my girl." He spoke low when Kendra and the others got out of earshot and he brushed off the kid's T-shirt with his hand, a shirt he'd given him that was too big for the ten-year-old.

"Now, go on. Git," he told him.

The kid didn't say another word. He kicked at the dirt and made a big show of hating every step he took, but little man did as he was told. Rafe jumped back into the van and drove it miles away from the tunnel entrance. When the cops found it, the stolen vehicle wouldn't lead back to them.

Rafe ran to catch up with the others. Alone in the dark, he looked over his shoulder until he felt satisfied no one followed him. Until he met Kendra, he didn't know that L.A. had miles of abandoned tunnels under its downtown streets. At the turn of the century, she told him, they used them to connect different sections of Los Angeles to downtown, but when superhighways got built, the old railroad and car tunnels were abandoned. They even filmed movies under the streets of downtown. *The Matrix*. *Planet of the Apes*. Kendra knew stuff like that. She was real smart.

Once he got deep in the tunnels, Rafe picked up his pace and used a shortcut. He had a small flashlight with him, but he rarely needed it. Using it meant his night vision would be messed up. He followed familiar metal railways and climbed rusted spiral stairs to catch up to Kendra and the others. The musty, dank smell used to stink to him. Now it didn't.

In the dark, the mysterious painted murals on the chipped brick walls were unmarred by graffiti, reminding him how old the tunnels were. Sometimes he'd sit and look at them alone, like they were his private museum. Rusted old machinery, encrusted in dust and cobwebs, had been abandoned long ago. He liked them, too. They were landmarks for him to know which way to go. Some people would be afraid, but to him the tunnels were home.

As he got closer to Kendra, he sensed something wasn't right up ahead. Something moved, out of place. A smell he hadn't counted on. *Something.* He'd quit second-guessing his nature long ago. He trusted it.

"Argh!" A little voice growled like a tunnel beast, and a small shadow leaped from behind a fallen brick wall. The giggling gave Benny away. Rafe pretended to be scared.

"Oh, man. You really got me, dawg." He grinned. "You waitin' for me?"

Benny jammed a tiny shoulder against his leg and gave him a bump. Rafe never had a little brother. He never had a use for one until Benny came along. The kid wouldn't have lasted on the streets of L.A. alone. The way Rafe saw it, he had no choice but to let the kid hang with him. Taking care of Benny, he didn't feel like such a loser.

"You should've let me come with you." The kid kicked at the dirt and hung his head. "No one sees me unless I want 'em to. You know that."

"Yeah, I know, but I needed you to stay with Kendra. You know how it is." Rafe shrugged. "When I'm not around, all she's got is you, little man."

When he first came to live in the tunnels, Benny knew he wasn't like Rafe and the others. He didn't have special skills. Rafe felt bad for him until the runt came up with his own gig. Benny turned into a superhero-ninja dude. He didn't see the harm in letting the kid believe he could disappear *whenever*. Rafe grabbed Benny and swung him up high, letting him straddle his shoulders. The kid liked that.

Without a word, Rafe let Kendra know where he was when he got close enough for her to read him. *I'm on your six. Don't sic the twins on me.* When he caught up to her, he had a smirk on his face as he carried Benny.

"Hey, Benny." Kendra grinned up at the kid on Rafe's shoulders before she said, "I see your shadow found you."

"Yeah, he did. As always." Rafe lowered Benny and ran a hand through his hair. "I'll catch up with you later, chump. Right now I gotta help my girl, here."

The kid made a face and gave him a sly smile before he puckered his lips in a fake kiss and left. Rafe narrowed his eyes at the kid without saying anything. When he was alone with Kendra, he couldn't help but talk about what happened. He felt jacked up by it. They were all getting stronger. Working their skills, instead of always hiding them, felt good—like lifting weights and pumping up.

"Glad the Effin brothers are on our side." Rafe grinned. "Those guys practically wet themselves runnin' away from the mutts."

From the glow off his flashlight, he saw Kendra smile. She

got off on scrambling the brains of the Believers' meat army. The twins had a way of making a lasting impression that would keep those chumps running scared, pounding each other and scarfing food like they were starving. By the time the effects wore off, they'd have to turn in their man cards.

All of that would buy Kendra time—to get the new kid stashed and back on his feet. Even though the new guy couldn't feel it, Kendra held his hand as the others carried him. She always got real protective of the fresh-picked ones.

"The twins are a wonder. No doubt," she said.

The twelve-year-old identical twins scared Rafe with their freakish blue eyes and pure blond hair, but he'd never said that aloud. The Effin brothers were never apart. They did everything together. Rafe had never heard them say much. Their choice. Except for Kendra, no one really communicated with them—not in any way Rafe understood—but he could tell the boys had other ways to entertain each other.

Kendra had nicknamed them the Effin brothers because of what they could do. Rafe didn't understand the science of it like Kendra did. She said the twins could tap into a gland in the human brain—something like a hippo-talmus—that controlled the four F's of human behavior. Feeding, fighting, fleeing and hooking up, something like that. Those twins were short and skinny, but they could seriously mess with anyone's head and make them do whatever. Like a puppet.

Those men found *that* out.

Rafe didn't know if Effin was their real last name. It sounded French the way Kendra pronounced it. She had to spell it for him. Sometimes she laughed when she called them that, but real names didn't matter much to her, or maybe she liked the idea of starting over fresh.

When they got to the deepest part of the tunnels, Kendra had the new kid put into her room. Rafe had never seen her do that before. He wasn't sure he liked it, but it was hard to argue with her. He had to work double hard to block his thoughts so she wouldn't know. Secrets were exhausting.

"Put him on my mattress. And get me rags, a bowl of water and a med kit. He may need stitching."

While the rest of them scrambled and brought her what she needed, Rafe stayed out of her way and watched Kendra from a distance. She lit candles to see and stripped the kid of his ragged clothes after she searched his pockets.

"No ID," she said. "I only found a phone number written on scrap paper. No name."

"I could find out who it belongs to. I gotta hit topside tomorrow. I got something to do. I can call the number. Want me to try it?"

Rafe fought a smile as he thought about what he had planned for tomorrow. A surprise. Kendra looked like she could use something special.

"No, don't worry about it." She stuffed the paper into her pocket. "Not yet."

"I'm goin' anyway if you change your mind."

Kendra didn't seem to hear him. She looked over the kid's body for bloody holes to plug. He had a mean gash on his back and arm and a knot the size of a baseball on the back of his head, too. She'd gotten good at playing doctor, but something in the way she took special care of this kid made Rafe... *worry*. He waited for things to settle down and for the others to leave before he had her alone.

"Those men. They saw our faces this time. You even gave them a taste of what you can do. What were you thinking?" he asked.

Rafe asked a question he already knew the answer to. Kendra had gotten more over-the-top on everything she did. It was like she dared anyone to stop her.

"We've talked about this, Rafe. I got a plan, remember?"

Rafe knew Kendra had a mission to save kids like them, but in the latest confrontations with the Believers, she got in their face in her quiet and controlled way. He didn't know what to think.

"It's like you're rubbing their noses in it," he said. "That could put us in their crosshairs on their timetable, not ours. You picked that old garage to meet this kid because there weren't surveillance cameras, but why show our faces to those assholes?"

"We pulled it off. That's all that counts."

"You wanted them to see us…to feel your power." Rafe narrowed his eyes at Kendra when he realized what she must have done. "Is that why you waited until the kid made it to the rooftop…while there was light enough for those men to see? This kid got hurt because you waited, Kendra."

"I had no way of knowing that would happen. If I thought he'd get hurt, I never would have done that." Kendra's voice cracked. "I'm tired of being a victim when we have every right to exist as they do. In the open. Free."

She turned back to the new boy and dabbed a bloody, wet towel across his forehead, tending to his wounds. The kid hadn't opened his eyes yet. She took a deep breath and heaved a ragged sigh.

"We're human beings, Raphael. We're just…different. We're better than they are and that makes them afraid. They hunt us, yet we're the ones they treat like unworthy animals. It isn't right."

"I didn't mean to accuse you of anything. I know what happened to this kid was an accident. I just get…afraid for you sometimes. You take on too much. I wish you would let me help you more." He knelt by her side and stared into her watery eyes.

Her lips curved into a sad smile and she said, "I couldn't do any of this without you. You know that, right?"

After Rafe nodded, she handed him a bowl of bloodstained water and he took it.

"I could use fresh water," she said.

"Is he gonna die?"

"Don't know." She brushed back the kid's hair. "I can't feel him anymore. Don't know what that means, but it scares me."

"You'll fix him. You're good at that."

"I gotta get to the garden. Figure stuff out," she muttered. "He's gonna need the best I got."

Rafe didn't know how Kendra knew the things she did. She had a thing for plants and healing, but what she did with her mind made her different, even among them.

"The Believers send their hunters, and each one is like a rabid pit bull on two legs," he said. "This time, we had a gun shoved in our faces. These guys are crazy."

"I had everything under control. You saw that."

"Yeah, and I got pumped seeing it. No lie, but maybe next time you won't be in control, Kendra."

Rafe hadn't planned on stirring things up with her again, but the words were out of his mouth before he could stop. Kendra always pushed. It was what she did, but the more chances she took, the more she threatened what they already had. Rafe and Benny had found a home in the tunnels, but he felt a clock ticking down to a detonation he couldn't stop— not without Kendra, the girl who had lit the fuse in the first place, torched it with a damned flame thrower.

"Every time the Believers take one of us, it should make you angry like it does me," she argued. "We have a right to be the way we are. We have a right to question their world. All I want to do is put our mark on it. That's how movements start, Raphael. Don't you want to be part of something bigger than we are?"

"Yeah, sure. I guess."

Rafe couldn't argue with her. If Kendra hadn't found him and Benny, who knew what would've happened. There were worse places than juvie and foster care, thanks to the church freaks. Kendra had been the one with a mission to save the world, a kid at a time. That was how she found him and Benny and the others. She made them feel like somebody, not a piece of throwaway garbage. She gave them a family and treated them like they mattered.

Kendra was only seventeen, a year younger than him. He didn't know how she got to be brainy and pigheaded at the same time.

"We've been lucky, but if you keep snatching these kids out from under their noses, they could focus on us. That's all I'm saying," he cautioned. "From what you said, they got money and powerful people in their back pocket. Doesn't that scare you, even a little?"

When she didn't answer or look at him, Rafe lowered his voice. He reached out his hand to touch her shoulder, but stopped.

"Because of you, we're getting stronger," he said. "But I'm not sure we can handle whatever they throw at us. How long before they target you, Kendra?"

Rafe didn't tell her how much that would kill him. When she didn't say anything, he did as she asked.

"I'll get you fresh water."

Rafe brought back a bucket of water and set it down near her makeshift bed, along with fresh rags. He didn't say anything. For that, Kendra had been grateful. He only shot her a worried glance and left her alone with the new one, the pretty one—*the special one.*

She drenched a new rag with water and wiped his face and chest. Combinations of medicinal herbs raced through her head. She dismissed them as fast as she thought them up. She couldn't afford to guess. Not with this boy. Every bruise, every gash on his body hurt her, too. Rafe had guessed right. She had stalled getting to the deserted parking garage. This boy got hurt because of her. She'd messed up and he'd paid the price. The crack on his head worried her most.

Everything bad happened because of her.

She touched his cheek and felt his fever. A concussion was serious and a brain swell could kill him. Treating the wounds on his body kept her busy, but patching him up on the outside wouldn't fix what kept him from opening his eyes.

She didn't know if she'd done the right thing—for him.

I'm so sorry. This is my fault.

If she'd made the decision to take him to a real doctor, she knew what that would've meant. To run the risk of exposing her street family would have compounded their problem, and the Believers could've found the boy easily. Without anyone knowing, he'd disappear and never get a second chance at freedom. The Believers had a far reach and she'd learned not to trust *anyone,* but how *she* felt about stuff didn't mean he believed it, too.

Living different and free had become precious to her and not something to take for granted. Her kind had become perfect victims. The very act of speaking out would bring on what they feared most—people knowing what they were becoming. A spotlight would make their struggle worse on a global scale. Kendra knew how *she* felt about that. She'd rather die than be anyone's slave or lab rat, but did this boy feel the same? Would he risk death for what he believed?

Without thinking, she'd taken that decision away from him.

There were times—*like now*—that Kendra didn't feel strong enough, or smart enough, or old enough to take care of her new family. Some of these kids were children. They looked up to her—and she put on a good show—but sometimes she didn't feel worthy of their loyalty. With the stakes escalating, so were her doubts. She felt part of something bigger, yet completely unworthy of it.

She woke up scared and heard things in the dark that reminded her she was still only a kid—a kid who had screwed up and gotten someone seriously hurt. She brushed back the boy's hair and touched a trembling finger to his pale lips, something she never would've done if he were awake.

I just found you. Don't…leave me, please. I can't do this on my own anymore.

Kendra prayed he heard her. If he died, she wouldn't even know his name.

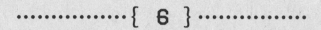

{ 6 }

Downtown L.A.
Hours Later

Pain gripped Lucas long before he opened his eyes. It slithered from his throbbing head down his back, inflicting damage wherever it went. Even his fingertips hurt. He felt the heat of a fever behind his eyes and through his chest. When he finally cracked his eyelids open, shadows spiraled like smoke in front of him. The blur, dotted with pinpoints of light, triggered his memory of being on that garage rooftop when he gazed at the stars before everything turned black.

He felt sick and fought the urge to puke by taking deep breaths. When his mind cleared enough to question what had happened, he looked for answers in the room where he lay. A flicker of light made shadows move on a wall across from him. It took him a while to realize the faint glow came from a burning candle.

Thick and muggy, an odor hung heavy in the air and made it hard to breathe at first, until he got used to it. He couldn't tell where it came from, but as he breathed it in, it calmed him. When he looked down, his arm had a bandage of gauze loosely tied. He saw the edge of a wet poultice under it. Green stuff that looked like crushed plants.

He felt the strong presence of a healer, although he'd never met one.

When his vision cleared enough for him to see farther, he looked up and got lost in what he saw over his head. A faded mural of an old railroad station stretched across a high wall. It had passengers dressed in turn-of-the-century clothing, and the wall painting had been done over red bricks that had chipped off through the years. The damage made an odd pattern, sparking his mind to look for animal shapes in the missing pieces like he did when he saw clouds drift across a summer sky.

It reminded him of the elaborate street graffiti painted on the tunnel walls at the old Griffith Park Zoo, only the vast mural looked like something found in a museum.

Beautiful, isn't it? Like you.

The girl's voice whispered from inside his ear.

I thought you weren't…going to make it.

Slowly Lucas turned to look for her. He squinted into the candlelight and found her in the shadows, sitting on a wooden crate. She pulsed in a cobalt-blue aura and looked as serene as the deep blue of the ocean. He recognized the curve of her lips, the soft pink of her skin, and the odd mix of defiance and vulnerability in her dark eyes. He'd seen her before in the crystal fragments of his mind, but because she'd been his first, they shared an intimacy of mind that connected them deeper than anything Lucas had ever felt. It was as if he had *always* known her.

Fighting his pain, he cleared his parched throat. He could have sent her a message without using his voice, but speaking aloud made her real and not just a distant voice in his head.

"You're…the one," he said. "The girl…in m-my head, aren't you?"

She came with water for him to drink and knelt by him

with a fragile smile. When he saw her eyes filling with tears, he had his answer. Even though it hurt to move, Lucas reached for her hand.

Don't cry, he told her. *I'm here.*

Lucas Darby. He'd told her his name and she shared hers. In that instant, a faint melody played in Kendra's head, sweet white noise that calmed her. She wondered if he heard the music, too. She saw the pain in his eyes that he tried to cover with a smile. Touching him, talking and hearing his real voice as she looked into his pale gray eyes had made their bond stronger, something she hadn't known would be possible.

"I can't be certain, of course…" she began. "I'm pretty sure you have a concussion, but I'll take care of you."

I'm sorry you got hurt.

Having him with her, Kendra used her voice to speak to him in private, mostly. Thoughts slipped from her to him that she really should have controlled better, but she couldn't help it. She was excited to be with someone like him, someone more powerful than she was.

"You're the healer." He didn't ask. He knew.

"Yes." She smiled. "I'm learning."

"Good. Being here with you, it's like nothing I've ever felt before. It's gonna take practice…for both of us." Lucas smiled. "The drugs they gave me at the hospital, they screwed me up. I got lost. They made me feel like I drowned. I don't feel as strong as you."

"Oh, but you are," she answered in a rush. When she laid a hand on his bare chest, she yanked it back as if she'd touched a flame. "I…I c-can feel it. The way we connected. That was you."

Lucas sighed and winced in obvious pain. She gave him

water, a little at a time. When his eyes became heavy, she knew he needed to sleep, but she could tell he had questions.

"Will you show me…what you do?" he asked. "Be my…teacher?"

Kendra reached for his hand and laced her fingers in his. The minute she touched his skin with hers, she felt a surge of energy up her arm and through her body. *That* had come from him, too, not her.

"Do you feel that?" she asked him. When he only shook his head, Kendra squeezed his fingers and said, "You will. Your body is weak now, but you have no idea what you're capable of."

"All my life, teachers and doctors acted like what I am is…wrong. Like I'm defective and it's my fault," he told her. "But hearing you inside me, it feels like I can finally breathe on my own. I don't know how to explain it."

"That's just it. Here, you don't have to explain anything. You belong…with us, Lucas."

A smile tugged at his lips for only a second before he shut his eyes. She knew the comfort of being with her kind, and he would, too, when he got better. Connecting to the hive mind for the first time had been a powerful and profound spiritual awakening that had given her life purpose. Kendra made it her mission to share that experience and nurture the lives of those like her. She found it hard to define the intimacy of the act, even to another of her kind. That connection had to be felt by each Indigo soul.

From the first moment she linked to Lucas's essence and experienced the breadth of his life force, she knew he was different. She'd never felt anything like him before. Kendra had been right to risk everything for him.

He was their future.

She blew out the candle and let him be. When his breathing changed and she knew he was asleep, she rested her head on his chest and shut her eyes, listening to the gentle pulse of his heart.

Kendra didn't let go of his hand. She needed the connection more than he did.

Burbank
The Next Day

"Where the hell have you been? I expected you to nab the kid yesterday."

When O'Dell saw his man Boelens for the first time since he'd assigned him the Darby kid, the guy looked rough. Even on a good day, Boelens had a lizard stare. He never blinked. *Ever.* Now with his disheveled hair, wrinkled clothes and a crazed glare, the man looked like a *Stars Gone Wild* booking photo.

"I don't know what happened." Boelens had gotten back his blink—and an annoying twitch to his lips. "You got anything to eat? I'm starving."

"Eat on your own time," O'Dell said, but Boelens ignored him.

When the man had the audacity to rummage through O'Dell's personal desk drawer, he flexed his snake tattoos and punched Boelens in the arm. The man yelped and blinked like a freak.

"What the hell is the matter with you?"

Before he got an answer, Boelens raced to the small fridge O'Dell had in his office to keep his power-drink supplies and other stuff. When he flung open the refrigerator door, he found O'Dell's private stash of Chinese takeout. Foam containers were marked by date and stacked from top to bottom in chron order.

O'Dell had an unhealthy obsession with Chinese food. He

knew it and didn't care, so when Boelens targeted his General Tso's, O'Dell had to draw the line. He wrestled Boelens away from the fridge and shoved him into a wall, jamming his elbow against the man's throat.

"Talk to me. Tell me what happened," O'Dell demanded. "Don't make me ask twice."

At the sudden show of violence, Boelens cried like a girl. He even drooled. The guy was a total wreck. Eventually he told O'Dell about what happened at an abandoned garage in West Hollywood.

"Where are your men, the ones you took with you?"

"Don't know. They ran. Haven't seen 'em." Boelens turned blue.

"And the MS-13 crew? They were supposed to track the other sister. What happened to them?"

"Don't know that, either. I left messages."

"Hell, why didn't you say so, man? You left messages. Problem solved." O'Dell leaned his body into the guy and limbered up his snake. "Would you recognize the girl who got in your way, if you saw her again?"

"Yeah. Definitely." The man's eyes bugged out like a pug on meth.

"Did she do this to you?"

"Do what?"

O'Dell rolled his eyes and shoved his elbow tighter against the man's windpipe.

"I don't know wh–what happened. I…s–swear," Boelens blubbered. "She had…m–more kids with her. A mind-freak militia."

Boelens had crossed the line into pathetic. O'Dell backed off a little and let the man breathe. He'd gotten everything out of him. The guy was clearly under the influence of something. If those kids had the power to scuttle a man's brain as bad as

Boelens had it, they could be like the Darby kid. Maybe his employer would appreciate his initiative to round up more kids than he was assigned.

The fact that this girl had amassed her own misfit menagerie made him wonder how she connected with them. Maybe this freak could lead him to more of her kind. O'Dell made up his mind. His reputation within the organization would be on the line if he didn't corral the Darby kid soon. He'd pull everyone in and focus his whole operation on Darby. How long could it take to round up one scrawny fifteen-year-old kid? And for good measure, he'd clean out this new girl and her nest of head cases.

"When you get your head on straight, I want you looking through our database for the face of that girl…and any other kid you saw with her. We'll take on our *own* assignment. I can't have those little cockroaches getting in my way."

When his man nodded, O'Dell let Boelens go, after he turned a fine shade of sapphire. He expected the man to do the rational thing and take his bruised ego home until he sobered up before he came back to hit the computers, but that was not what he did. Boelens went straight for O'Dell's fridge and dropped to his knees. He ripped open containers and stuffed handfuls of food into his mouth, paying no attention to the dates written on the cartons.

"Ah, man. At least respect the chron." He threw up his hands and shook his head.

Boelens had lost his mind—and O'Dell had lost his lunch.

Griffith Park
Midnight

At the stroke of midnight, Gabe pulled his sweatshirt hood over his head and grabbed his knapsack, filled with his art supplies and his sketchbook. He left the safety zone of the maintenance shed to head into the night. In the dark, he hiked his way to the tallest hill in Griffith Park—a familiar path—to gaze over the golden lights of the city.

After Rayne left, Gabe couldn't shake her from his mind. Her eyes haunted him with an accusing stare. She had every right to resent his refusal to help her search for Lucas. He hadn't told her why he couldn't risk it, but he had begun to believe that no justification made a good enough excuse. If her brother's life was on the line, Gabe didn't want to be the guy who sat back and did nothing.

"What's up, boy?"

He felt Hellboy with him before his ghost dog made an appearance. When the dog did, Gabe almost lost it. Plain as day, Hellboy hunkered near him, taking care of his personal grooming.

"Dogs lick their junk even after they die? Good to know." He shook his head. "I know guys who'd never leave their room if they could do that."

Despite Hellboy's practical and persistent hygiene efforts, Gabe had grown accustomed to the presence of his phantom dog and craved being around him—especially after he discovered by a fluke what they could do together.

After he'd crossed paths with Rayne and had a dream about her brother, his usual tether to Death and Hellboy had hit a new level of intensity. That was why he'd come. Rayne might have triggered his need to help her, but tonight he'd been drawn to high ground with a greater urgency than ever before. He had to come. He was restless and his skin felt zapped by a strange surge of energy. Even Hellboy looked more alert. Sniffing the air with ears up, the dog paced the ground, listening for sounds carried on the wind that swept through Griffith Park.

"You feel it, too, don't you, big guy?"

The dog stared into the blackness and crept closer to Gabe. In protective mode, Hellboy growled as if he saw something. Part-wolf and all loner, his ghost dog gave off a brutal kinetic energy. Gabe felt the punch of it down his spine. Something was very different tonight, but that wouldn't stop him.

"Let's do this."

With the dog staying tight to his side, Gabe put his knapsack on the ground and gazed up at the stars. He slowed his breathing until the beat of his heart throbbed soft and steady in his ears. Under the vast inky-black umbrella of the night sky, he felt the first wave of assault on his shoulders and his belly. It almost doubled him over in pain. His muscles went taut as a slow-brewing rage swallowed him whole. Flashes of his past stoked the fires of his anger. His father's cruel voice became an undercurrent to his darkest memories when he hid under the covers as a kid, hearing his parents argue late at night when they thought he couldn't hear them.

They only argued over one thing—*him.*

He hated his father for what happened. That hatred sparked a fire in him, but as his rage spread, it always came back to him. That was when his anger kicked into high gear. When the blame came full circle, he felt it in every muscle of his body. He was stoked and ready for what would come next.

Hellboy yelped and circled at his feet with a contagious excitement. Gabe didn't have to open his eyes to know the dog sensed his mind probe. The first time had been by an accident triggered by Hellboy, but since then, each incident allowed him to push the envelope on his newfound ability.

When Gabe felt every molecule in his body break apart and drift—as weightless as the gray, velvet ash swept by the wind off a cold fire pit—he welcomed the unsettling experience and let it happen. When he couldn't contain his rage any longer, he let it blast out in a million pieces. Within seconds, he felt his awareness shift to a trusted and familiar place where he felt whole and calm again.

He saw through Hellboy's eyes after his mind entered the essence of the animal's spirit.

When his two legs felt as if they'd turned into four—and the earth rose up to meet him—Gabe let go of his humanity and imagined Hellboy's animal instincts to be his own. An addictive rush of adrenaline swept through him, and with that feeling, his sense of hearing and smell heightened to an acute awareness, but the feeling carried a message of danger that hit him hard.

Hellboy had understood that, and now he did, too. Something felt different.

Channeling through his dog, he forced his consciousness to reach out beyond where he stood—beyond Hellboy. Pushing his limits, Gabe tested his abilities, feeling stronger and more whole every time he did. In an instant, the dog linked to other creatures of the night like a catalyst, making Gabe's stomach lurch as if he rode a fast-moving roller coaster barreling down a dark track. His arms turned to wings and he felt his body soar across the night sky when he spotted movement below with the nocturnal eyes of a predator.

Still anchored through Hellboy, he catapulted to a great horned owl and felt the essence and power of swift, silent death as the bird stalked a creature in the brush. He sensed the rush of the hunt as the gray ghost swooped low in the dark and extended its talons to snatch its prey off the ground. He felt the tug and weight of the weasel as it struggled to pull free of the claws that tore open its back.

"Oh, sweet Jesus. This is unreal."

Tingles surged through his body and Gabe felt the chill of the blue fire off Hellboy. It whipped through his hair like gusts from a preternatural wind, and his breath turned to vapor from the cold. Connected to everything at once through his dog's spirit, he gorged on the rush of his consciousness hurling from one creature to another. He didn't feel like a messed-up loser on the run. What he experienced through Hellboy and Death made him special.

But when he focused his mind on finding Lucas and using Death and other animals to search, unexpected flashes replaced the owl's hunt in his mind—disturbing imagery that interfered with everything. The whole thing felt wrong. Tonight something sinister lurked in the darkness of his extrasensory world and ambushed him. A head-splitting ache behind his eyes sent a jolt through him.

"Ah," he gasped.

When Gabe collapsed to his knees, Hellboy yapped and licked his fingers, not leaving his side. Gabe winced and grabbed his head with both hands as stabs of bright light blinded him. Even the wind carried punishment. Every gust shot needles across his skin that he felt under his sweatshirt and down his back.

He had no idea where his mind had taken him and felt powerless to control what he saw. He only knew it was important—something he needed to witness and feel. This time it hadn't been a dream. He wasn't asleep. He had one foot on either side, straddling the precipice between the living and the dead. The owl and its prey were gone, replaced by another face that came into focus with crystal clarity. A girl he'd never seen before. Strange, disruptive visions had happened before, but nothing like this. Gabe had to move. *Now!*

He forced his legs to work and stumbled like a drunk through a growing darkness, barely able to see as images battered him. In a blind stupor, he found his rucksack and tore through it by feel. He grabbed his sketch pad and charcoal pencil and collapsed to the ground. Without looking down,

Gabe stared into a vision only he could see and drew what came to his mind.

But memories of his own dark past flooded his head, too. *Pure torture.*

Psychic obstacles forced him to sift through his vision and draw what he sensed would be important. He filtered through the hallucinations and struggled to separate Death's message from his past as his hand raced across the paper. In unfaltering strokes, he filled one blank page and flipped over to add more as he rocked in place. His breathing came in rapid pants and sweat trickled down his spine.

When he sensed that the vision had run its course, he stopped drawing and the pain of his blistering headache left him exhausted. Gabe held up the sketchbook and let the lights of the city shine on the pages. This time he'd done two drawings. One of a girl and another he didn't understand at all.

"That's...weird," he muttered.

As he gazed down at what he'd sketched, a voice made him jump—and Hellboy burst into swirling blue dust that dissolved as it hit the ground.

"What did you see, Gabriel?"

With a shocked expression, Rayne stepped out from the shadows and kept her distance. Her voice sounded shaky and she looked scared...*of him.* This time, even if he wanted to, there'd be no need to lie to her.

Rayne had seen *everything.*

Griffith Park—Overlook

"What the hell was that?" Rayne couldn't control the shake in her voice or the chill over her body that even deadened her toes and fingertips. "I mean…I don't even know what to ask. You caught fire, but everything turned…cold."

She'd seen Gabriel turn into a human torch before, but what remained of her rational brain made her doubt what she'd seen. Maybe Gabe's ghost dog had more to do with the weirdness than he did. She sort of believed in ghosts. Why couldn't dogs hang out in the afterlife? But now, after standing close to Gabe when everything went to *bizarre town,* the magnitude of his transformation scared the hell out of her. It rattled her insides and sent a biting chill racing over her skin.

Gabe wasn't normal. Not even a little bit.

"I want to ask about wh-what you saw…and look at what you sketched, b-but…" she stammered. "I gotta ask. What… are you?"

The minute those words came out of her mouth, Rayne knew she'd hurt him. She saw it on his face, but she couldn't help it. She had too many serious questions that his jokes or vague answers wouldn't satisfy. He'd scared her so badly this time that she thought about running down the hill and never looking back, but Gabe had drawn Lucas's face.

That kept her standing there, shaking in her boots like a lump of Jell-O. The blue kind.

"I don't…know exactly." Gabe didn't look her in the eye. He said the words so low that she almost didn't hear him. When he turned toward her, she backed up a step.

"I know you must be scared over what you saw, but…" He took a deep breath. "I won't hurt you, Rayne. This thing I do, I feel it inside me, but I've never hurt anyone or anything by doing it."

"And the visions? The faces you draw?" she asked.

"Like I told you, I thought they were only harmless dreams, not visions. But this time when I focused on Lucas, it felt different." He got excited as he tried to figure stuff out. "I wasn't asleep and the connection I had with him felt stronger, like it wasn't one-way. He linked back to me too, Rayne. I've never had that happen before. I don't know if it came from him or me, but something weird happened. You were right. I have… visions, I guess."

She stared at him for a long time, not sure what to believe, until she broke the silence.

"What did you draw?"

When he stepped closer, it took all of Rayne's courage not to back away. He handed her his sketchbook, flipped to the page of his first drawing. A girl's face, someone she'd never seen before. She looked asleep, lying on the bare chest of a boy. Only a part of his chin showed, but that glimpse had been enough to trigger Rayne's memory. She turned back a page to see if she was right.

"What is it?" he asked, looking over her shoulder.

"I think this is Lucas." She showed him two pages, bent so he saw both. "See how his lip is cut…and that bruise on his chin and the wound on his arm. The marks are identical and his arm is bandaged in the same spot."

"Oh, wow. You're right." He flashed a quick smile. "Guess it worked."

"What worked?"

Gabe winced. It looked like he would clam up again. Sharing didn't come naturally, that was for sure.

"I came here…to look for your brother."

"You did?"

"Yeah, I kept my focus on him and I guess I got a glimpse. I've never done that before. So cool."

"I thought you weren't gonna help me," Rayne said. "That you didn't care about him."

"Yeah, well. That's what I needed you to believe." He jammed his hands into his pockets. "I got…stuff goin' on, that's all. But it doesn't mean I don't care what happens to your brother…or you."

"Yeah?" Rayne fought to keep a straight face.

"Yeah." Gabe did his best shy boy.

"If you were plannin' on helping me on the fly, does that mean you're in?"

"Don't read into this, Rayne. I still got problems. I could be an epic fail for you and Lucas."

"I think he's already there, Gabe. I need to find him." She took a deep breath. "Whoever this girl is? She's with Lucas and maybe she bandaged his arm. At least he's got someone. He's not alone."

"Yeah, maybe, if my drawings are real, but we don't know that."

Rayne looked at his sketch again.

"What's this? You did another page. This is strange. Did you actually see this?" She held the page up to the city lights to get a closer look. "It looks historical, like you tripped out on a time machine. What's with the missing chunks?"

She pointed to a detail in the background that looked like an old train engine with people in vintage clothing, but there were blotches cut out of it. Even though the damage seemed deliberate on Gabe's part, that didn't make sense.

"I don't know." He shook his head. "I get flashes. Impressions. Sometimes it's hard to figure out. I had to draw it separate. It seemed important, but it could be nothing. When I see stuff, it gets jumbled. I have to make choices on what I draw."

She could tell Gabriel wanted to help, but he looked frustrated.

"Sorry. I know this sounds crazy," he said. "You're trying to find Lucas, and all of this could be nothing but a major waste of time. I don't even know what I'm seeing exactly."

"It's more than what I had." She touched his arm. "I've got to believe you're seeing my brother. You're tuned in to him. Whatever's happening between the two of you, I think you need practice. You're like a radio on static. All you need is… channel tweaking."

"I don't think my problems can be fixed with a tweak." He shrugged, not looking her in the eye again. "My static runs deep. I came with it. It's not goin' away."

"Please. You've gotta help me. I have no one else…no one that understands, anyway."

Although Gabriel narrowed his eyes, this time he didn't say no. He nodded and heaved a sigh.

"I don't know what I can do, but I'll give it a shot," he said. When she smiled at him, he shook his head. "I'm not doing you any favors. Believe me. I'll do what I can do, but if I tell you I'm out, you have to respect that. No questions asked. I've got my reasons and it won't be because I'm being a jerk. At least, not on purpose. Agreed?"

He held out his hand to seal their deal.

"Oh, hell, yeah. Agreed."

With a grin, Rayne closed the distance between them and hugged Gabriel. A handshake wouldn't do. Feeling his arms around her sent a different kind of tingle down her body, from the prickles in her scalp to the tips of her toes. Gabe's strange power over his ghost dog and his link to the dead had nothing to do with it.

"The other day, when I saw you catch on fire at the tunnels, I felt something," she said, still in his arms.

"Like what? An urge to run out for marshmallows?"

"I'm bein' serious." She fixed her eyes on the glittering horizon. "I got a rush of memories from my past, people who have died. It felt real, like they were with me. Did you have anything to do with that?"

Rayne pulled away and looked up at him. She felt crazy even bringing up the weird connection she had experienced to her family, alive and dead. Memories from her past had collided in her mind as if they'd been real and happening in the present. Given the intensity of the sensation, she couldn't let it go without asking him, but she didn't feel like telling him about both her parents being dead, either.

"I don't know, Rayne. You're the only one who's ever been close enough to see me do this." He stared off toward the city, and the glow of it touched his face. "But with Hellboy being on the wrong side of the dirt, and me linking to him on the Fringe side, who knows?"

"What happens to you when you channel through him?" she asked. "I mean, you look so…angry, like you're about to explode. Like it hurts."

He had a hard time looking her in the eye. She wasn't sure he'd answer her.

"Not sure I can explain how I stir it up exactly. Guess I really don't want to." He shrugged. "Physically, I don't think much happens, but inside it feels like—"

"Like what?"

"Like every molecule of my body is blasted apart and they float. It doesn't hurt when *that* part happens, just the opposite. It's a total rush."

"I get that way with chocolate."

Rayne had no clue, not even when he explained how his awareness blasted like a shotgun from creature to creature, alive or dead. He could zone in on one, or feel the essence of all of those experiences at once. A total mindblower. Rayne's eyes grew wide and she forgot to breathe until he finished.

"That's…insane," she said. "I mean, not that you're crazy. I'm no one to judge. I have trouble bein' in just *my* head, but that sounds seriously…awesome."

"Yeah, it is." He grinned.

Epic cuteness. Rayne smiled. She felt closer to Gabriel than she ever had before. This time it felt as if he'd trusted her with a fraction of his truth. Could she trust him with more of her story? It might have been a perfect moment to explain her situation and tell him more about Lucas and Haven Hills and Mia, but she was afraid of losing him. Their alliance was still fresh. When she thought about her dysfunctional family, it reminded her that Gabriel had secrets, too. Out of the blue, she blurted out what had been on her mind since she saw where he slept.

"Why are you living at an old zoo? Are you running from something?"

Gabe stopped grinning, and it took him such a long time to answer her that she thought he wouldn't.

"I promised to help you with Lucas, but there's stuff about me that's off-limits," he said. "How I live and why? That's *my* business." He'd said it plain. No anger.

"Yeah, okay."

Rayne understood dark corners and secrets and things too personal to share. She wasn't sure she could let go of the mounting questions she had over Gabriel, but she could definitely give him space.

"And, Rayne?"

"Yeah?"

"If for some reason, I take off and clean out my stuff at the zoo—no explanation, I'm just gone," he said. "Please don't hate me."

In shock this time, Rayne stared into his eyes before she wrapped her arms around him again. She held him tight until she felt the warmth of his skin through his sweatshirt. This time she wasn't scared for Lucas or herself.

This time she was afraid for Gabriel.

Mia had run out of luck searching for Lucas on her own. Given the years between them, she hadn't been as close to Luke as Rayne. Stepping into a parent role and legal guardianship when she was only eighteen had been a lot to handle, but she'd done the best she could. Now she had new worries.

Her last call to O'Dell, she could tell by the cold tone in his voice that he had stopped buying her excuses, and he quit returning her calls when she tried reporting in. He'd lost faith in her, the last thing she wanted or needed. Everything had escalated beyond her control. With Lucas missing, unwanted attention could make things worse for her—and now she knew Rayne would be a wild card.

Mia had only one option left. Balancing her duties at the church, she decided to follow her sister when she could slip away from work, and gamble on Rayne's devotion to Lucas and her mile-wide stubborn streak.

Rayne had spent the day on her Harley, taking a tour of

her past with Lucas and visiting old family haunts while Mia drove her Lexus sedan at a safe distance and tailed her. She didn't have to read lips to know that Rayne questioned everyone she met about Luke. As the day went on, she got more and more discouraged, judging by her body language.

Mia felt sorry for her. Rayne's growing desperation showed, and seeing the places she visited had been hard on Mia, too. It reminded her of what they'd all lost and how fractured they were as a family. She could understand Rayne not trusting her. She'd made mistakes when she was too young to know better, but Mia didn't see how she'd ever make up lost ground.

As night came, Mia almost gave up on tracking her sister's moves, but when Rayne rode her Harley onto the grounds of the old L.A. zoo before midnight, that got her interest. With headlights off, Mia followed her onto Crystal Springs Drive, a dark, winding road that led to the old zoo entrance. She had to admit that she got off on the adrenaline rush of sneaking around in the dark.

This time it felt as if she'd finally done it.

With such a clandestine location, she felt sure Rayne would meet up with Lucas here. Maybe Rayne's search had finally turned up something, but when Mia got to the upper parking lot, near the old front gate, Rayne's taillights had vanished. Her bike wasn't anywhere to be seen. There had only been one way into the park. Where could she have gone? Her sister had either figured out she had a tail and got cagey or she'd taken her bike off road where Mia couldn't follow her.

Damn it!

"What the hell are you up to, little sister?" she whispered as she gripped her steering wheel. "Why did you come here?"

Mia stayed parked in the shadows for a long while, waiting for Rayne to show up again. When that didn't happen, she gave up and drove home. She felt sure she'd stumbled upon an unexpected piece of the puzzle and she wasn't about to let Rayne's meddling jack with her plans. She'd be back and better prepared. Whatever or whoever had brought her sister to Griffith Park, Mia was determined to find out Rayne's secret.

She had a feeling it would matter.

Burbank
2:17 a.m.

O'Dell never kept regular hours. He worked by the job, for the results. If he needed a workout, he took one at a gym down the street from work. If he got hungry, he scarfed whenever he felt like it. Regular hours and punching a clock were for suckers.

When he left Operations, the parking lot had only a few vehicles for the on-duty night crew. His SUV was parked under a security light in executive parking. With his car keys flipping on his finger, O'Dell had his gym bag slung over his shoulder as he approached his SUV and noticed something didn't look right.

"What the hell?"

He heaved a sigh and tossed his bag down, gripping his keys tight in his fist. Shards of glass on the asphalt caught the light and his vehicle listed to one side from two flats. Someone had broken into his car and trashed it.

"I can't believe this!" He cursed as he surveyed the damage.

From what he saw inside, they hadn't taken much except his stereo, but whoever did this had balls. The lot had a secured cyclone fence with a keycard gate. One way in, one way out. When he gazed up at the closest security camera, he cursed louder. Whoever got to him took out the surveillance, too. Operations had no signs posted on the small lot. They kept a low profile on purpose, like utility companies did for their critical operations stuff. A big show would only draw unwanted attention.

O'Dell stood alone in the parking lot and considered his options as he reached for his cell phone, but when a taxi pulled up to the curb near the entrance to Operations, he stopped everything. He watched the driver get out and head for the door. The idiot acted like it would be business as usual at this hour—like *duh,* why is the door locked?

"It's after two in the morning, jerk wad," O'Dell muttered under his breath and shook his head, but before he messed with his phone again, he yelled at the taxi guy, "Hey, buddy. You're not getting in there. The place is closed."

With his gym bag over his shoulder, he walked toward the man as he flicked his keys.

"Someone called for a cab," the driver told him. "Dispatch sent me here."

"Maybe they got the wrong address." O'Dell shrugged. "But you don't have to go away empty-handed. I could use a lift…and you could use the fare. What do you say?"

"I say…you're on. Get in."

O'Dell gave him a cross street close to where he lived. Since cab drivers recorded their fares, he didn't want his residence to be on any log. He'd walk a few blocks. No big deal. The driver called Dispatch, and O'Dell watched as he turned the cab around.

He let his mind wander—thinking about Boelens and Mia and that Darby freak—as the taxi made its way to a freeway. But when the driver didn't hit the on-ramp, O'Dell tapped the Plexiglas shield that separated him from the front seat.

"Hey, pal." He raised his voice. "Why didn't you get on back there?"

The cab driver only glanced in his rearview mirror before he hit a switch on the front dash. Every door locked at the same time and a mechanized privacy panel inched its way up the Plexiglas—the kind that he'd seen on high-end limos. In minutes, he wouldn't see or hear the driver. O'Dell tried both doors and yanked at the handles.

They wouldn't budge.

"Hey, what's happening? You can't do this." O'Dell pounded on the shield as his rear windows faded to black, too. The lights of the city were disappearing. In seconds, he'd be in pitch-black, unable to see anything.

What the hell?

"Sit back, sir." The driver's voice came over an intercom. "Don't hold your breath. You'll only get worked up over something you can't change. Stress is a killer."

Over the drone of the taxi's engine, O'Dell heard a soft hiss and smelled humidity in the air, tinged with a medicinal odor. Despite what the cab driver had told him, he held his breath until his lungs were on fire, but that didn't last. In heaving gulps, he sucked air into his chest, and the fire in his airways spread. He felt sick and dizzy, and when he couldn't hold his chin up, he leaned forward to pound on the shield again but couldn't lift his arm.

"Hey..." he slurred.

O'Dell slumped to the seat in a thickening mist that felt cold on his skin now. Listening to road noise, he fought to stay conscious—and lost.

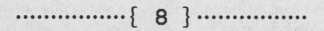 { 8 }

Downtown L.A.
Morning

Kendra had fallen asleep from sheer exhaustion and didn't see Lucas get sicker. He'd taken a bad turn during the night. After she woke from a restless sleep, curled up on the concrete floor with a jacket for a pillow, she found him thrashing under the dank sheets of her bed, delirious. She rushed to him and put a hand to his forehead, feeling the heat off his skin before she even touched him.

"Oh, no, you're burning up," she gasped.

She hadn't asked anyone else to stay because of her guilt over what she'd done. Now she felt as if she'd made things worse for Lucas and the only family she ever really had. She doused a rag in a bucket of cool water she had close by and wiped him off. Water trickled down his face and over his bare chest. Lucas looked ghostly pale. Seeing him like this, she didn't know what else to do. She'd used her best herbal medicine and even resorted to giving him aspirin four hours ago when he was coherent enough to swallow the pills. Fevers sometimes got worse before they broke. She'd seen it, but what if that didn't happen?

Lucas? Can you hear me? she pleaded to him and only got a frightening silence in return.

She could haul him to a clinic and make up a story about him, but that scared her. She could ruin everything—for all of them—if she risked that. Rafe would go with her and help carry him. She knew he'd do it if she asked, but what if the doctors got the cops involved?

Rafe would be unpredictable. If he thought she'd be in danger, he could do anything. *Risk anything.* That meant the others might have no one left to take care of them, and she didn't want to imagine what would happen to Lucas or Rafe or her if the Believers got ahold of them. None of her scenarios ended well.

The more she thought about what bad stuff could happen, the more those dark thoughts knotted her stomach. As much as she wanted to do right by Lucas, Kendra had others to think about, too. She kept the washrag cool and stroked him with it. She had to hold him down so he wouldn't get hurt when he flailed his arms.

That was when she heard it.

Lucas mumbled something. She'd been so worried over him that she nearly missed what he said, but the words he spoke in his delirium caught her attention and held it like an icy fist at her throat.

"I didn't mean to do it, Daddy. It just…happened. Please don't hate me."

Her face flushed hot as if Lucas's fever had become hers. Those words had been hers, years ago. Hearing them again shoved her right back there, as if it were yesterday. It was as if he'd read her mind, down to her darkest secret.

No. Stop, Lucas. You don't know what you're saying, she told him. *Please don't…*

She tried to reach him in the only way she knew how—

with her mind—but he didn't stop. He said stuff over and over. Everything he mumbled brought back a terrifying crush of memories like a tormenting strobe that flickered an exposing light onto her worst nightmares.

How could he know what had happened? She hadn't told anyone. *No one knows!* Not even Rafe when they had one of their marathon confessions late at night after neither of them could sleep. Kendra felt sick and all she could do was tend to Lucas as he blurted out her secrets without knowing how much he hurt her.

"Shh. Please, be quiet," she whispered. *Shh!*

The fever made him do it—and maybe the mental tie she'd made to him had triggered the bond she couldn't break with him now. Kendra touched his lips with her trembling fingers as tears trickled down her cheeks.

"Please. You can't know what happened. No one can."

She knew Lucas had a powerful mind. If she guessed right about him, he was evolving into a Crystal child, a rare thing for an Indigo kid to become. She'd searched some websites before she ran away from home. Kendra had prayed to encounter other Indigo psychics, the first line of evolutionary warriors that would fight and surpass mankind to pave the way toward a future where their kind would be plentiful. But reaching out and finding a Crystal child like Lucas—the future, more advanced evolution of the Indigos—had shocked her. Linking to him, touching him, knowing he was real had lifted her soul.

Putting a name to what they all were explained so much. It gave her hope that what she'd read and wished for might come true, if they could survive those who hunted and destroyed what they didn't understand. She didn't feel like such a freak. What she was—what they all were—was *blessed*.

They had a duty…to become. Evolution had picked them to plant its seed.

The first time she sensed Lucas, only days ago, she knew he'd be special, but if he could see into her mind, through the walls she'd built to hide her worst terror from Rafe and the others, Kendra didn't know if she could take it. After the fever went away, would Lucas remember? If he did, how could she look him in the eye again? If he knew—if he'd actually seen what she did—*he'd hate her.*

But an even darker thought hit her. Could she trust him not to tell?

Two Hours Later

Rafe Santana rushed through the shadows of his underground home. He knew how to move in the tunnels without flipping on his small flashlight and wasting the battery. His eyes and his nature sensed the dark. Even the darkest corners had glimpses of light if he looked hard enough. Maybe that had more to do with his mood than anything. He had a small box in his pocket and he didn't want to crush the pink bow. He'd wrapped it. Even with his clumsy hands, it came out pretty good.

But he had one stop to make before he gave that box to Kendra.

"You seen Benny?" he asked Little G.

"Not if he doesn't want to be seen." The kid smirked and nudged his head. "Yeah, he's playing down at the old engine. Saw him two minutes ago. The twins are with him."

The scrawny kid with a dirty face barely looked up. He carried two buckets of sloshing water, doing his job of restocking their drinking water and filling the system that kept Kendra's garden going. They got their fresh stuff from a water main they'd hijacked—like the city of L.A. would miss what they stole.

"Thanks, man."

Rafe picked up his pace and turned down a corridor to walk on old railway tracks. As he rounded a corner, he saw a familiar sight in the murky darkness. A huge shadow blocked the dim light behind it. An old steam locomotive engine rose from the gloom like a hulking monster with a metal grill that looked like bared teeth that hovered over the rail. Its broken headlight looked like a cyclops eye and its black body looked fierce and powerful. A massive creature without a soul.

That was what he thought when he first saw the steel beast.

Benny had a thing for that old rusted train engine, though. He knew every inch of it and had played with every gauge and lever. The first week he came to the tunnels, the kid hid in the dark there. Wouldn't come out. Rafe had to bring him food and water and stay with him until Benny figured out he wasn't being punished and that Kendra and her crew were okay. That old engine wasn't a basement with a locked door. The kid could come and go whenever he wanted. He and Benny had found a home where they could stay together.

"Yo, Benny. It's me." Rafe picked up a stone off the ground and flicked it at the monster's teeth. It pinged and echoed in the dark. "I got something for ya."

"For me?"

A little head popped out from the engine compartment—then two more—and Rafe heard footsteps clang on the stairs. Benny liked hanging out with the Effin twins. They never talked to him. They didn't talk to anybody, but that didn't matter to a stealth ninja.

"What is it?" The kid jumped to the lowest step and sat down. The twins took the steps above him. The Effin brothers' lips twitched into their version of a smile.

But another face edged from the darkness like a mist. An old face materialized in a slow swirl, with wrinkles that cut deep into its skin and sad, watery eyes. It took all Rafe's concentration not to jump and scare Benny when he saw the bleached skin that glowed in the dark and a head that hovered without a body until the spirit finally showed. An old dead guy, dressed in soot-covered overalls, stood over the boys and looked down at Rafe.

The dead don't speak if they don't want to. Not to him anyway. The Effin brothers probably could do it, but he'd never been strong enough to hear what they had to say.

A weathered hand reached down to pat Benny on the head—a callused hand with dirt under the nails, a hand that had seen plenty of work in its day. The kid grinned up at Rafe and scratched his head where the dead guy had touched him. Rafe looked at the twins, who only shrugged. They had the ability to see the spirit world like he did, but Benny had no idea the old locomotive had its own ghost—one that watched over him as if he were a grandbaby.

Rafe figured it was tough enough for a kid to sleep belowground. No sense telling him about *everything* that lurked in the dark. Where he came from, Benny had enough to be scared of, for real. With a subtle nod of his head, Rafe greeted the spirit and shifted his focus back to Benny.

"I got you something to bring you luck. Your own piece of magic." Rafe held up a silver charm tied into woven black leather. The trinket was in the shape of Kendra's lucky number—eight. If that number was good enough for her, he figured he'd borrow the good luck for him and Benny, too.

"Friendship bracelets are made of string. You seen 'em, right?" When the kid nodded, Rafe knelt down and said, "Hold out your wrist."

Benny's wrist was so small that Rafe had to double wrap it. The kid didn't notice.

"This one's in black leather," he said as he tied the brace-let on with the twins looking over Benny's shoulder. Their mouths were gaped open. "That means we got something stronger than friendship. We're family now."

He expected the kid to say something, but he got real quiet and didn't look up at him. Benny kept his head down and stared at his lucky charm. Rafe ran a hand through the kid's hair and smiled before he let him be.

"I gotta see Kendra." He stood and took a step back the way he'd come. "I'll catch up with you later, little dude."

"Rafe?"

"Yeah?"

As the kid sat on the steps—with his mirror-imaged silent friends looking at each other—Benny stroked his bracelet with tiny fingers. In a shaky voice, he said, "No one's ever gotten me anything before."

Benny had a way of breaking his heart and making him feel good at the same time, even when the kid reminded him of stuff he didn't want to remember, either.

"Don't think that's cuz you didn't deserve something nice, Benny," he said in a quiet voice. "Some folks shouldn't have kids. No one knows that better than us."

Rafe didn't say anything more. With his hands in his pock-ets, he nudged his head at the dead guy in overalls, who never took his sad eyes off him, then headed through the darkness to Kendra. Rafe knew where to find her without asking any-one. She'd be playing with her new toy, Lucas. The new kid would eventually lose his shine to her and become like the rest of them. It would happen, but not soon enough for him.

He pulled the gift box from his pocket and looked at it as he headed for Kendra's. Today he'd worn his favorite Raiders jersey and best jeans. *Look sharp, be sharp.* She always made him want to be his best. When he came into her room, she had her back to him as she sat on the edge of her mattress with a washrag in her hand. She hovered over Lucas. He looked real sick, but with her candles burning, the glow of them made Kendra look like his guardian angel. If she could look prettier, he didn't know how. Her candles brought light to the shadows, like she'd done for him.

Before today, he'd always loved seeing her in the flicker of her candles. Now that sight put him on edge. A dark premonition triggered inside him when he saw Kendra with this new kid. A cold stab of truth he couldn't pin down.

Kendra saw Lucas as a savior—a new kind of human being that she thought of as the next coming of Christ—but when Rafe looked at Lucas, all he saw was a threat to what they had. A kid that could tear down everything from within. When Kendra first felt Lucas's presence, she got all excited and spilled her guts about this kid to him. She got all religious and stuff, like a higher power had a hand in everything. She didn't think much of organized religion. In her mind, this world and the universe had a natural order that made more sense to her.

Rafe didn't believe in a Supreme Being or a master plan. If someone like that existed, why would he and Benny have been dealt such a shitty hand of cards? How could God let bad stuff happen to a sweet kid like Benny? But Kendra believed in something bigger than people turning into worm food. It was what got her through the dark in her life. Who was he to mess that up for her?

"Hey, Kendra." He nudged his chin as she glanced over her shoulder. "Got a minute?"

She hesitated and looked at Lucas before she said, "Is it important? I think his fever is down, but I don't know."

"Uh, guess not. It's…nothing." When he turned to go, she stopped him.

"Wait." She ran a hand through her dark hair and sighed. "I could really use a break."

Rafe heard her get up, but he didn't watch her, something he normally would have done. Instead, he stepped into the dark tunnel outside her place and waited. He clutched the wrapped box in his hand with his eyes shut tight as he listened for her.

He could have used his ability to sense her mood— something she might not detect him doing—but he wasn't sure he really wanted to know. The new kid needed her doctoring. He'd been hurt, and Rafe knew she blamed herself for that, but shit happened. Everything turned out okay. No big deal. He wanted to see things like Kendra did—that big-picture stuff she always talked about—but that would never be him.

All he saw, or ever wanted to see, was Kendra. When she rounded the corner, he stood straight and faced her. She looked worried. Distracted.

"I got you something." He forced a smile and flicked on his flashlight to shine it on the box he had in his hand. The glow off the shiny paper reflected onto her face like candlelight.

"Oh, Raphael. You don't have to keep doing this." She tucked a strand of hair behind her ear and heaved a tired sigh again. "I thought we agreed you'd stop."

"You agreed. I didn't." Heat rushed to his face. "Open it."

She narrowed her eyes at him, but when she touched his hand to take the box, she made him feel better. As she usually did, Kendra undid the paper and peeled off the bow to save it. She used it for the kids at Christmas. Her small fingers trembled as she pulled off the top of the box and lifted the white cotton. The light caught the silver charm as she held it in her fingers. It dangled off woven black leather.

"You told me once that eight was your lucky number, so I got you and Benny one. Me, too. See? We all match." Rafe grinned and held up his wrist to show his larger one. He'd scored the matching friendship bracelets made with black leather.

"Silver plated," he told her. "This won't turn your wrist green."

When he saw the eight dangling off the bracelet, Rafe knew he had to get it for her. He knew her favorite number because he remembered stuff she told him. He liked the idea that he'd bring her luck, and every time she looked at her new bracelet, she'd remember who gave it to her.

"Yeah, it looks like an eight, but you see how flat and stretched out it is?" she said, holding the bracelet up so he could see. "This is an infinity sign, Raphael."

Rafe flinched for only a second, before he shrugged.

"Yeah, I knew that. I was joking," he said. "Infinity, that's like how big outer space is and stuff. Or Little G's stomach when he scores a burger, right?"

"Yeah," she said. Her soft chuckle stabbed at his heart. "But infinity is also a symbol that means forever."

Forever. He liked that even better.

"You like it?" he asked.

"It's beautiful, but why… How did you…?" Kendra always had questions about where he got stuff. Like usual, she dropped it quick. "Never mind. Can you help me put it on?"

She handed him the bracelet. In one smooth move that only girls knew how to do, she held up her small wrist and asked for his help. She could be strong one minute but need him the next. He liked that.

"You looked like you need cheering up," he told her. "Maybe it'll bring luck to…that kid in there." He said that more for her.

His fingers were too big. Everything he did went slow, but that was okay, too. Her hair smelled like coconut, a shampoo he'd stolen for her. When he got the bracelet on her wrist, she smiled at him and played with the dangling trinket, wearing the infinity he'd given her.

"This had to cost you money, Raphael."

Yeah, money. Kendra had never accused him of stealing. Not outright, but she never faced the truth about him, either. His old man had been the opposite. To him, Rafe had always been something stuck to the bottom of his shoe. A piece of shit no one wanted. Being with Kendra had changed all that, and if he wanted her to have something special, he'd find it and get it for her.

"I didn't steal it," he said. "I saw it and thought of you."

"Well, thank you." She stood on her tiptoes and kissed him on the cheek. "You're always so good to me. I'll catch you later, okay? I gotta get back."

"Yeah, later." He jammed his hands into his pockets. "He's lucky to have you. We all are."

She left so fast he didn't know if she heard him. Rafe stood in the shadows with his eyes closed, still feeling the touch of her lips on his cheek and smelling coconut in the air. He stayed in the dark long after she'd left him to go back to Lucas.

A blaring buzzer jolted O'Dell awake from a dead sleep. It hurt his ears, and a red light spiraled through the dark, washing him in its color as it spun.

"What the hell?"

O'Dell jerked his head up and winced. He'd jump-started a headache and his neck hurt like hell. He couldn't turn without pain shooting down his shoulders. When he tried to get comfortable, he found his arms were strapped to the armrests of a metal chair, but even more disturbing, he had an IV punched into his left forearm and the whole contraption was plugged into a digital box like he'd seen on TV when a guy got axed on death row. If he had to guess, his future might depend on who controlled the remote.

With the ear-piercing alarm and infuriating red light, O'Dell let the intimidation get the better of him.

"Stop it! I'm up—I'm up already," he screamed. "You have no idea who you're dealing w—"

The siren came to an abrupt stop, leaving his ears ringing as O'Dell squirmed in his chair, fighting the ties cutting into his wrists. The red alarm rotated without sound now until a mechanized voice came over a microphone from speakers above his head.

"We know exactly who you are, O'Dell."

The voice filtered through software that disguised whoever spoke. It could be a man or a woman of any age. Mr. Roboto sounded like the Terminator had a love child with a supercomputer.

"What's with the IV? What do you have in that thing?" O'Dell couldn't hide how he felt. Tension oozed from every word.

"That depends on your cooperation."

What the hell does that mean? O'Dell felt his head pulse with a badgering headache.

"Why the cloak-and-dagger?" he asked. "Show yourself. We can talk. Man-to-man."

All this macho bullshit had to come from another guy. The high-tech, spy-craft gear and all the 007 tactics smacked of turf pissing, one guy impressing his superiority on another. The jerk had hijacked him and wasn't about to flip on the lights and play nice. While O'Dell waited for a response, he peered beyond the bloodred taint spiraling through the gloom and used the faint light to catch a glimpse of where he was.

A small room. One chair for him, and the digital box on a table. One door. Without windows, he had no idea what time of day it was or how long he'd been knocked out. A mirrored panel stretched across one wall, positioned above where he sat facing it. He had no doubt whoever had taken him from his life stood behind that observation window—a faceless coward.

That pissed him off, but when the never-ending red beacon assaulted his eyes, his head hurt too much to do anything about it.

"You were assigned Lucas Darby. We expected results, but so far you've failed. How do you plan to rectify that?" Short and to the point, the voice demanded an answer.

"I don't know what you're talking about." O'Dell took a risk. "Who's Lucas what's-it?"

Whoever hid behind the two-way mirror had funded his kidnapping with flair. The taxi setup had to cost money. None of this smelled like feds or cops. They didn't have the brains to pull off something like this. He figured the guy with all the questions had to be a player higher up the food chain in the church.

They were testing him.

"You kidnapped me, but if you let me go now, I won't report this to the cops." Yeah, if they were testing him, he'd give them a good show of smarts and a dose of loyalty.

"We both know you'd never go near the police. Quit wasting our time."

A blinding white light seared his eyes. It pointed at him from above and burned a ghost image on his retinas. He couldn't see, and when the blaring alarm sounded again, it scared the hell out of him.

"Shut that damned thing off." He squinted and yelled. When his ears popped, his eyes felt as if they were being stabbed with needles.

"Answer my question. What will you do about the boy?"

Under the blinding light, seconds felt like an eternity to O'Dell and everything hurt. After the intense lights and the racket from the alarm, he couldn't open his eyes, and his eardrums felt busted. He wanted to hold out to show the bastard he wouldn't be a pushover, but somewhere amid the noise and his exhaustion, he couldn't muster his usual attitude.

"What's the big deal about one kid? You've never questioned me like this before," he yelled above the racket. "I've never failed you."

As suddenly as the chaos had started, it stopped again and left his ears ringing.

"Yes. That's precisely why you are here, O'Dell." In the eerie quiet, the disguised voice sounded more macabre.

"What does that mean?" The sound of his own voice was muffled in his ears. "You hijacked me. Busted my eardrums. Is this your idea of a pat on the back for a job well done? You could've just given me a bonus. Money works."

"Not good enough. The Darby boy is vital to our cause."

"Then maybe you'll want to hear what I got planned." O'Dell decided to take a risk.

"We're listening."

O'Dell told what he knew about the encounter Boelens had with a mystery girl and her crew. If he could line up the head girl's ID and run her known associates or other faces his man Boelens had seen, then he'd have some real leads, but he added one more thing.

"But the way you got us working in territories, with me not knowing what others are doing, that could be a problem," he said. "If you want me to run down the leads I have, I can do that, but I need more…authority."

O'Dell waited for a reaction. He didn't have to wait long.

"Ah, I see your point, but with more authority, there will

be increased responsibilities and greater expectations from us. But that's precisely why we've brought you here. We want to impress upon you the significance of a new task we're giving you. Think of this as a…promotion."

"What new task?"

"As you know, our structure is segmented for a reason. Each target-acquisition team works independently. Secrecy has been the key to our success, but with this boy, we have reconsidered our strategy."

For once O'Dell kept his mouth shut. He wasn't sure he liked where this was headed.

"From this point forward, you will be our lead acquisition team. We won't split up the intel to other teams or limit your search area. You'll have full control. The Darby boy will be your first test. If hunting down this girl helps with that objective, then so be it. Are you up for the challenge?"

"Hell, yeah. One hundred percent." Instinct told him to answer straight up. To hesitate would be a sign of weakness.

"Good. You will be given the resources you need to broaden your search and you will answer directly to me through an encrypted phone. Don't disappoint us."

Before he could say anything, the box linked to the IV in his arm whirled into action. Red digital numbers flashed. After a long moment, he realized he'd been holding his breath—waiting to see what the box would do.

"We're placing our faith in you," the voice said. "If you fail, there will be no place for you to hide. You of all people know what we can do."

The mechanical voice sent a shiver down his body when meds flooded his system to remind him how vulnerable he was. A remote signal switched on and the IV pumped something into his arm. Strapped down, he couldn't stop it. He slumped into his chair and struggled to hold his head up.

O'Dell hadn't given his job much thought except for the money. In truth, it helped not to have a conscience and he felt eminently qualified in *that* department, but as his body shut down and the lights faded into shadows, he knew things would have to change. Without his say, the organization had moved him up to the big leagues where losing wouldn't be an option.

It couldn't be business as usual. Not anymore.

Before he gave in to the dark, the voice jolted him with a question.

"Do you know what we do to these children?"

O'Dell could only answer with a shake of his head.

"Fail us and you'll find out."

Not even those chilling words kept him awake.

Behind the observation window, a man took off his headset and tossed it onto a nearby desk as he sat in a leather chair. Alexander Reese watched his men haul an unconscious O'Dell from the room below. He loosened his silk tie and undid his shirt collar as he considered his options. He could still back out of his plan to include O'Dell, his most ruthless team leader, before he initiated his most ambitious hunt yet. Even though the old reporting structure afforded his organization greater anonymity, he'd grown impatient.

He had personal reasons for bypassing protocol. No one knew that but him.

"Do you trust him?" A woman's voice pulled him from his thoughts. The scent of her expensive perfume wafted toward him as she came closer.

"I don't trust anyone," he said.

"Not even me?"

Alexander didn't answer. He let his practiced smile say it all.

"I suppose it's not a matter of any *real* trust," she said. "You don't let many see behind the curtain of Oz. Out of necessity, what we do must be kept secret. Mankind's destiny depends on it. We must save the masses from a future they aren't capable of understanding."

Her arrogance knew no bounds, but Alexander certainly understood the massive ego it took to achieve everything she had in such a short amount of time. Ambition and drive for power had played a part, too. The woman imagined her involvement in his organization as nothing short of essential to their cause. She glorified what she did and had appointed herself savior, salvaging humanity from a future she had plans to shape.

Whatever justification got her through the night, he didn't care as long as she did what he told her.

"Under your new strategy, we should see more immediate results," she said. "But surely you have other men working on your behalf. Redundancy wouldn't be a bad idea. You can't possibly mean what you told this O'Dell character, that he'd be in charge of the whole recovery operation for the Darby boy? That's not like you, Alexander."

"With men like him, stroking their ego is part of the game." He swiveled his chair to face her. "But no, he will not be my only pawn on the chessboard. There's too much at stake."

When he didn't tell her more, her face tensed, but she didn't push him for his strategy.

"How do you feel about him chasing after this mystery girl?" she asked.

"If he acquires the Darby boy, I don't care what it takes. The girl and these other children are of no consequence. If O'Dell has to get more aggressive in his tactics, they'd be collateral damage to our cause."

"We've never killed on a hunt before. That could get messy with a man like O'Dell. He lacks finesse. Are you prepared to clean up after him?"

"That goes without saying. Yes."

Anyone else would have realized the gravity of what he'd just said, but he saw the soft flicker of a smile on her face.

"I'm pleased that you have such faith in my recommendation on the Darby boy. We make a good team, you and I," she said.

She wore her blond hair loose, not pulled back the way she wore it on the job. Her stunning blue eyes and exquisite Scandinavian features had drawn him to her, but her devious mind, excellent credentials and her need for control had made them coconspirators.

"Yes, we do, but make no mistake. I'm in control when it comes to target acquisition and resources," he said. "No need for you to fret over such things, my dear."

The woman forced a smile. When he saw the tightness in her jaw, he appreciated her self-control when she didn't push him for more. She didn't like being cut out of the loop, but that couldn't be helped.

"See to it that O'Dell gets the encrypted phone," he told her. "I'll consolidate and send the information that we have on Lucas Darby from the other teams. The electronic file will include your anonymous medical assessment of his capabilities and recommendations. O'Dell will have everything he needs when he wakes up."

"Yes, of course." The beautiful woman grabbed the phone O'Dell would use to report in. Before she left the room, she looked over her shoulder. "Anything special you need from me? I've built a rapport with the Darby boy's sister Mia. She trusts me."

"That could be quite useful. Manipulate that connection to the sister as you see fit. With your influence and cunning, my dear Fiona, you are my rock."

"I believe in your cause, Alexander. Our cause."

This time she smiled for real before she left him alone in

the darkened room. Being head of psychiatry at Haven Hills Treatment Facility, Dr. Fiona Haugstad had proved to be a worthy ally and she'd given his organization a perfect cover under the patronage of a church. They could commit and test patients, identify their most promising young targets and operate in complete anonymity, all under the guise of treatment.

Lucas Darby had somehow escaped facility grounds before Fiona had made her final assessment and been justified to transfer him to Ward 8 where she could have complete control over him, in secret and without prying, judgmental eyes. She'd seen enough to know that the drugs he'd been given had masked his full capabilities. The day she had reported her findings, he'd never seen her so excited.

"I did it. I found a Crystal," she told him.

Fiona acted as if she'd invented the Darby boy. If she proved right about him, though, Lucas Darby had evolved into a Crystal child at the unprecedented age of fifteen. Either the boy had accomplished a remarkable feat or the evolutionary process had escalated and there would be more of his kind to come.

Alexander had to know. The boy had to be tested and studied beyond the usual protocols. The teachings of his church demanded it. This was not the time to doubt or question their long-standing beliefs that mankind should dominate and forestall the rise of this evolutionary mistake. These children were a plague on humanity—a test of man's faith—nothing more.

He shuddered at the urgency of the situation, but not Fiona. She'd become too blinded by her own achievement and taken full credit for "discovering" him. For whatever reason, because of her efforts, the boy had landed in his lap as if he'd been a gift—one that Alexander wanted back at all cost.

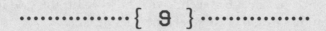

{ 9 }

Griffith Park Zoo
Dusk

"Take a ride with me." Straddling her bike, Rayne tossed her father's old helmet to Gabriel and he caught it as he stood in the doorway of the maintenance shed. "I've got an idea and I need your help."

Even though her Harley had announced her arrival, he still took precautions to hide his face under his hoodie. He stayed in the shadows of the shed, not letting the evening light shine on him. In case someone came after him, he could bolt real easy. Seeing his practiced maneuvers made her feel sad for him. She understood him being wary, but it made her all the more curious about why.

It had taken all her patience to wait until dusk to pick him up. She'd done that for him.

"Where are we going?" he asked.

Rayne didn't miss the fact that Gabriel hadn't budged from where he stood. He had to be convinced.

"That historical sketch you did. I have an idea where to look for it. You game?" When he shrugged and didn't say no, she smiled. "Grab your sketch pad, Picasso. We're gonna need it…and your memory of that vision."

He tossed back his hoodie and stared at her. Trust definitely didn't come easy for him, but as he sized her up, Rayne felt heat shoot to her cheeks. She gripped the handlebars as a distraction from his penetrating stare. Rayne had never met anyone like Gabriel. He scared and excited her at the same time. He felt like an adventure—a memory she'd always carry with her—but she had a bad feeling that he lived off the grid for a reason that would always keep her at a distance.

After Gabriel put on his helmet and locked the shed, she watched him walk toward her with his backpack on his shoulders. Every step he took and every move of his muscular arms and legs sent tingles through her stomach. She hadn't given much thought to what it would mean for him to ride with her. She held her breath as he straddled her bike with his long legs and slipped his big hands onto her hips.

He leaned close to her until she felt the heat of his body on her back. In a low voice, he said, "I'm all yours. Don't get us killed."

With a smirk, Rayne gunned the Harley, and when it lurched forward, Gabriel grabbed her waist. On the off-road trail, he held on, but as they hit the winding part of Crystal Springs Drive, Rayne leaned into every curve and waited to see what he would do. When he fought her with an insecure shift of his body, she knew he'd never ridden on the back of a bike before, but as his trust in her mounted, he followed her lead and mirrored her moves. By the time they left Griffith Park and hit a freeway on-ramp, Rayne felt Gabriel relax as he held on to her.

Too bad she couldn't say the same. The motorcycle engine vibrated every muscle in her body—a fraction of the shudder that he made her feel—for a very different reason.

Minutes Later

Her Lexus had been parked on the frontage road under the shadow of the Ventura Freeway. Mia had tailed Rayne before and when her sister rode her motorcycle toward Glendale, she had a pretty good idea where she'd go. She'd followed her to the abandoned L.A. zoo in Griffith Park once before and lost her on the grounds near the zoo entrance.

A really weird place to go, especially at night.

With only one main road though the park, it would be too easy to get caught following her this time of day. Mia had lost Rayne once and wouldn't make that mistake again. She decided to wait for Rayne outside the park and not take a chance that she'd be spotted. From a safe distance, she used high-tech binoculars to watch. She'd bought the surveillance gear at a specialty shop that catered to the paranoid. The military-grade binoculars had a night-vision zoom lens, a feature she thought would come in handy, but it also shot 1080p HD video and took high-quality still images with audio, if necessary. The gear would be more than she'd need, but it'd be worth it if it helped her find Lucas.

This time she'd be more prepared to follow Rayne, day or night. When her sister came out with a guy on the back of her bike, Mia's heart lurched in shock.

Lucas. It has to be him.

"Oh, my God," she whispered as she adjusted the focus on her new binoculars. "She's been hiding him."

Mia recognized their father's old helmet. As she started the Lexus, memories rushed to her mind when she remembered how much that Harley had meant to both her brother and sister. She pulled from her hiding spot to follow the motorcycle onto the freeway, resisting the urge to gun the car and speed up. She had to be patient and careful. One careless move could cost her.

She might never get a better chance than she had right now.

As she hit the on-ramp, Mia made a hands-free call through her Bluetooth system. She hadn't talked to O'Dell for hours.

Not knowing what he was up to worried her. Somehow she had to stay connected to O'Dell, even if he creeped her out. The Church of Spiritual Freedom had assigned the man to Lucas, to search for him without calling attention from authorities outside of the church's control. With Lucas missing, she felt the urgency of their escalating tactics to find him.

Mia had called O'Dell earlier, but he didn't pick up. When the call clicked as if it would roll into voice mail, she nearly ended the connection, but a voice stopped her.

"Mia? This is Dr. Haugstad. I heard a cell phone ringing and I saw your name on the display. I hope you don't mind that I answered. I wanted to find out how you were doing."

"No, I don't, but how do you know O'Dell? Is he there with you?"

"I can't be certain, but I believe he's stepped away. Is there anything I can do?"

The doctor was new to Lucas's case, but Mia hadn't expected her to pick up. She had a hard time processing the link between someone like O'Dell and such a credentialed and noted psychiatrist. After Mia overheard nurses discussing Lucas and his potential transfer to Ward 8, she panicked. She'd heard of kids getting reassigned there, but none came back out. Ward 8 had special security protocols. No one she knew had access and no one in the church talked about it. That section of the hospital felt like a one-way trip where the worst, most hopeless patients were sent. How could Luke deserve that? Dr. Haugstad had evaluated him to intervene on his behalf. The woman seemed earnest in wanting to help, but when timing didn't play in her favor and the transfer looked inevitable, Mia had lost hope that her brother would ever leave Haven Hills on his own.

Mia had her reasons for being involved with a man like O'Dell—to try to get to Lucas before anyone else—but anytime she had dealings with Dr. Haugstad, she hated keeping things from her. The woman had it together and seemed very sincere. For Lucas's sake, she would have to trust her gut on how she handled his doctor. If he ended up back in Haven Hills, she would need an ally, someone with influence.

"Uh, no. I already left him a message. I don't want to bother him again. Sorry I disturbed you."

"No bother, my dear. We are all concerned for the whereabouts of your brother. His safety is foremost on our minds. I can assure you we are doing everything in our power to locate him," the doctor said. "I've heard you're doing a commendable job juggling your work hours at the church with your search for your brother. Has something happened? Have you got a lead on him? Is that why you're calling?"

"Not...exactly."

Before she said another word, Dr. Haugstad told her, "I sense you're holding something back. Please, do not attempt to confront your brother alone, Mia. Off his medication, he is a danger to himself and anyone around him. Please, for his sake and yours, tell me. Where are you?"

L.A. County Museum of Art
Thirty Minutes Later

"A museum? What are we doing here?" Gabriel asked as she drove past a row of tall palm trees and pulled the Harley into a parking spot.

The public parked in a muni-garage, but after she'd volunteered one summer, Rayne knew of a smaller lot closer to the library archives building, reserved for exhibitors and volunteers. Although the museum campus was spread out, the location she wanted to go was near her favorite part of the complex, the white modern structure that always reminded her of a human backbone with its modules strung together and distinctive roofline jutting up.

"Not just any museum. It's the main one for L.A. County and it's got a research library that specializes in art archives."

"Ah, smart girl."

Rayne had to smile. He had trusted her enough to go along for the ride, without knowing where she'd take him. She called *that* progress. When she turned off the motorcycle and removed her helmet, she waited for him to get off before she told him her plan. It didn't escape her notice that the minute he removed his helmet, he pulled his sweatshirt hoodie over his head. He covered most of his face in shadow—*Assassin's Creed* revisited.

"Your art-history lesson got me thinking. Something in your train-station sketch reminded me of a class I took once. Who knew such a lame field trip could pay off? I gotta check out my hunch."

"And why am I here?"

Okay, he had a good question. If she had her way, she'd spend time with him anywhere. Be a girl hanging out with a cute boy, but he was a human torch who channeled through a dead dog and she had a missing brother and an iguana. Things were far from normal.

"You're the one who saw the vision. I thought if we found something useful it would trigger another memory that could get us closer to Lucas. It's worth a shot, right?"

"Yeah. Guess so." He shrugged and kept his head down as he talked to her, hiding his face from the light. "Being in public like this, it takes getting used to, that's all."

Before they took another step toward the front entrance to the library, Rayne stopped him by touching his arm. When he didn't hide his face from her, a sliver of light shined across his hypnotic honey-brown eyes and she almost forgot to breathe.

"I know this is hard for you." She slipped both her hands in his. "Thank you, for everything, Gabriel."

"I haven't done anything yet." He grinned. "I don't even have a library card."

She stepped closer to him.

"You being a legit card-carrying geek doesn't matter. You can't check out books here. It's not *that* kind of library. What matters to me is that you're here. With me."

Looking into his eyes, she felt a lump in her throat. Her fears for Lucas, and every dark thought she'd had about finding him, came rushing to the surface. After losing her parents overnight, the thought of never seeing Lucas again had crushed her. Searching for him alone reminded her how lonely and solitary her life had become. Gabe had secrets to his nature like Luke, but he was living his life on his own terms, without being imprisoned and drugged in a hospital.

Everything about Gabe gave her something to look forward to. She hadn't lost everything. She had Gabe, and maybe Lucas wasn't a lost cause.

"Before I met you, I didn't have much of a chance at finding Luke in a city the size of L.A.," she said. "Now I feel like I have hope…because of you."

She stood on tiptoe to kiss him on the cheek. His skin felt warm on her lips and she loved how he smelled. Even with half his face covered in shadows, up close she saw him blush and it made her smile.

"Rayne?" He kept his voice low.

"Yeah?"

"I gotta warn you. I'll be on the lookout for security cameras and people staring, stuff like that. Once we get inside, I'm gonna be weird."

"And that's different…how?" She grabbed his sweatshirt

with both her hands and leaned against him, nuzzling into his arms.

"Don't say I didn't warn you."

Rayne wanted to stay with him like this, feeling the warmth of his body, listening to the softness of his voice meant only for her. But she knew none of this would last. Somehow, with Gabriel, she felt every moment with him would be precious.

They'd crossed paths for a reason, but that same reason would eventually take him from her forever. Even as she smiled up at him now, a twinge of sadness nestled around her heart and stayed.

The L.A. County Museum of Art maintained significant research on art. Rayne remembered that from a field trip she'd taken to the place. For once a class had done her some good.

When she got inside, she hit the computers to do an initial search, using keywords like *mural paintings* and *turn of the century* and *Los Angeles* and stuff like that. She saw Gabriel shrug out of his knapsack to carry it on one shoulder and felt him with her as she went online. But as she got into her queries, she didn't feel him standing near her anymore. She looked around and didn't see him, either.

The library part of the museum campus had smaller research wings that specialized in different stuff. She could lose him if they weren't careful. She made note of books she wanted to find and went looking for them, but one in particular seemed really good—on mural painting and decorations in Los Angeles County.

It didn't take her long to find the right stack, but the book she wanted wasn't there. She stared at the catalog number on the paper and made sure she had found the right shelf.

"Damn," she muttered.

"Did you strike out already? Lightweight."

She recognized Gabriel's voice, but when she looked around, she didn't see him.

"Where are you?"

"No wonder you can't find the book," he whispered. "You're blind."

Torch boy was in the next aisle, peering through the book stacks at her. She only saw his amazing eyes.

"You were right," she said.

"About what?"

"You are acting weird," she teased. "Or should I say… weirder."

"Did you find anything worth looking at?"

Besides you? she wanted to say, but didn't. She didn't know how to flirt, but Gabe made her want to try.

"Yeah, but I'm having trouble finding my first choice."

She glanced at the note she'd made and rechecked the book numbers on the shelf in front of her for a fourth time. When she looked up again, Gabriel had vanished. She pushed aside books and looked through them, but he was nowhere in sight.

"Hey, where did you…?"

"I'm here."

She jumped when she heard his low voice right next to her. The guy moved like a damned ghost. He'd learned something from Hellboy.

Putting his backpack down on the floor, Gabriel grinned and grabbed the paper from her hand. When he gave it back to her too quickly, she thought he'd given up, but she'd been wrong. Backing up one slow step at a time, Gabe ran his fingertips along the spines of the books. With his arms spread across the aisle, he touched both stacks. Hoodie boy kept his head down, so she knew he wasn't looking at anything except his boots or he had his eyes closed, even weirder.

Rayne almost made a joke, but when he slowed down and

shifted one hand up a row without looking, she didn't say a word. Her breath caught in her throat when he pulled down a large picture book and finally looked at it in his hand.

"Is that it?" she asked, unable to hide the excitement in her voice.

"Oh, hell, no. Who do you think I am? That *Mindfreak* dude?"

She grimaced and punched him in his rock-solid arm. The guy had totally scared her with his magic act, but her heart raced even faster when she looked at the book he'd handed her.

The right book.

"Oh. My. Gawd," she gasped, and Gabriel smiled. "If this whole dead-dog-trainer thing doesn't pan out, you can always become a resource librarian."

"Good to have a solid backup plan."

Rayne had other books to look for, but the one she had in her hand looked promising. It had plenty of pictures. She grabbed Gabriel by the arm and pulled him toward the first table she found to flip through the pages, but he stood his ground and wouldn't budge.

"Nope, sorry. The tables are too open. I'm staying in the stacks. Flip through that book quick." He grabbed the list she'd made. "I'll get these others if this one doesn't do anything for you."

"What if I find something I want you to see?"

He smiled and asked, "I don't know. What trick can you do? Something you only do in front of a mirror when you're by yourself."

"Come on. I'll just cough or clear my throat."

"Boring." He shook his head. "Lacks imagination. Creativity points, zero. You gotta do better."

She glared at him and sighed.

"Okay, there is one thing, but I'm not saying it out loud."

"Then how will I know?"

"Believe me. You'll know."

Rayne turned and rolled her eyes, not waiting for his answer. Sitting at the closest table, she opened the book with a shake of her head. Because of Gabriel's goofy game, she had mixed feelings about turning up something that would help her find Luke. Yeah, she needed that to happen, but now making an ass of herself had become part of the equation. So not fair.

She only had one unique talent, something inspired by Floyd Zilla, her pet iguana.

When she got into the book's table of contents, it didn't do her much good except to narrow down her initial search to the meaty middle. She flipped through those pages and skipped anything that didn't look like an old mural train station. One section totally grabbed her interest.

"Bingo," she whispered. One image looked like Gabriel's drawing. She recognized the style, but she needed to see his sketchbook.

Unfortunately, that meant…

Oh, brother. Rayne looked around, hoping to wave him over and back out on her promise to signal him, but when she didn't see his eyes staring back through the stacks, she let out a moan. *Only for you, Luke.* She put her fingers to her mouth, stretched her lips tight across and poked her tongue through them in a sweep. One lick. Two.

Her version of "lizard lips."

When she didn't see Gabriel, Rayne did it again and pointed in different directions. She ignored the strange looks people gave her, but when she heard Gabriel laughing behind a bookshelf, she knew when to stop.

Gabriel had forgotten what it felt like to laugh. Really laugh. Doing it in a library hadn't been optimal, but Rayne had a way of reminding him what normal felt like—and that his life had strayed far from it.

In a heartbeat, the smile left his face.

"What did you find?" He sat down next to her with his head down.

"This," she said. "Is it the same?"

She shoved the picture book open and showed him a page with a large mural on it, painted on brick. *My mural.* In a flash, his vision came back to him. The rush of it forced him to close his eyes, almost as if it hurt. He felt a dank cold on his skin and shadows clouded his mind as if he'd slipped into another reality. He couldn't put his finger on the sensation of that distant feeling, except that it reminded him of…*a cave.*

Without answering her, he unzipped his backpack and pulled out his sketchbook. When he flipped it open to the right page, his eyes grew wide. The details were amazing. He'd never seen the real mural. Never knew of its existence, yet he'd drawn it.

Rayne looked eager for an answer. To her this meant she might be one step closer to her missing brother. To him, it only reminded him what a freak he was—and what a messed-up loser he'd continue to be long after she went on with her life.

He hadn't asked for this. *None of it.*

"Well?" she asked.

"Dead ringer."

Rayne grabbed the book and read from it.

"Did you know there were tunnels under downtown L.A.?" She shook her head, not expecting him to answer. "Eleven miles of 'em. What does this have to do with Lucas?"

"I don't know, but just now…" He swallowed and couldn't look her in the eye. "I got a feeling like…I was in a cave."

"Like in a tunnel?"

"Yeah, could be." He nodded and half shrugged.

"We gotta look for these tunnels, Gabriel. We have to go there."

"Eleven miles is a lot to cover."

"Yeah, but maybe Hellboy can help us." She put a hand on his arm. "I got a flashlight on my bike. The book gives cross streets. I got a pretty good idea where they are. We could do this."

Before he could answer, Rayne did a double take at the commotion near the reference desk. She didn't look happy.

"What's she doing here?" she muttered and used him like a shield to hide behind.

"Who?" Gabe looked up to see a woman at the information desk. She looked like a Hollywood type. Not a hair out of place, classy duds and a picture-perfect face all made up.

"My sister, Mia," she said, peeking over his shoulder. "She's been spying on me. She thinks I'm hiding Lucas."

"Why would she think that?"

"Long story."

Gabe didn't have time for long stories. Not here, not now. He had his share of secrets. He guessed Rayne had hers.

"I haven't told you everything about my family," she admitted. "It's complicated."

Gabe didn't like the sound of this. Without thinking, he stuffed the library book in his unzipped backpack and shoved it next to his sketchbook. He took Rayne by the hand and rushed her behind the closest bookshelf.

"I'm listening." He crossed his arms and stared at her with his rucksack slung over his shoulder.

"My parents are dead and I don't trust my sister." She sighed. "Neither does Lucas. He told me something spooked him about her and the hospital she had him committed to."

"Whoa, back it up. Your brother...what hospital?"

"Yeah, about that. Lucas escaped from a mental hospital. Haven Hills."

Gabriel rolled his eyes and let out a deep sigh.

"Well, he doesn't really need to be there." Rayne shrugged. "Lucas is just different."

"Thanks for the explanation, Dr. Darby. When did you get your psych diploma?"

"You don't know him," she argued. "Besides, what's with the attitude? Aren't you afraid of OD'ing on irony? You're not exactly on the right side of normal, Gabriel."

"Touché." He pulled the hoodie down over his face and didn't look her in the eye.

"Mia works for the church that funds the treatment facility where Lucas got committed. I think she's hiding something about that church and Lucas from me. Like I said, it's complicated."

"What church?"

Rayne narrowed her eyes. His question had taken her off guard. Of all the things he could have asked, the name of a church would've ranked pretty low for most people.

"The Church of Spiritual Freedom. Why?"

"Come on. We gotta get out of here," he said. "No questions, remember?"

When his survival instinct kicked into high gear, Gabe checked out their situation in a hurry. Two major shelving units had bordered the tables where they'd been. That area had been too wide open. His only choice had been hiding in the row of books, but now they had only two aisles to hide. Both of them led in the wrong direction, back toward the main desk, and exit signs lit in red were across the room. Either way, they'd be seen when they showed their faces. They were cornered.

They needed a diversion, fast. Scratch that. *He* needed the diversion.

It pained him to think like this, but he had to. It made no sense to drag Rayne into his screwed-up life. Even though he'd hoped it wouldn't happen, he'd warned her that he could take off in a rush without a word and leave his stash behind at the zoo. He hadn't realized how fast that would happen, but like a chess player, he always played scenarios in his head and moves in advance. He had a backup plan that didn't include Rayne.

She'd be better off without him. At least she had a place to look for her brother—the tunnels under L.A. It would have to be enough.

For her sake, Gabe had to ditch her. *Now!*

Following her sister, Mia had pulled into a parking lot on the L.A. County Museum of Art grounds in time to see Rayne head into one of the smaller buildings on the complex with the boy she had brought with her. With the sun going down, the light had played a factor and interfered with the night vision of her high-tech surveillance gear. She hoped to confirm Lucas was with Rayne, but seeing through binoculars into a fading light, Mia couldn't make out much.

Why would Rayne take Luke here?

She got out of her Lexus and jockeyed to a better position to zoom in and videotape them, but the boy in the hood never showed his face. After she stopped recording, Mia kept her sister in sight and followed from a safe distance. She didn't have much of a plan, except to ID Lucas. If it was him, she'd have to confront both of them.

Mia had been to the museum before, but never this building. From what she'd seen, Rayne hadn't gone toward the bigger exhibit halls, auditorium or café. She went the opposite way and Mia followed her steps into a library. The minute she stepped into the quiet setting, she walked past a front information desk and searched the faces of the people inside. She looked down aisles and her heart beat faster whenever she saw anyone who looked like Rayne or Lucas.

She'd almost given up on finding them when she caught movement and a shadow through the book stacks. Mia had to get a closer look.

"Please. Let it be Lucas," she whispered.

They were cornered. They had two rows of books for cover, but to get out either way, they had to go through Mia. Rayne didn't see any other option. If her sister stayed put near the front desk, it would only be a matter of time before she'd see them. For Gabe's sake, she couldn't let that happen. The guy had only tried to help. The last thing he needed was to get questioned by her meddling and judgmental sister.

"I swear, I don't know why she's here. She gets off on spying on me these days, but I can talk to her and see what she wants," Rayne offered as she watched her sister through the books, crouched low to the floor with Gabriel. "She doesn't have the police with her this time."

"Cops. Great." He winced.

"I'll distract her and give you a chance to slip out. She can't be after you. She doesn't even know you," she said. "If she doesn't force me to go with her, we can meet at the bike when I get rid of her."

"Yeah, okay."

Gabriel agreed too fast. He looked totally distracted. Hunkered down next to her, he shifted his eyes between Mia and a way out, but he never argued or asked her more about cops or why she felt the need to hide from her own sister. Rayne had a bad feeling about why. Trust. It had come down to trust and she wasn't sure Gabriel would be waiting in the parking lot. If he took off now, she'd never find him again. The guy seriously knew how to bail.

"Gabriel? Look me in the eye and tell me the truth."

He shrugged and had trouble doing as she asked. "What?"

"If I do this, will you be waiting outside for me?" She put a hand to his shoulder. "You know how much this means to me. Lucas is in trouble, I know it and I think you do, too. If you tell me you'll be there, I'll believe you."

Even as the words left her mouth, Rayne wasn't sure she hadn't lied. It all came down to her ability to rely on someone else—and her faith in Gabriel.

Rayne had a way of looking into his eyes that felt like a lie detector. Right now she looked hurt. Gabe wasn't sure she'd buy anything he told her. He had a weird way of connecting to a ghost dog, but Rayne possessed a natural gift with living, breathing people—one he didn't fully appreciate at the moment.

She had called him on his bullshit and now she wanted an answer to a question that should have been simple for him. In another life, he wouldn't have hesitated.

He'd promised to help her find Lucas. Could he lie to her now, even if it was for her own good? Yeah, ditching her would be best for her, but what about her brother? His instincts told him this kid was in real trouble. It was one thing to keep secrets and not tell stuff, but lying straight up to Rayne when she needed him made him feel like a jerk.

Did he want to turn into "that" guy, a liar who didn't give a shit? No. His answer had to be no, if he didn't want to turn into a total dick.

"There's stuff about me that you don't know," he said. "I can't risk that your sister won't mess things up for me, too. She may have done that already."

"What? But..."

He touched her lips with a finger.

"I'm sorry. I gotta expect the worst. If she found you here, she could've followed us from Griffith Park. I have to assume my place there is compromised. I can't go back."

Rayne kept quiet and looked miserable. He had no idea how much trouble her sister could bring down on him, but that didn't matter. He had to play it safe.

"I've really messed things up for you, haven't I?"

"Not your fault." He reached for her hand. "Do you trust me?"

A fragile smile returned to her face and she nodded. A spark of hope had come back to her eyes, but this time he had to earn her trust by showing her.

"No matter what happens, no matter what you see, be ready to move and stick close to me."

When Gabe looked toward the desk, he saw Rayne's sister walking straight for them. In seconds, she'd cross their only way out. If she looked down the bookshelves, they'd have no place to hide. Whatever he had planned, he had to do it now.

Gabe let go of Rayne's hand and distracted her.

"She's coming," he whispered.

When Rayne turned to look for her sister, Gabe stood and ducked into the next aisle. Because he didn't know she'd followed him in Griffith Park, she'd seen him go through his transformation, from his seething rage to the rush of the blast when he let it go. He saw in her eyes how much he'd frightened her.

Having a choice now, he didn't want her to see the ugliness he had to conjure to make things happen. In the farthest corner against a wall, he dropped his backpack to the floor at his feet. He shut his eyes and flexed his arms to awaken the power and stir the anger that fueled him. He'd never summoned it this fast before.

Seconds. All he had was seconds.

★ ★ ★

When the lights flickered and Rayne felt a tremble under her boots, a familiar panic swept through her. *Earthquake.* Mother Nature's timing sucked. Tremors happened in L.A. and she'd experienced her share. She looked for a safe place to hide, but when she reached for Gabe, he wasn't with her.

He'd disappeared.

"Gabriel?" she whispered, but he never answered.

She turned in time to see a fierce glow coming from behind her. Spears of blue light nearly blinded her and shot through the books like a laser show. Before she could move to see what was happening, Rayne cursed and covered her head. A book had smacked her on the shoulder. The shelves quaked and stuff fell to the floor. If she didn't move fast, she could be crushed under a massive shelf full of books.

But in a sudden rush, she felt a swell of fear that gripped her hard. Not even when those jerks stalked her at the zoo in that hellish tunnel had she been so afraid. Stranger still, she had an overwhelming hunger, as if she'd been starving for days. Tears stung her eyes and her belly tightened into a knot. She had no idea why she felt such a crippling flood of emotions and strange cravings. All she wanted was to curl into a ball and cry, but one thought forced her to fight through what had seized control of her.

Gabriel.

When she heard the commotion of glass breaking and people yelling and running, she dared to look up. She had to find him, but everything she saw confused her. The glass doors to the museum entrance had shattered. Shards of glass were strewn on the tile floors, but with all the weirdness going on inside the library, something else shocked her.

Cats and dogs of all sizes ran through the museum building. They leaped over chairs and shoved into library tables, making a racket with their barking and mewling. Pigeons flapped overhead, looking for cover. These animals should have been running in the opposite direction, away from the danger. Instead, they ran toward it as if they had no choice. It reminded her of what Gabriel and Hellboy had done the other night in the tunnels, but this looked much more chaotic. Had Gabe drawn them into the library, like he'd done in the tunnels?

Something different had taken over and it scared her more. It didn't feel like Gabriel had control, not like the times she'd seen before. Her sister cowered near the desk and looked paralyzed with fear as she clung to another woman. Somewhere Rayne heard a big dog barking and growling and whining. The noise grated on her raw nerves like listening to old-people jazz, but the barking wasn't the only thing that stressed her out.

Two guys were fighting and beating each other to a bloody mess. *Why?* What would make them ignore the danger to stay and fight instead? The whole scene looked like a disaster flick in a cheesy movie. People caught in the library looked too struck to move or they'd let anger or a strange insanity take over. They should have run out, but they didn't.

Whatever had happened, Rayne felt it, too.

It was as if she'd been zapped with crazy juice and dumped into an alternative reality. The worst fear she'd ever felt had a grip on her. Part of her wanted to run as far as she could get, but she couldn't leave Gabriel, not when he'd sacrificed so much for her. She felt his familiar power as it sent a ripple of chills across her skin, and every hair on her head tingled with energy, but the strange sensation felt much stronger. Her stomach heaved as if she would be sick, especially when the dog wouldn't stop yelping.

Breathe. Just breathe.

Trembling, Rayne kept low and crept closer toward the next row. The blue laser light pulsed brighter as if it breathed.

Under flickering overhead lights, the whole library had been cast into a frenzied strobe show. She had to see Gabriel. She had to know he was all right. With tears stinging her eyes, she winced at the kinetic energy that jolted through her body like needle pricks as she peered around a shelf to find him.

The closer she got, the worse she felt. She got sicker and the excited dog got louder, too. When she peeked around the corner into the next row, the first thing she saw made her cringe. The freaked-out dog had been Hellboy. He scratched and leaped and yapped, trying to break free of something that boxed him in. He wasn't in icy flames this time. His ghostly silhouette came in bursts of cloud puffs and faded to a vapor mist. Wherever he was, a barrier held him back from Gabriel.

That was when Rayne saw Gabe and she gasped. Still standing, his body shook as if he had a seizure, and his beautiful eyes had rolled back into his head. Alone and engulfed in raging blue flames, he looked as if he'd collapse any second from the weight of the power surging through him on overload. Something had gone horribly wrong. Rayne shoved aside her instinct to run and got to her feet. Ignoring Hellboy and her fear of him, she raced to Gabe and reached through the blue flames with her bare hands and arms.

Her skin prickled in pain and her insides were in agony, but she wouldn't let go of him.

"Gabriel. Can you hear me?" She did her best to hold him up, but he was too heavy.

She staggered under his weight and lowered him to the floor in a heap, but his tremors wouldn't let him rest. He rolled and pinned her to the floor, mumbling things she couldn't understand. A strange heat mixed with a chilling tinge that radiated off his body like an energy force. It raged through her, too. With his face next to hers, she held him tight in her arms. She breathed in his gasps as if she could take away his pain.

She could tell he wasn't with her anymore. Whatever power radiated from his body had taken over and consumed him.

"I'm here. I won't leave you." Rayne didn't know if Gabriel heard her, but she wouldn't let go. "Stay with me. Please!"

Hyped on adrenaline, raging fear and something out of control, Rayne did the unexpected. She kissed Gabriel. Not a sweet and shy first kiss. She pulled him to her as if they'd made out plenty of times before and pressed her lips hard to his. At first, he didn't react. The shakes still had control over him, but eventually his body relaxed and he gave in to her. She kissed his lips, his neck, even his eyelids until he collapsed into her arms and his shakes stopped.

Rayne looked at his slack face. His eyes were closed and she felt his full weight on her. He'd stopped moving. She didn't even know if he was breathing.

"Gabriel?" Her eyes burned with tears. "Are you...okay?"

The noise in the library became muffled. The voices, the animals and birds, and a distant alarm faded and went dark in her mind. She even blocked out Hellboy. All she could think about or care about was Gabriel.

His eyes blinked open as if he'd awakened from a long sleep. When he finally saw her, he moved an arm as he lay next to her on the floor. Looking worn-out, he reached a trembling hand to her face and ran his fingers through her hair. A smile nudged his lips when his drowsy eyes fixed on her. She could've stayed in that moment forever, breathing in his same air, comforted by his touch and the feel of his body next to hers.

"What...happened?" he asked in a raspy voice.

Such a simple question. She wanted to kiss him again, only this time on her own, without being under the control of the power he had unleashed, but she had fallen under the spell of a different influence now—one that came from her.

As much as she wanted to hold him and cry—happy that he was okay—she resisted the urge. Something terrible had happened. She had to focus on getting him somewhere safe that wasn't Griffith Park.

She had to fix what she'd done to him.

"Good question." She smiled and kissed him quick.

"What was that for?" he asked as he tried to sit up. "Not that I'm complaining."

Oh, my gawd. From the look on his face, he didn't remember that first hot kiss. At least, it was hot and unforgettable for *her.* Rayne only shrugged. How could she explain that kiss to him when she didn't understand it herself?

Something in Gabriel—and in her—made Rayne want to protect him. Her obsession with him had grown beyond his connection to Lucas. Everything about him baffled her. She pulled the hood up on his sweatshirt and covered his head and face as much as she could.

"Can you stand? We gotta go."

"Think so."

On shaky legs he stood, but not without her help. He put his arm around her shoulders and she held him. They crept down the aisle strewn with books, dodging stray cats and one foul-tempered Chihuahua.

"Don't step in pigeon poop," she told him.

"Good call."

Hellboy had vanished. She didn't see or hear him anymore and Gabriel hadn't asked about him, either. The questions she had in her mind over what had happened to his phantom dog would have to wait.

When they got to the end of the row, Rayne peeked around a bookshelf to find her sister. Mia looked stunned as she helped another woman to her feet. They both were distracted by the men who were still wrestling on the floor with their arms and legs flailing. Rayne would have only seconds to get Gabe out.

"Go. Now," she told him.

Rayne didn't turn her head. She held her breath, praying her sister wouldn't see them leave out the side. She walked him to the exit door that gaped open. The door alarm had been the blaring sound she'd heard before. She rushed him through the door and into the cool night air, thankful when they finally reached the darkness beyond the lights of the municipal building. The cops had arrived. Their red-and-blue lights spiraled across the front of the building, cutting through the night sky. They had to get out of there before they were questioned.

As they approached her Harley, Gabriel slowed and stopped.

"I know I haven't given you much reason to have faith in me, Rayne. After what happened in there, I'm not sure I can count on me, either, but I *do* want to help you find Lucas."

She nodded and watched him struggle with more he wanted to say. She waited for him to find the words. Whatever doubts she had about him, they had vanished under the weight of her unexplained yet undeniable need to look after him. Something in this runaway boy felt important, and the fact that he had a bond with Lucas made it easy to trust him.

"Right now, the way I am, I'm a danger to me…and you, if you stay." He stuffed his hands into his pockets. "I could even be bad for your brother. The thing is, I need answers. I need to know what's happening to me."

"How are you going to do that?"

"I have a place I can go, but I've never brought anyone else. It could get tricky."

"You don't want me to go with you?"

"No. I didn't say that." He grabbed her hand. "But I'm giving you the choice."

Before he said another word, she squeezed his hand. "Then I'm in."

He looked worried and had trouble looking her in the eye. That should have triggered questions, but she only had one.

"Will this place have food? 'Cause I'm starving."

"We'll see. I think I could scrounge you a PBJ." He smiled and kissed her on the cheek. "I feel the urge to thank you."

"If it helps, you owe me big." She grinned, but that faded fast when she saw the look on his face.

"I don't know what happened in there." Gabriel got serious. He even looked scared. "Ever since I first saw your brother in my vision, this thing I do has felt weird. I'm not sure I'm in control anymore. That's why I want you to think twice before you come with me."

"What do you mean?"

"This time I shotgunned without Hellboy. It all happened so fast, I never felt him and I definitely didn't go through him."

Rayne thought about what she'd seen of Hellboy. Gabe could've shut him out to protect him, and that was why the dog couldn't break through.

"But I thought *he* was your power. Doesn't everything happen through him?"

After Rayne thought hard, she remembered that the blue flames had consumed Gabe in the library. If he didn't feel Hellboy and hadn't gone through him to summon his ability, then the strange, chilling fire had always been his.

Gabe stared at her a long time until he finally shook his head.

"Whatever I connected with in there, I think your brother had something to do with it. I felt the others, the ones in my sketchbook. It's like…they've become a part of me I can't shake. I reached out this time and something grabbed me back. It wouldn't let go."

Rayne touched his arm.

"Did you feel Lucas? Because he wouldn't hurt you, Gabriel. I know him." She ran a hand through her hair. "God, listen to me. I don't understand this. How could any of it come from Lucas?"

Rayne couldn't move. She stood in the parking lot next to her Harley, staring up at him. All she had wanted was to find Lucas. If Gabriel was right, his bond with Luke might've forced him to cross a line, a point of no return. His mind link to her missing brother had triggered something in him—something dangerous.

If he couldn't control it anymore, what did that mean?

"I don't know what to think, either, Rayne. I can't remember everything, but this was something major. I didn't like it. Not even a little. It was as if all those faces in my sketchbook suddenly came alive, like I knew 'em."

She pictured his drawings, and the faces haunted her mind, too.

"Oh, hell," Rayne gasped. "Your sketchbook."

"What?"

"Your backpack. Where is it?"

Gabe stared at her with his eyes wide and shook his head in stunned silence. They both knew the answer as they turned toward the museum when another police cruiser pulled into the parking lot. No way could they go back inside.

Not now.

Dr. Haugstad drove her Mercedes down Wilshire Boulevard. In case they found the boy, she'd come with two of Alexander's men, and one of them sat next to her in the front seat, trying to get a fix on the GPS location they'd been given. The coordinates were for Mia Darby's cell phone, but with a complex as large as the L.A. County Museum, pinpointing the exact location would not have been easy until Fiona saw the flashing lights of several police cruisers. She didn't bother with locating a suitable and legal parking spot. She followed an ambulance onto the property.

"This has to be it," she said. "I don't believe in coincidences."

"Close enough." The man nodded.

The minute she parked and saw the damage, the busted front door and the strange animals and distraught people running from the building, her heart elevated to an alarming rate. If Lucas had been cornered in the building, she had a suspicion of what might've happened if he felt threatened. She hoped he hadn't been arrested. That would only complicate things.

"Quickly, we must find Mia Darby," she ordered her men and got out of the car. "She could prove to be an invaluable asset, but not if she talks to the authorities. And you…" She pointed to one of the men. "See if there are any surveillance cameras inside. We need those recordings, at least a copy of them. Pay whatever you must."

Fiona picked up her step and followed her men. When she got inside, she stood in silence as her eyes took in the shocking aftermath. She wanted to remember everything. She had a feeling what happened here would be of great significance.

She didn't have to look for Mia Darby. The girl came to her with trembling hands and shaky voice.

"You should have seen it. I don't know what happened. I can't find my sister and Lucas…." Tears fell now. The girl looked as if she'd collapse.

"Mia, please focus." She took the girl by the shoulders with a firm grip and looked her in the eye. "Tell me what you saw. Every detail, no matter how trivial."

The Darby girl rambled about blue lights and animals and people fighting in the middle of an earthquake. If Fiona didn't know any better, she could have sworn the girl had experienced a psychotic break. Shaking with adrenaline, Mia recounted her story, sounding as if she suffered from post-traumatic stress disorder. Fiona had many questions that would have to come later.

Now they had to assess the situation quickly and mitigate damages. She'd overheard witnesses talking about it being an earthquake, and another person thought it had been an underground gas explosion because of the color of the flames. But without books being burned and no other building in the complex affected, Fiona felt satisfied the police would need time to sort things out. They may never come up with an answer, but she had her own theories. Although she had to get the Darby girl out of there to question her under a controlled setting, one question could not wait.

"I need to know more about this blue light you saw. Could you pinpoint where it came from?" Fiona had to whisper. She didn't want anyone else to hear, especially the police, who were questioning others.

"Yes. It came from over here. The back corner."

Mia Darby led her down two rows of shelves to a spot where books were strewn on the floor in a heap. Something had definitely happened where they stood and Fiona found a backpack on the floor. The bag was unzipped and she saw a book and a spiral notepad inside, but she didn't have time for anything more than to grab it before the authorities did.

"Thank you, Mia. You've been a great help." She embraced the girl and let her cry for as long as it took to give the illusion that she cared. "Unfortunately, my dear, we must leave now. It's not a good idea for you to mention any of this to the police. I hope you understand."

"Uh, y-yes." The girl nodded and wiped her face.

"I've got my car, but give me your keys. One of my men

will drive you home and I'll follow. You're in no condition to be behind a wheel. We'll talk more while things are still fresh in your mind, but afterward I can give you something to help you sleep."

After she got the girl's car keys, Fiona wrapped her arms around Mia and walked her outside. By noon tomorrow, she'd have a full report for Alexander Reese and she'd have time to examine the contents of the backpack. Thanks to the Darby girl, Fiona had a pretty good idea what might've happened. Her mind raced with possibilities. She could barely contain her excitement.

A Crystal child could have done this. She desperately wanted that to be so and she wanted it to be Lucas, the boy she had discovered. All of her testing and experience through her studies with the church gave her the instincts to recognize these human abominations. Being a doctor, she wanted to better understand what had made them mutate, but through her beliefs, she passionately held that these children were another plague on mankind.

Only a very powerful Indigo could have accomplished this level of chaos—an evolving Crystal child of great magnitude was in the process of "becoming," but what had triggered him? She had to know. Perhaps Mia could fill her in on more, and the backpack could also hold answers if she got lucky.

She should have been alarmed by what she had seen in the museum and heard from the Darby girl, but a peculiar adrenaline raced through her veins like ice water that made her hyperalert. Everything she and Alexander had undertaken for the sake of humanity lay ahead of her. The Darby boy. It had to be him. They were getting closer. She felt it. Soon she'd have the boy under lockdown in Ward 8 at Haven Hills—completely under her control.

Before she got into her car, she gave an order to the man who had stayed with her.

"Get a team to hack into the traffic cams for the parking lot and the surrounding streets. Unless the Darby boy and the other sister were on foot, we could find something useful."

Fiona breathed in the night air and stared back at the museum exhibit hall with the spiraling police beacons strafing the entrance of the building. She wanted to remember this moment. It felt like a significant turning point—one that she had instigated with Lucas Darby.

Lucas struggled to open his eyes and be free of a familiar torment—the nightmare that had escalated and forced him to run away from Haven Hills. Trapped in a twilight sleep, he felt his consciousness lift from his body. He could look down and see his thrashing arms and the sweat that clung to his skin, but he remained tethered to the body that had failed him and kept him a prisoner.

It hadn't been the fever that kept him from opening his eyes. It had been the dream.

A red-and-white sign posted over secured double doors made him flinch. Ward 8. He felt his arms and legs tied down to a cold gurney. Stern men dressed in white ignored his pleas for help. They took him to a cold room with bright lights. His heart pounded loudly enough for him to feel a punishing throb in his brain. He knew what would come. The dream never wavered. A faceless woman dressed in white always brought pain. Even her voice made him cringe, yet it came muffled as if she spoke underwater.

"No!" he cried, but no one ever rescued him.

Lucas didn't know what he saw. It could have been stirred by a memory struggling to surface, or someone else's panicked vision or a dose of paranoia over his uncertain future. In the throes of the dream, that didn't matter now.

He would have to endure it as if it happened to him.

{ 11 }

Outside L.A.
10:30 p.m.

Rayne filled up her Harley with gas, and with Gabriel directing her where to go, they left L.A. behind. When wide highways turned into two-lane roads, he got quiet and slumped against her back with his arms around her. She knew he had to be exhausted and needed to sleep. He still hadn't told her where they were going, but simply being alone with Gabriel felt like enough.

Before they'd left the museum parking lot, he'd asked her again if she still wanted to come with him. Her answer hadn't changed, but she'd had plenty of time to think. Miles of night road, with flashes of Gabriel convulsing in blue flames, had their way of niggling at her insides. Rayne felt good that he still wanted to help her, but she knew that his demons had caught up to him.

Nothing about their situation felt right or good. Whatever Gabe's problems, they'd collided with her search for Lucas. She understood why Gabe needed answers. He didn't want to make things worse, but she couldn't help be worried for Lucas, too. She prayed she'd made the right decision to stick with Gabe. Not knowing how bad things were for Luke made it easy for her to picture terrible things.

Darkness made a perfect canvas to imagine her worst fears.

City lights and concrete gave way to a canopy of moonlight and stars over her head, and the wind buffeted her body. Her headlight swept past tall grasses that whipped by her in a blur alongside miles of fence posts. Painted center stripes dotted a never-ending ribbon of asphalt that led farther away from towns and people. She had no idea where he would take her, but the drone of her engine lulled her into thinking they were safe for now, even though she had a bad feeling it would only be the calm before the coming storm.

Something had happened to Gabriel and they couldn't leave that behind or deny it or ignore it. He was right about needing help, and if he had a place to go where he could get answers, he needed to do it. They'd both brought their troubles with them, and it would only be a matter of time before they had to go back and face them.

Near Ludlow and the Bristol Mountains, she felt a distinct chill in the air as the elevation changed. Gabriel had her turn off onto a narrow road. She didn't catch the name of it, only that signs marked with the name Devil's Playground made her feel uneasy. She knew the Mojave Desert wasn't far, but in the dark she'd gotten turned around. When they drove up to a dirt road and a gate with a lock on it, Gabriel had her stop and he got off the bike. Without hesitating, he entered a code that opened the gate. For a moment, he looked surprised that it worked.

"What is this place?" she asked.

"If things don't check out, we may not stay," he said. Before she asked anything else, he said, "I lived here for a while when I was a kid."

That was all Gabe said before he climbed onto the Harley

and waited for her to hit the gas. But when a cloud drifted over the moon, it blocked out the stars and cast them deeper into darkness. Even under her helmet, Rayne heard the haunting wail of a coyote in the distance and she knew exactly how the animal felt to be isolated and alone.

The private dirt road had no-trespassing signs posted as they first rode in, and her headlight caught the glint off the eyes of animals in the pitch-black. She never got a clear look at what they were before they bolted, but she felt them watching. When the road took a turn up a hill, she felt the strain on her Harley and had to lean into the climb. Gabriel did, too, and he tightened his hold on her.

Enormous trees lined the side of the road, and boulders had been split to cut the pathway up the mountain. In daylight, she had a feeling the view would be breathtaking. But at night, her headlight captured the sheer drop-offs hidden in shadows, and that made the ride more ominous.

As the dirt road flattened out, they rounded a curve and she got a glimpse of lights on the horizon. When they got closer, she slowed down for a better look. A massive stone wall surrounded the biggest estate she had ever seen. Gabriel had taken her to a mansion in the middle of nowhere—a compound that looked more like a menacing fortress. She gripped the handlebars tighter. When she'd first met Gabriel, she got the impression he came from money. Real money. If he had any history with this place, she had guessed right about him, but that didn't make her feel any better.

Gabriel yanked off his helmet as she slowed to a stop at the crest of a hill, and she did the same. Rayne breathed in the night air and felt a soft breeze through her hair. She stared at the stone front filled with dark windows that looked like eyes and eerie spires that reminded her of only one place.

"Hogwarts. You've brought me to Potterville."

"I thought you trusted me, Rayne."

When she heard the smile in his voice, she took a deep breath and glanced over her shoulder. The moon had painted Gabriel in its bluish haze and made his eyes more haunting.

"Yeah, I do. Especially now that I know you and Harry are BFFs."

Being a smart-ass helped her deal with the wad of fear knotting in her belly.

"Follow my lead and no questions. Remember?" He put his hands on her hips. "I may not be welcome here."

Not asking questions had suddenly turned into the impossible, but she kept her mouth shut and handed him her helmet. She wanted to feel the wind on her face as she rode toward the impressive front entrance with its wooden doors made for a giant.

She trusted Gabe, but whoever lived in a place like this, they'd be another story.

Downtown L.A.

Having Lucas in her bed when he was injured and sick had been necessary. Kendra wanted him with her, for many reasons. He'd been delirious and plagued by nightmares. He needed her. In his more lucid moments, he didn't remember the dreams, or perhaps he didn't want to talk about the hallucinations that had tortured him. She certainly understood that.

But after the fever broke and he was getting better, she felt the flash of heat to her face whenever she touched his bare skin to dress his wounds. The way he watched her, comfortable in their silence, Lucas stared at her with eyes that seemed older than his fifteen years. He was physically beautiful, and from what she sensed of his gentle nature, he had a soul to match. After he connected with her—when their bond went both ways—she felt an addictive rush that she never wanted to end.

But on the night of his fever, all that changed. *Everything changed.*

The reality of her past closed in on her. At first she felt shock at his ability to get past her mental barriers. Her anger over his lack of respect came next, but her final spiral into misery had been a self-inflicted wound. Being reminded of her darkest secret by Lucas had been a harsh slap that she'd never be able to hide anything from him.

And, even worse, she'd never be worthy of the future she wanted for all of them.

"What's wrong?" he asked.

He reached for her hand, a gesture she would have wanted before he'd probed her darkest memory. Now she only pulled away, struggling with what to say.

"You can see the past," she said. "You read secrets in anyone's memory. I've never known anyone who did that. It's... frightening." She sighed, letting her pain show. "How long have you been able to do that?"

"I don't know what you're talking about."

When she clenched her jaw, he must have sensed her frustration.

"What happened? What did I do?" When he sat up and winced, she saw he still hurt.

"You don't remember?"

Flashes of her past rushed back to her, things she wanted to forget but never could—things she felt certain that Lucas had seen. She hid those memories from him now, but knowing he could delve into her mind even with a raging fever, she didn't know if her usual blocking tactics would work with someone like Lucas.

The not knowing was killing her.

"No." He shook his head. "Did I do something wrong?"

When his eyes locked on hers, he looked innocent. She

still felt violated and betrayed, yet whenever she looked at this boy, she wanted to believe that he had no reason to lie to her. She hadn't imagined what he'd done, but perhaps under the influence of such a high fever, he really didn't remember.

"You have no idea how strong you are or what you can become," she said. "You asked me to be your teacher, but it's me who should be learning from you."

She reached for his hand and felt him connect to her mind, too. Feeling him, inside and out, made her feel stronger. Better.

"There is so much potential in you, but you frighten me, Lucas. Connecting with you has affected me in a way I never could've imagined. I'm not sure I'm strong enough, but I feel a sense of duty toward you, even if it scares me."

"Are you saying that *I* scare you?"

She didn't know how to answer him. She wanted to reassure him that her idea of their future frightened her more, but that would be a lie. Right now, being with someone as powerful as Lucas, a boy who could slice through any mind blocks she could muster, scared her far more than the bleakest future she could imagine.

She touched his cheek.

"We must embrace who we are and who we're becoming, even if it scares us. We owe it to our kind."

"Our kind?" he asked.

"I read about us. Have you ever heard of Indigo kids or Crystal children? It's what they're calling us."

When he only shook his head, she said, "We're special, Lucas. We feel instead of think. We trust our instincts and use our minds the way they were intended. We see and feel things they don't—or can't—because they only use a fraction of their brainpower. Animal species evolve and change in order to survive. It makes sense that we do, too. We're the future, Lucas. Mankind 2.0."

She smiled, but he didn't.

"No one ever treated me special. Even my parents acted like something was wrong with me," he said.

"That's my point. Your family dosed you, teachers acted like you were in special ed and doctors treated you like a lab rat. They made you feel like you weren't normal. They fear what they don't understand, what they can't control. The future lies with us, not them. We must fight for what is ours."

Kendra knew how she must have sounded to him. No kid talked the way she did, not even Raphael, who was oldest. Her unique Indigo nature made her different. She felt the weight of duty on her shoulders, for a future she hoped that she'd live to see. She didn't have time to be a kid in a world that needed change, even though there were times that she yearned for the childhood that had been taken from her. She'd never truly known what being a child was, not like Lucas had. She could see by his innocence—and his unquestioning trust in strangers like her—that Lucas had been loved by someone, despite the hospital and medications he had endured.

With every question he asked her, his inexperience showed.

"Why can't we learn to exist *with* them?" he asked. "Fighting for dominance is their mistake. It shouldn't be ours."

"You've seen how ruthless the Believers are. They're only the first. Think of how bad things could get once the word really gets out about us. Right now people chalk us up to the lunatic fringe, but don't be naive that they'll leave us alone when they finally believe we exist. I named that damned church and its fanatics the Believers for a reason."

When she saw him flinch in pain again, she took a deep breath and calmed down.

"The way I figure it, you're a Crystal child, Lucas. You've

blown past being an Indigo like me. It's natural that you'd want peace, but that's exactly why you need someone like me. Indigo kids are fighters. We don't settle for how things are. We get angry. We fight. Someone has to do it, but you…" She touched his cheek and said, "You're our future."

She had to get him to see how things were, not how he wanted them to be.

"Trust me when I say they understand fighting far better than you do," she said. "They will not allow us to exist among them. They fear us now. What will they do when we get stronger and our numbers grow?"

"But you can't know that will happen." For the first time, he raised his voice, and it looked as if it hurt him.

Kendra sighed and ran a hand through his long hair. She leaned over and kissed him on the cheek.

"No more talk of fighting. First, you'll eat. I've made you a vegetable broth." She smiled to hide her worry. "I've washed your clothes. When you feel up to it, I'll show you your new home."

She hoped Lucas would choose to stay with them—with *her*. If they were meant to survive, they'd need him, but Kendra didn't have the strength to resist what he could do.

If Lucas wanted to, he could know everything about her.

Bristol Mountains
11:10 p.m.

Dead leaves swirled at Gabe's feet and whipped into the air, casting shadows as they moved under the dim light of a single lantern fixed to the stone wall outside the door. The littered front entrance, with its cobwebs and mounds of dust, told him things had changed from what he remembered of the grandeur of the estate. He felt the weight of isolation and an unshakable gloom.

Now, as he stood at a door he never thought he'd see again, he worked up his courage. Seeing this place through a kid's eyes, it had once looked huge and magical. Every room held a mystery. Every old storage trunk told a story. Being here again had tapped into a part of his childhood that would always be special. It surprised him that despite the years—and all that had happened—the place still felt the same. It hadn't changed much.

He had been the one to change. He wasn't a kid who believed in magic anymore.

When a spark of guilt kept him from knocking, he glanced over his shoulder at Rayne. She only shrugged and didn't push. She even forced a strained smile. She seemed to sense how hard it had been for him to come here. If his gut didn't feel like a pretzel, he would've kissed her.

As he reached for the buzzer, the door moved on its own. It opened with a loud, rusty creak.

"Holy shiitake!" Rayne cried out and jumped. She grabbed him by the arm and wouldn't let go.

The heavy wooden door with its ancient metal hinges inched open and sucked dried leaves into the gaping mouth of the mansion. Gabe stayed put. He stared into the darkness and waited to see who had opened the door.

But before he saw anything, he heard a familiar growl. Hellboy blocked his way and wouldn't let him cross the threshold.

"Sorry about that," he said to Rayne. "He's a little… protective."

Clutching his arm, she said, "If that's a problem, call the Dog Whisperer."

Gabe put his arm around her and walked inside with Hellboy leading the way. The dog's massive body hovered off the ground and moved with a ghostly grace. Every muscle that once had been his rippled through his back and legs under fur that held together like a swirl of dense fog. With ears back and head low, Hellboy glared into the darkness and crept slowly. His growl trailed in his wake and echoed into the emptiness of the foyer until he stopped and sniffed the air.

Before Gabe felt a presence, Hellboy wagged his tail and stopped. A voice came from thin air.

"It is good to see you again, Gabriel."

Gabe couldn't help it. He jumped and turned at the familiar sound. What he saw was not what he had expected. The ghost of the estate's butler spiraled from the gloom like a glittery tornado. His eyes came first, followed by his floating lips and his round belly. Dressed in the formal attire he had worn when he was alive, he let Gabriel see him.

"Frederick?" Gabe's throat went as dry as the Mojave. "You've looked…better."

"I can honestly say that I am not presently at my best." Frederick raised an eyebrow. "But I haven't let Death stop me, sir."

"That's the spirit."

"Who are you talking to, Gabriel?" Rayne asked.

Before Gabe could explain, Frederick took a shot. "Oh, dear, I'm sorry. How rude of me. Is this better?"

The dead butler closed his eyes and stuck a thumb in his mouth and blew it like a horn. He popped like a puff of smoke and crackled like a fire until his form took shape enough for Rayne to see him.

She yelped and would've fallen if Gabe hadn't caught her.

"I gotta sit down," she said. When Hellboy cocked his head and whined, Rayne sighed. "Does anybody actually *live* here?"

It suddenly occurred to Gabe that he didn't know the answer to that basic question. He turned to Frederick, who smiled and waved a hand toward another part of the mansion.

"Your uncle Reginald is in the great room, sir. He doesn't

sleep well these days, I'm afraid, but I'm sure your visit will cheer him. I'll announce you and your guest."

After the butler vanished to the sound of a cork pop, Gabe took a deep breath. He wanted Frederick to be right, that his uncle would be pleased to see him—but he couldn't see how that could be. Too much had happened between them.

The one person they both loved most had paid the price for Gabe being different. He couldn't help but feel that his uncle would be reminded of that every time he looked at him.

It was why Gabe had left in the first place.

With Hellboy at his heels, Gabriel headed down a shadowy corridor of ornate rugs and old paintings that hung on wood-paneled walls. Before Rayne followed him, Frederick popped back and waved a hand to stop her. As he stepped closer, the ghostly butler smelled of dust and cinnamon. One smell reminded her that the man was dead. The other trailing scent told her that when he was alive, Frederick liked cookies.

"Forgive me for noticing, my dear, but your stomach has the rumbles. I believe Cook always has something appealing in the icebox. Have Gabriel show you to the kitchen after your visit with his uncle."

Frederick winked, but before she thanked him, he vanished. The essence of his shape drifted to the floor like glitter that dissolved at her feet. Rayne stood in silence with one word on her mind.

Weird.

She picked up her pace to catch up to Gabriel. When she joined him, Gabe took her hand without saying anything. The crackle of a blazing fire and the rhythmic pulse of a grandfather clock drew her into the murky great room, a cavernous space filled with books and antique furnishings that looked centuries old.

Without any other lights burning in the room, the fire cast eerie long shadows that danced across the walls. An older man with a full head of gray hair sat in a wingback chair uphol-stered in royal-blue-and-red velvet in a rich tapestry pattern. He sat near a massive stone hearth and gazed into the fire until he finally looked up. He stared at Gabe with his eyes filled with tears that caught the glow of the fire. Rayne let go of Gabriel's hand and stayed behind. When Hellboy sat next to her, she felt a tickle from the phantom dog's presence as he brushed against her jeans.

Even a dead dog could tell they needed space.

When Uncle Reginald stood, Rayne's eyes trailed up his long legs to his aged face as the man lumbered from his chair. Gabriel was tall, but this man dwarfed him.

"After you left, I looked for you." His uncle spoke first. His gravelly voice cracked.

Gabriel only nodded. He didn't move. He didn't say any-thing. He waited.

"I don't know why you're here, but I prayed this day would come," the old man said.

"I didn't think you'd ever want to see me."

A single tear trickled down the man's cheek. He didn't wipe it away. "My dear boy, how wrong you are."

In two steps, Uncle Reginald closed the distance between himself and Gabriel and wrapped his arms around his nephew. He lifted Gabe off the floor in a monster hug. Rayne fought the lump in her throat. If love were a pie, she could've served a heaping portion and had plenty to share. Seeing Gabe with his uncle, she thought of Lucas and her father and mother, and even Mia.

She ached for the family she lost, but she was happy for Gabriel.

Uncle Reginald Stewart made her feel welcomed after she

was introduced to him. The big man reminded her there would be food in the kitchen and told her that Frederick would ready the rooms where they could sleep. Getting ushered to a bedroom by a dead guy—no matter how nicely he dressed—would take getting used to. In this mansion where the living walked among the dead, Rayne would have to accept the way things were. She had stepped into bizarro world with Gabriel as her guide. She had a feeling she'd only scratched the surface of the many secrets Gabe had.

With a smile and a nod, Rayne left Gabriel to his reunion. Hearing his uncle's thicker British brogue, she now understood where Gabe's accent had come from. His parents must have been Brits. It took every ounce of willpower she had not to listen as Gabe and his uncle spoke by the fire.

The room could have fit her apartment in it ten times over. She put distance between herself and Gabriel, to give him privacy and to check her cell. In the library, she'd switched her phone to vibrate and felt the tickle of a message countless times during their road trip. She didn't have to check her phone to know who'd been calling her. Mia had left several messages, nothing that couldn't wait until she figured stuff out.

An amazing display at the other end of the room made a better diversion.

Rayne hadn't noticed before, but the übertasteful decor was oddly paired with huge faded posters mounted on frames along the back wall. *Circus posters.* Trapeze artists and elephants and strange clowns covered the walls and towered over her head. Shadows cast from the fire undulated over the promo pieces and made the enormous images come alive.

With her mouth open, Rayne stared up at the colossal illustrations that looked more like exotic and mysterious billboards from a circus carnival. She wanted to ask Gabriel why they were displayed the way they were. They seemed out of place, but when she looked back at him, he'd stopped talking to his uncle.

In that moment, Gabriel made her heart bleed. The sadness on his face gripped her and made her look at the posters again—*closer.* This time she saw what had made him look miserable. A young boy wore a hooded cape that covered his head and most of his face. He had his arms outstretched in a way she recognized, but the boy's captivating eyes were unmistakable. A stunning woman named Lady Kathryn, dressed in a cape and a tiara, stood by him and a large dog that looked more like a wild wolf.

Hellboy and the Third Eye had been printed across the top of the billboard and below it appeared the words *Letters from the Dead.* Rayne saw the similarities before she had to ask. Gabriel looked like his mother, and he and his ghost dog had a long history. He'd known the dog when Hellboy had a beating heart.

Gabe's link to the dead had deep roots to a past she wanted to understand.

Downtown L.A.
The Next Day

Lucas felt weak and his head still hurt, but he couldn't stay in bed. Without seeing daylight in the tunnels, he'd lost track of time. Kendra had fed him and he drifted in and out of sleep, but when he awoke to find he was alone, he had to find her. As she'd promised, she had his clothes washed and dried and folded near his mattress. They were laid out on a crate. After he dressed, he went looking for her.

He tested his abilities by sensing where Kendra was in her tunnel stronghold. He didn't reach out to her in their usual way. He merely pictured her face and trusted his instincts on how to navigate through the darkness. He'd never done that before. After meeting Kendra and feeling the presence of the others, he realized that what made him a freak in one world made him strong in another. That gave him the courage to try new things here, without hiding or fearing who he was.

He found Kendra working in a garden. The color of her aura had tinted to a soft bluish-green. It oozed from her, rather than pulsed. Her contentment showed. Seeing the unexpected beauty underground stunned him. She must have created it, an oasis of fresh herbal aromas and a heady floral scent. When he stepped into the light, he had to shield his eyes until they adjusted to the brightness. Greenery draped down, bathed in streams of sunlight from a grated opening at the surface above. Vines stretched their leaves toward the light, and bees and butterflies flicked from flower to bud. Kendra and her children cultivated their harvest by using metal scaffolding between the tiers of crops, and plastic tubing dripped water down the walls. The air smelled of humidity and rich soil and the sweet aroma of her garden.

Lucas knew Kendra had envisioned this and made it happen. She had cultivated her garden in the same way she had plucked each child from danger and brought them here to become her family. She nurtured each one as she wanted to do with him.

Kendra's ability with her mind paled in comparison to the beauty of her heart.

"This is…magic. You did this, didn't you?" He stared up into the rafters of plants that spiraled up the wall over his head.

"I started it so we'd have food to eat," she said. "The excess I sell to local grocers and a health-food store buys my medicinal herbs so we have spending money. Rafe and Benny take care of that end."

When she kept working, he sensed something had changed between them. He had to make her understand how he felt about being with her.

"I'm new to all this," he told her. "You tell me that I have a place here with you…that I belong, but I need time. It's like I've been in a coma for years. I don't know who or what I am. All this time, I thought I was defective. A lifetime of feeling damaged can't be fixed overnight."

When Kendra stopped working, he felt the lurking shadows in her soul before she even made a sound. She *let* him feel her darkness.

"I used to hear the voices, so many voices. I heard them

most when I worked with flowers. Plants helped me channel them."

"That's beautiful."

"But time has taken those voices from me, Lucas. Time and the Believers. One by one, our gifted children have been taken and their voices silenced. I don't know what has happened to them, but I feel their loss in a way I can't describe. Our children could be dead or silenced in other ways. The Believers are interfering with what should be the natural order."

"We could get help…to stop them."

She shook her head.

"Who can we trust to help us? We're perfect victims for anyone who preys on us, because we can't speak out. We can't afford to be put under a microscope for the world to see. If we go from weird New Age websites to government-funded scientific studies, there'd be no place safe for us."

She lowered her voice and her expression softened. Her aura drifted to a darker hue and vibrated.

"Do you remember the joy you felt to finally be connected…to hear my voice and know my words were meant for you?" she asked. After he nodded, she said, "Well, think of how much it hurts to have those voices taken from you, one by one."

Her eyes glistened with tears.

"I don't have to know them, or meet them face-to-face, to feel they are a part of me." She stood and turned to him, taking off her gloves to throw them onto a scaffold. "You ask me for time when all I see are lives destroyed forever. We don't *have* time. We're in a war for our very existence and our future. I need you with me."

When she stepped closer and put her hand to his chest, he heard the music from his childhood playing softly in his mind as if it had always been with him. Looking into her eyes made everything perfect, as if he'd come full circle. He smelled the scent of lavender and herbs and something uniquely Kendra. She balanced the strength of her cause with the vulnerability of her secrets. She was a mystery he wanted to understand. As she touched his cheek, he breathed her in and cradled her face in his hands before he kissed her.

Sweet. Pure. Perfect.

He stayed in the moment with her, feeling her warmth and the press of her body next to his. She pulsed in brilliant blue again, the way he'd first seen her. In the midst of her garden with its mist and flowers and the hum of bees—that blended in perfect harmony with music only he could hear—he understood what she wanted of him. He had to let go of the life he had before. She had drawn him to her for a purpose, one that she hoped he would eventually embrace. He felt unworthy of her belief in him, but maybe one day he would measure up.

After they kissed, he held her.

With his eyes closed, he thought of what she'd said. She had such unwavering faith in him—maybe too much. How could she know him when he didn't know himself? After their minds had linked, he felt a dependence on her. She had opened his eyes to a world he might never have known, but she wanted her cause to become his.

That scared him, but not enough to leave her. Kendra had a drive and a purpose she would die for. He wanted to believe in her cause as much as she did. Maybe one day he would, but for now—all he had was her.

Haven Hills Treatment Facility—L.A.
Morning

Dr. Fiona Haugstad hadn't gotten much sleep last night. Her mind wouldn't let her. Even now, as she headed down a hospital corridor of Haven Hills, her interrogation of Mia

Darby played on her mind. The young woman had witnessed something amazing, yet the whole event at the museum had been wasted on her. Mia Darby was ordinary. Although the girl was employed by the church and officially involved in recovering her missing brother, she would never attain Fiona's level of security. She simply did not have the skills or the drive. She was weak.

She only had her brother. Lucas was the real prize.

As Fiona used her keycard to unlock the staff entrance to Ward 8, she puzzled through what she had found. Once she'd obtained the traffic-cam surveillance and pictures her security team had acquired from the museum, she had assessed everything and had one image enlarged. When that digital photo had come back, she was shocked at what she found. She compared the face in the photo to the file she had on Lucas Darby to be sure, but she had her answer.

The boy at the museum with Rayne Darby had *not* been Lucas.

Impossible, she thought as she grabbed a clipboard of medical history that hung outside another locked room. When she got inside, she quickly flipped through the pages of the health records of the drowsy boy strapped to a gurney. He'd been drugged for the procedure, but that seldom stopped them from trembling when they realized they were completely in her hands. A plastic bag of fluids fortified with an anesthetic hung near his head. She upped the dose and waited for his eyes to shut.

"This will be a big day for you. Very significant, I would say." She stroked his cheek and looked into his eyes.

"Just one last procedure, then I'll be done with you. I promise." Fiona tousled his hair and forced a smile. "Now, close your eyes and let me get to work. I've got a busy day."

It would be the last time this one heard her voice. She'd

done all she could do with him. Some simply did not conform to her standards or cooperate in any way to make themselves useful to her or the church. This one had taught her all he could.

She hadn't lied to the boy. Today *would* be significant for him. All that remained was one final procedure—one that required a sacrifice on his part for the good of science. She would make better use of his brain than letting him keep it. One way or another, she got what she wanted from each of them. The best they could give her. When a nurse entered the room, Fiona looked over her shoulder and gave an order.

"Prep him for surgery. And arrange for disposal of his body. This one won't be staying with us. We could use the bed."

"Yes, Doctor."

While the nurse prepared the boy, Fiona turned the final page of one boy's life in favor of another more interesting case. She replayed the library images in her mind, assessing everything again, especially the gem she had found in the backpack. The aftermath of the scene had felt like the product of a Crystal child. Her instincts couldn't be wrong. She had believed that the boy in the sweatshirt, who had done a great deal to hide his face, had been hiding something more than his identity.

She'd been right. Fiona smiled as she headed in to scrub for the harvesting surgery.

Her instincts on the backpack had proved correct. When she had unzipped the bag and dumped the contents to look over them, she felt disappointment in what she'd found at first. It looked like an art student's bag. It had a sketch pad and a library book on L.A. County art inside, but little else. She had almost given up until she got a better look at the drawings and recognized a face.

The face of Lucas Darby. There were two sketches of the boy.

Fiona had made copies of each sketch. She had a plan and wanted to surprise Alexander Reese with it once she made progress, but she had to tell him something today. He was expecting a full report of the incident at the museum. She had enough to tell him for now, but she would save the best to savor later.

After surgery, she would run each sketch through the Tracker program. If she got hits on their database of targets, that would tell her a great deal about the boy who had drawn the images. If the drawings were significant, the library book the boy had planned to steal had to be significant, too.

She needed time to figure out the puzzle this mystery boy had left behind. Fiona had no intention of presenting only half a theory to Alexander. She'd wait until she had more on the importance of the library book and the Tracker results. Alexander would expect no less than perfection from her, and she felt up to the task.

She also had confidence that she'd found another Crystal child, one even stronger than Lucas Darby. If this boy could draw the faces of other special children, then perhaps he had the ability to see them in his mind and track them. She could use a boy like that.

Fiona had to know more.

Bristol Mountains

Rayne opened her eyes and thought she was still dreaming. Under warm linens and a plush comforter, she gazed in a sleepy stupor at a lacy canopy. The four-poster bed had elaborate carvings in the wood that had an old-world feel to it. When she heard a fire burning in the hearth of the bedroom, she stretched and sat up to gaze around the room that had been hers for a night. She wanted to remember everything. No way she'd ever get a chance to sleep in luxury like this again.

Giant doors and oversize furniture made her feel like a little kid in the biggest bedroom she'd ever seen, even in the movies. Last night a girly nightgown and robe and slippers had been laid out on the bed. It looked like silk, and when the ice-blue color shimmered in the light, she ran a finger across it to make sure it was real. Wearing something that fancy felt weird, but in a place like Hogwarts 2.0, she didn't think anyone would laugh.

She threw back the covers and jumped out of bed to put on the robe and slippers. Gabriel had a bedroom down the hall. She got the impression that the room had been his when he lived here before and his uncle had kept it the same, hoping he'd come back. Guess Uncle Reginald hadn't wasted his time.

Rayne went to her private bathroom and flipped on the lights. Everything glittered in tall mirrors that dwarfed her. Fancy soaps and scented stuff were there for her use and the soaker tub awaited, but when she thought about not having clean clothes to wear, she turned out the bathroom light and went back to the bedroom. The reality that she didn't belong here hit her hard until she saw an envelope pushed under her door.

A note had been written on stationery. She smiled as she read it.

Anything you like in the armoire, it's yours.
Gabe

Rayne didn't know what to expect. She turned to see the ornate wardrobe closet across her bedroom and opened the doors. Clothes in different sizes hung inside with lingerie drawers filled with new things that still had price tags and were in unopened packages, ready for any unexpected guest of the estate.

"Oh, wow."

She'd never seen so many beautiful things, not even in Mia's closet.

The Church of Spiritual Freedom Headquarters—L.A.
Noon

After Fiona had shown Alexander Reese everything she had on the incident at the museum, the man sat in silence looking down at the stills she'd printed for him. His jaw tightened as he held up the blurred picture of a boy in a hooded sweatshirt, the best one they had. Everything in Alexander's body language set her on edge as she waited for him to speak.

In her mind, the boy was clearly not Lucas, yet he had been in the company of Darby's sister Rayne. She'd done her homework on the family, and Mia had talked about her sister, too. There was a definite connection between this mystery boy and the Darby family, something worth pursuing. Yet Alexander did not look satisfied.

"Are we any closer to finding Lucas?" he asked.

Fiona furrowed her brow.

"No, but I thought you'd be pleased. We may have found another boy like him, maybe more powerful. This one is an artist." She flipped to the sketch of Darby and shoved it over to him. "Perhaps he draws what he sees in visions. I recognized the face of Lucas Darby from this sketch without running it through our Tracker software. Doesn't the implication thrill you? We could use this boy to hunt them."

Alexander stared at the drawing in uncomfortable silence before he finally spoke.

"I want the Darby kid." He shoved back the sketchbook and the picture of the boy in the sweatshirt. "You've tested

Lucas. He's a sure thing, you told me. This boy could be no one, a boyfriend to the sister. You don't even know if these drawings are his. I don't want us chasing another target until we have Darby. Do I make myself clear?"

"I understand your concern, but I thought we could acquire this boy, too."

"It's not your job to manage our strategy and resources, Fiona. That's my responsibility." He swiveled his chair to face her. She had to admit it—the man intimidated her when he got like this.

"I appreciate your enthusiasm," he told her. "But let me worry about this new boy when and if I see he is a viable target. Now you have your assignment. Get to it. I want Lucas Darby."

Fiona clenched her jaw and stood to leave. When she reached for the knapsack, Alexander stopped her.

"Leave the bag," he ordered. "Leave everything. I want you focused."

Fiona did as he told her. She left his office without another word, but if he trusted her as his rock, she had to follow her instincts on this new boy. She'd asked his permission to pursue him and that had failed. Now all she had left would be to ask for Alexander's forgiveness after she did what she *had* to do.

He'd left her no choice.

Bristol Mountains

Even with gowns and designer clothes to choose from, Rayne picked out the simplest outfit to wear, because the borrowed clothes weren't hers. Mia would have no trouble playing dress up, but Rayne couldn't do it. She'd bathed and washed and dried her hair, using all the fancy products they had, but the clothes were too much.

Dressed in dark slacks that fit her as if they'd been tailor-made and a powder-blue, long-sleeved blouse, she crept down the hall to Gabriel's room. After she knocked softly on the door, she put her ear to it and listened. No answer.

"Gabriel?" She tried again, whispering his name.

When she didn't hear him, she turned the knob and slipped into his room, with a peek over her shoulder to see if anyone watched her do it. In his room, she turned to see Gabriel. He was still in bed, sound asleep.

She inched toward him, unsure what to do until she got close enough to see him breathing. With his chest bare, she realized he could've been naked under those covers, and a rush of heat warmed her face. Rayne knew she should have turned and walked out, but seeing him like this, it wasn't easy to leave.

Despite Gabriel's powers and strength, she saw him as vulnerable, too. Maybe those feelings had started and been grounded over the guilt she felt about not protecting her brother enough, but she knew that whatever she felt for Gabriel now, those feelings were real and about him.

His childhood home had brought out his soft underbelly that she never would have seen if he didn't allow it. When she first met him at the zoo and he'd let her see how he lived, she sensed that he'd been lost. Something was missing. If anyone knew that lonely feeling, she did, but Gabriel belonged here. He had his uncle and a past he couldn't outrun. Whatever haunted him, the answers would be in this place. She watched the gentle rise and fall of his chest and resisted the urge to brush back the strand of dark hair that had fallen into his eyes.

She wanted to touch him, to kiss him. Every second she spent with him felt like a dream that she'd wake up from and he'd be gone. Watching Gabriel sleep, Rayne had no trouble seeing the child he had been—the extraordinary boy who had lived an odd adventure with his mother in a traveling circus.

But Rayne knew his story wouldn't be that simple. Something had made him run and an unmistakable misery colored his eyes. Without waking him, she backed out of his room and shut the door behind her.

Alone in Gabriel's childhood home, she felt the mystery of him everywhere.

Minutes Later

Rayne had a strong urge to wander the hallways of the vast estate on her own, but without leaving a trail of bread crumbs, she believed getting completely lost was a distinct possibility. Even though she wanted to eat, she retraced her steps downstairs, back to the great room, and stood under the circus posters of Gabriel and his mother.

She stared into the eyes of Gabriel as a boy. It was as if he stood before her now. He had a way of captivating her, and his mother must have had the same ability. Even now Rayne couldn't turn away—from mother or son.

"Good morning, my dear."

Rayne jumped at the sound of a loud male voice and footsteps behind her.

"Uh…hello." She gulped a breath and turned.

Uncle Reginald appeared and didn't notice that he'd startled her. The man wore dark slacks and an open-collared white shirt with rolled-up sleeves. He looked happier—and younger—than he had last night.

"Is he still sleeping?" the man asked. After she nodded, he said, "That's not like him."

Rayne could have told him what happened at the museum—that Gabe had a right to be tired—but it wasn't her place to tell him.

"When he was a boy, he haunted these halls on his own in the mornings. Every day was a big adventure. Before I knew he had the gift, I thought he had a vivid imagination that kept him entertained for hours, but I soon realized his fanciful friends and peculiar pets weren't of this world. He's a special boy."

Rayne had to grin at how Gabriel's uncle talked in such an openly amused way about his abilities. She couldn't imagine saying stuff like that to Mia. Her sister would lose it. When Lucas used to say he saw their mom and dad after they died, Mia told him to stop. She acted like he'd been cruel. At the time, Rayne figured that was Luke's way of dealing with his grief, but if he was like Gabriel, maybe he had really seen them.

In truth, she wished they would've come to her, but they never did.

"Are you like him?" she asked. "I mean, you live here with Frederick. Can you shotgun through animals, too?"

"Shotgun? Is that what he calls it?" Uncle Reginald smiled. "I see he's confided in you. Not having anyone to talk to can make this existence lonely."

"I didn't exactly give him a choice. Seeing him lit up like a Bunsen burner was a real icebreaker."

When the man laughed, really loud, the sound echoed through the estate and nearly made her jump. She'd gotten used to the quiet, but she had to admit that she liked the sound.

"For the record, I don't 'burn, baby, burn.' We all manifest in different ways." He winked and slumped into a chair near her as she stood under the circus billboard. "I'm afraid I'm rather boring and old-school. Gabriel surpassed my abilities long ago. He's an absolute marvel."

"Did he get this way from his parents? I see that he traveled with his mother in the circus. Did his dad go, too?"

Uncle Reginald's expression changed as fast as a dark storm blowing in. His jaw tightened and his brow furrowed. Rayne thought she'd done something wrong. She sat in a chair across from him, but the man had a hard time looking her in the eye.

"Kathryn, his mother, was my dear sister. Our side of the family had the gift. Gabriel's father never understood." He crossed his arms and shook his head. "I've said too much. Gabriel is a deeply private boy. I'm afraid that revealing any more about him, without him being here, feels like a betrayal. I'm sorry, my dear. Nothing personal. I quite adore you, actually."

"Ditto."

Rayne returned the smile that eventually warmed the man's face, but with every question she asked him about Gabriel, she had misgivings about going too far. Above all, she wanted Gabriel to share his life with her because he wanted to.

She hoped one day he would.

"I know you must be hungry. Come on." He breathed in the air and said, "Can you smell that? I'm famished."

Rayne hadn't noticed before, but the amazing aroma of food made her stomach grind. She smelled fresh-baked stuff and bacon. When she actually saw the buffet set up in the dining room, she couldn't wait to dive in. A long serving table held chafing dishes of hot food, bowls of fresh fruit and pitchers of juice, with the aroma of coffee in the air. When Uncle Reginald let her go first, she grabbed a plate and filled it. She picked a topic to talk about that she hoped would be neutral. She didn't want to intrude on Gabriel's privacy.

"Letters from the dead? What was that?" she asked, as she sat at the table with her loaded plate and juice. "If you can't talk about it, I understand."

Uncle Reginald's face clouded over as he thought about the past. He set his plate and coffee on the table and sat across from her.

"He and his mother created an astonishing act. Quite touch-

ing, in fact. I'd never seen anything like it before or since."
His deep voice trailed off. "Kathryn embellished their act
with circus flair, and Hellboy did his part, but Gabriel became the real star."

"How? What did he do exactly?"

"Gabriel had always been a sensitive boy. Even in a crowd
of people, he found it hard to shut out their thoughts and…
especially their pain. One day, he simply stopped the act and
scribbled something on a piece of paper and handed it to a
woman in the audience. When she read what he wrote, she
hugged that boy. I thought she'd never stop crying."

"What did he write?"

"He never told anyone. He said later that what he'd written was meant for only her, but I heard from others that the
woman's daughter had committed suicide and never left a note.
Gabriel wrote what the daughter had always meant to say to
her mother. And so began his new act."

Goose bumps raced across Rayne's arms. She couldn't imagine being connected to the dead like Gabriel and hearing
voices that were impossible to ignore. How could he block
them out? Would he even want to? Maybe Lucas had been
like him, but the drugs and the doctors took his ability away.
A part of her felt sad for Luke, but another part wasn't sure if
he could've handled the torment.

If she had been in his place, what would she have wanted?
Rayne honestly didn't know.

Being around Gabriel, and seeing his version of normal,
helped her understand Luke in a way she never had before.
Love hadn't been enough. Her brother had always needed her
to fight for him and accept him as he was. Maybe not keeping Luke a secret would be a good first step in changing how
things were to how they could be.

"My brother, Lucas, is like Gabriel, I think. He's in trouble. That's how I found your nephew."

She blurted out the words as they came to her, like tearing the bandage off a cut. She wasn't after his sympathy, or his pity, but she had to get everything out into the open—including the big question she still had on her mind about Gabriel.

"My parents are both dead. If I could do what Gabriel can, I would've wanted to see them one last time."

Uncle Reginald didn't say anything. He only listened.

"Frederick stayed here…after he died," she said. "Is Kathryn still here?"

The man narrowed his eyes and opened his mouth to speak, but when he stopped, Uncle Reginald looked beyond her and another voice answered.

"No, I've never felt her." Gabriel had entered the room and must have heard enough.

Rayne turned in her chair. She wanted to apologize for anything and everything, but she didn't get the chance.

"Every time I shotgun, a part of me looks for her, but she never comes. I don't know why."

Bristol Mountains

"My dear boy, I know you must miss her. I do, too," Uncle Reginald admitted with a grave look on his face. "I suppose that's why I still live alone in this mausoleum. Every inch of it reminds me of Kathryn, but surely you can't want your mother's spirit to haunt you. I know you don't really want that for her, either, do you?"

Gabriel didn't answer his uncle right away. He stepped into the dining room and collapsed into a chair near Rayne. Dressed in jeans, a black T-shirt and a brown plaid shirt over it, he stared across the room and clenched his jaw.

"Maybe not for an eternity," Gabe said. "I'd settled for...a week."

This time his uncle grinned.

"A week. I'd love a week, too." The man shook his head. "You're right. Terribly inconsiderate of her, I must say. Always thinking of herself, that one."

Even Gabe smirked, a gesture Rayne found contagious.

"Rayne, please eat before your food gets cold," Uncle Reginald said. "Gabriel, load up, my boy. Have to keep your strength up. Off you go."

After a trip to the buffet table, Gabriel looked as if he

wouldn't eat much, until he took his first bite. Rayne almost laughed after that. Living at Griffith Park, he couldn't have eaten well. Now it looked as if he would scarf enough to last him. When he slowed down, his uncle directed the conversation to more serious stuff. Rayne and Gabriel caught him up on how they met. They told him everything, including the sketchbook visions and what happened at the museum library—his connection to Lucas and the others that latched onto him, too.

"What do you suppose happened to Lucas?" his uncle asked him.

"Don't know. I do sense danger. He was definitely scared. I saw him…beaten." Gabe stopped and turned to Rayne. "Sorry. I don't mean to worry you."

"No, go on. We have to talk about this. That's why we're here," she said.

"The second time I saw him…in a vision, he was with a girl. He'd been hurt. We think he's hiding in some tunnels in L.A. We can't be sure until we go there, but after my mental train wreck at the museum, I didn't want to make things worse for him."

"The thing is, my brother has been protected his whole life. Luke being on the streets alone scares me and we have no idea who this girl is. I have to find him."

"Of course you do, my dear." The man smiled. "Then it's a good thing you crossed paths with Gabriel. Quite fortunate, indeed."

Gabe had come to his uncle for answers. Now that Rayne met the man, she had a pretty good idea why. The guy knew things and he didn't hold back. He didn't treat either of them like kids. Uncle Reginald reminded Rayne of her own father, or maybe the guy he would've turned out to be if he had lived.

"Conspiracy theorists continue to weigh in on Indigos and

Crystal children. They even link the CIA, the Pentagon and other governmental agencies across the globe to the phenomenon," Uncle Reginald said. "Query the topic online and I'm told you'd get millions of hits. I prefer books over the internet, but I'm ancient."

"I've never heard of an Indigo or a Crystal kid." Rayne finished the last of her biscuit with jam.

"You wouldn't be alone, dear girl."

"So what *are* they?"

"From what I know and believe, Indigos are highly intelligent, gifted psychics. Most are your age. They're named for their bright 'indigo' aura and some have a fascinating, almost obsessive mission to save the world. Quite remarkable, really."

"Lucas. He saw our mom and dad after they died. I...didn't believe him, not really." Rayne shook her head. "My sister, Mia, had him doped up so she didn't have to deal with him. Eventually she had Luke committed to a mental hospital."

"Sad, but these children are frequently misunderstood. As with your brother, they're diagnosed by therapists and doctors as having attention deficit or behavioral disorders, and medication is too easy a solution, I'm afraid."

"I've seen what Gabriel can do, but are these kids for real?" she asked. "Are they like him?"

"Many people dismiss the phenomenon," the man said. "They attribute it to nothing more than overindulgent parents who prefer that their children be recognized as 'special' than label them as 'peculiar.' They'd rather their children be considered saviors of our planet than be called dysfunctional misfits."

Uncle Reginald shrugged and went on.

"Are they real? Since I believe that I'm an earlier version of Indigo, perhaps you shouldn't ask me." The man winked. "My duty is to protect those who come after me, if they will allow it. Despite what's best for them, some of these children can be quite stubborn and determined to be on their own, or so I'm told."

He raised an eyebrow at his nephew.

"So if Gabriel is a new-and-improved version of you, does that make him a Crystal child?"

"No, not with my temper." Gabe was quick to answer. "I'm an Indigo, like my mother and uncle."

"Your connection to the dead always made you the strongest Indigo I've ever seen, Gabriel, but from what you've told me about the museum and your undeniable connection to Rayne's brother, I think I've been wrong."

"Wrong? About what?" Gabriel asked.

"You're not an Indigo. Not anymore. I believe you're becoming what you were always meant to be. A Crystal child, but not like one I've ever read about. I'm not even sure what to call you. You could be a hybrid, of sorts. In an evolutionary process, it's not easy to see what lies ahead." Uncle Reginald leaned an elbow on the table and fixed his gaze on his nephew. "Your mother always said you were destined for greater things. Now I think I know what she was talking about."

Gabe's uncle sighed.

"Early on, Kathryn encouraged his abilities. That caused friction with his father, but she believed in her son," the man told them. "Perhaps she saw our side of the family in him and it excited her. You were always your mother's son. The Stewart clan had grown up with our peculiarities and had learned to embrace them. It made sense to us since all species evolve. It's the natural process. Why not for human beings, too? Are we so special that we're perfect just the way we are? I think not."

As the conversation shifted, Rayne saw Gabriel got quieter. His eyes almost seemed to change color, from honey-amber to darker. He'd stopped eating, too, but his uncle hadn't noticed and kept talking.

"Kathryn believed that children like her Gabriel, and perhaps your Lucas, are sensitive beings who rely and trust their feelings first, Rayne. Their psychic abilities can be quite powerful. They go with their gut instincts and what they sense, even if that flies in the face of what others accept as fact."

"Before they took Lucas away, I remember he questioned everything, especially when he was a kid in school," Rayne said. "That used to drive his teachers crazy, mostly because they didn't know how to answer him. They always wanted to put a label on him, like being different was a bad thing."

"Unfortunately, these children are frequently misunderstood," the man said. "Instead of being considered gifted, most are ostracized or recommended for medical treatment. They don't fit into the norm. Some actually see guardian angels, and as you've seen, we have an affinity with the dead. That's why the dearly departed seek us out. I have no doubt that Indigo children are the next progression of mankind."

"But kids like me are freaks. Haven't you heard? We're mistakes, broken beyond repair." Gabriel shoved his plate aside and crossed his arms. "I should be locked away. Controlled. I'm an embarrassment."

"Your father never understood, Gabriel."

When the conversation switched from Gabe's mother to his father, everything changed. Rayne had only seen him angry when he brought on his power, the time she'd seen him at the zoo and in Griffith Park. Everything else about him had been kindhearted and sweet. She chose to see him as the boy who could conjure the miracle of fireflies in L.A. to calm her. But seeing him flip out over his dad scared her.

"Anger is not the legacy your mother would have wanted for you," his uncle said. "I know it's been hard, but—"

Gabriel interrupted, "He took everything from me. He took *her* from me. How can you not feel rage at what he did to *us?*"

Uncle Reginald watched as his nephew left the table. Gabe turned his back and stared out a window that looked onto a courtyard. Rayne didn't know what to do. She wanted to help, but she knew nothing of Gabriel's pain. That was when it hit her.

That was why he had come to his uncle. Whatever his abilities were, they were also wrapped in a rage that had been with him for a long time. She had no idea what his uncle could do. One thing she *did* understand was anger and frustration over things she couldn't control. Mia had taught her that lesson.

Maybe she wasn't that different from Gabriel after all, but dealing with years of his pain felt hopeless.

"You asked for my help to deal with what's happening to you," Uncle Reginald said. "I've got an idea how I can do that, if you'll allow it."

Rayne did a double take. She hadn't expected optimism from his uncle. Gabe hadn't, either. He glared at the man as if he'd been punched.

Uncle Reginald had a plan. Gabriel looked skeptical as hell and Rayne got a vibe that wouldn't quit. Her cell phone had gone off again. She excused herself from the table and left the dining room long enough to check it out.

She'd turned the sound off because every message had been from Mia. She'd texted. She'd left voice mail. Before Lucas went missing, Rayne might not have heard from Mia for weeks, but Luke and the museum fiasco changed all that. Rayne hadn't sent one word in response.

She didn't know what to say. If she acknowledged she'd been at the museum, Mia would freak. If she denied being there, Mia would freak. Rayne saw no upside, but now her sister had resorted to lying. At least, that was what Rayne believed. She'd texted that she only wanted to make sure she was all right. In another message, she told her that she'd gotten into her apartment, this time through the property manager.

Mia had the gall to even forward Rayne's home phone so she'd get all her calls. Had she done that to spy on her, or had she hijacked her home phone with good intentions? Rayne didn't know. She didn't care about her sister fielding her calls. Mia already admitted to spying on her, but if Lucas tried her number again, he'd get Sister Dearest. What would he think? He could only believe one thing—that she'd turned against him and was now on Mia's side.

"Damn!" She could only imagine what her sister had told her apartment manager to play on her sympathies. *My baby sister is missing, blah, blah, blah.* Okay, so that part was true, but Mia was all about drama and she wasn't above slanting the truth to get what she wanted.

She even stooped really low on one of her texts. She used Floyd Zilla to get to her.

Fed your lizard. Should I call animal control?

Rayne knew how Floyd ate and she'd left her iguana plenty of food and water before she left. Plus she had a backup plan. A friend in her apartment building had a key to her place and owed her a favor. Since her cell-phone battery had run low on juice, she took care of Floyd. One text to her friend, one reply back, problem solved. She shut down her cell.

Mia had pulled out all the stops to make her feel guilty. Yeah, it worked, but still. *So not fair.*

Burbank

"Where the hell have you been?" Boelens bellowed as he stood at the threshold of O'Dell's office in the underground operations bunker. He had a file in his hand. "You look rough."

Boelens had his unblinking reptile stare back. O'Dell would've taken that as a good sign that the guy was back to normal, except that he was on the receiving end of that unrelenting glare. *Normal* wasn't any way to describe his man Boelens.

"Shit happens. Get over it." O'Dell had downloaded the extra file information he'd been sent from the head cheese, Mr. Roboto. "I got more intel on that Darby kid."

"Good. That kid pissed me off." He plopped down into a seat in front of the desk. "Think I found the girl, too."

O'Dell narrowed his eyes at the man until he remembered what girl Boelens was talking about. He'd ordered him to look for her in their database of targets. She had a face he said he'd recognize. He guessed he hadn't lied.

"You mean the girl who hijacked our boy out from under your nose? *That* little girl?" He smirked. "What about her?"

"Found her in our archives. She was a target that got away. Guess no one went after her. She got lost in our system or maybe she wasn't important."

"Until now."

"Yeah, until now." Boelens twitched his lip, his version of a smile. "I ran a report on her known associates, too. Only one name came up. Raphael Santana. Some punk with a rap sheet and a sealed juvie record, but he earned a spot on our hit parade. A loser *and* a head case."

Boelens tossed a file folder on O'Dell's desk. A photo spilled out, the face of a Hispanic kid and a young girl.

"He should be in a casting call. This kid could have a future in the movies with a face like that. Too bad." When he looked at the girl, he shook his head. "What a waste. She's smokin' hot."

As O'Dell printed out the information he needed, he said, "Load these kids into the Tracker. If they help us find Lucas Darby, we rank them with him. They're top priority now."

"Already ahead of you, boss. With you being on vacation, I figured you'd appreciate me taking some initiative."

O'Dell saw no need in explaining why he went missing. Getting tapped by the big boss was no one else's business.

"Vacation, my ass. Since when? I'm not a plaid-shorts, flip-flops jerk." He swiveled in his chair and grinned at Boelens, glad to have his number-one guy back in the saddle. "So spill it. Tell me what's in that file."

Boelens told him that traffic cams caught Santana, and some little kid not in their system, hoofing it between a health-food store and a small grocer down the block. Since they'd been caught doing both locations more than once, odds were they'd do it again. Weaknesses. Everyone had them.

"Put these locations on a city map. A big one. I want it in my office pronto, like how they do it on cop shows on TV."

"Speaking of cops, they found our stolen van. Not far from these stores."

"Put that on the map, too."

Boelens shrugged and stood. Before he headed out the door, he turned and asked, "What are you looking for?"

"Patterns. These kids think they're mixing things up to throw us off. They figure no one's paying attention and that they're smarter than us, but they make mistakes. When they do, it'll be in the patterns they keep and we'll be there when they screw up."

"Promise me that I'll be the one to look that Darby kid in the eye again." Boelens glared. "I got a score to settle with his girlfriend, too."

"You'll get your chance. Our job is to find them and turn

'em in for money. No one says they've got to have all their moving parts."

After Boelens left, O'Dell picked up the photo of Raphael Santana and smiled.

"Everyone's got a weak link. Looks like you're it, Raphael."

Downtown L.A.
Afternoon

Rafe served Benny a steaming bowl of potato stew from a kettle in the commons area of the tunnels. As he watched the boy head to a table to sit with other kids, he saw Benny's pants were hanging off his little butt. They didn't fit, but the way he'd sprouted, the kid wouldn't be the runt of the pack for long.

Any kid who outgrew their clothes got to pick from hand-me-downs hanging in the commons on old metal garment racks. Whenever they ran low on sizes, Kendra had him buy things at a surplus store, but she had him barter for what they needed, too. The stuff she grew in the garden had a value to folks, and Rafe knew how to hustle a good price.

"Any of you tunnel rats want more?" he said. "Raise 'em up."

The Effin brothers raised their bowls with a grin. They always ate like they had a tapeworm. One of them had a front tooth out, the only way Rafe could tell them apart. He grabbed their bowls and served them more.

Whenever he had kitchen duty, the little ones always ate first. Too many times he'd gone to bed hungry. That wouldn't happen here, not on his watch. When the tables got quiet and everyone had their faces in their bowls, he served himself and found a spot with a view.

The commons were close to Kendra's garden. That made cooking easy, and they used the light from the surface to give them a break from the dark when the sun was shining. Rafe watched Kendra pack up supplies from her garden as he ate alone, sitting near the stew kettle. He knew the drill. Soon she'd ask him to make a run to sell whatever. She let him feel a part of running things, but it was all on her.

Kendra did everything.

He would have helped her, but she already had her new *toy* working it. *Lucas.* That kid looked messed up when he came in—bloody and wearing clothes that stunk like a homeless dude had stepped in it—but he cleaned up real good.

Too good.

"Yo, Benny. Mind the store. I'll be back."

Rafe left his stew on the table and took off down a dark corridor. He knew what he was about to do would be wrong. He felt like shit, but he didn't stop. When he got to Kendra's room, he searched through her stuff, careful not to mess things up so she'd notice. It didn't take him long to find what he looked for. Kendra had a special box he'd given her before. She kept important stuff there—like the scrap of paper with a phone number on it, the one she'd taken off Lucas when he first got there.

He didn't know why the number had burned like a laser into his brain, but it had from the first moment he'd seen it. The number was Lucas's tie to the world he'd left behind. It meant he had a life outside the tunnels. He didn't *need* to belong here.

A guy like Lucas didn't understand kids without options, kids like him and Benny. He had a bad feeling that this new kid would screw things up for all of them, but he didn't know how or why. He'd learned to trust his gut. It had kept him alive.

He stuffed the scrap of paper into his pocket and headed back to the commons. He had no idea why he'd taken the number instead of memorizing it. He guessed he wanted to feel in control of something.

Lucas wasn't like them. Kendra was too blind to see it, but Rafe felt it in his bones.

Haven Hills Treatment Facility—L.A.

Dr. Fiona Haugstad received an encrypted report at her office at the hospital. She'd gotten several hits off the database for known targets, and the results of her Tracker scans were uncanny. The sketches she'd found at the museum library were perfect matches. That couldn't be coincidence. She'd seen too many of these gifted kids do amazing things. Drawing a vision or connecting to another Indigo through a sketch didn't seem out of bounds. Quite the opposite—the discovery of the sketches thrilled her.

But a flag on her report grabbed her attention, and not in a good way.

"What the hell?"

Someone had pulled two records, similar to her search results. The file on Raphael Santana and Kendra Walker had been retrieved a day ago. The boy had a sealed juvenile criminal record and the girl had been a target on their database before, but they'd lost her. She went off the grid. Fiona looked closer at the date and time stamp for file retrievals. Such information was only reported and flagged at her level of security clearance. Her inquiry would be kept confidential, except if Alexander had been monitoring *her* activity. She didn't think that was likely, but she'd have a perfectly good explanation for her search.

But who had pulled the files before her?

She found a numeric code on the inquiry and had to run a search on a separate employee-authorization database. What she found surprised her. O'Dell's man Boelens had searched for the information a day ahead of Alexander assigning Lucas Darby to O'Dell as his top priority.

How could O'Dell and his people be a step ahead of her? What did they know?

She should have been pleased that Alexander had found the right man to head up the hunt on Darby, but an inferior man like O'Dell had no right to be ahead of her. She had to know how he'd done it, but making contact directly with the man would break all their rules of protocol. Alexander would not be pleased, no matter what her justifications would have been. She'd already gone against his express orders by continuing to pursue this other boy.

But perhaps there was be another way.

If O'Dell had Lucas Darby in his sights, she could shift her focus onto this new boy, a Crystal child with equal or greater potential. That would please Alexander more once he saw her point. He had told her to follow her instincts. That was precisely what she intended to do.

If O'Dell made the hunt for the Darby boy into a race, she'd give him real competition. Why should he get all the credit? He had sole authority now, but the prize of capturing another boy, even stronger and different from Lucas, would give her the recognition she deserved. Fiona wanted to be more to Alexander than merely a credentialed doctor who identified these abominations.

She wanted him to see her as an equal—a partner.

Alexander was always talking about chess moves and playing a strategy that kept him many moves ahead. That was how she saw her role now. She had an edge on O'Dell with this new boy. She also had a library book that she knew still held significance. Fiona grabbed the book and her copies of this new boy's sketches. They would be her new priority.

If she couldn't stay one step ahead of a man like O'Dell, she didn't deserve to be Alexander's equal.

Downtown L.A.

Rafe Santana liked mixing it up when he picked his route out of the tunnels. Sometimes he came up through the county buildings near Temple and Broadway, but today he hit the streets near the King Eddy Saloon at 5th and Main. That part of the tunnel had been sealed off, but he'd found a way around it that no one knew about. The night his old man nearly killed him, that rat hole had been his home until he healed up.

He never told Benny that story. The kid had enough of his own.

Benny made good company. He could tell the kid anything and he believed it. Benny didn't look at him like he was a loser. Rafe almost forgot that part when he hung out with the kid.

"You could use a belt. At least for a while," Rafe said. "You wanna hit the surplus store later?"

"Nobody wears a belt. You don't." Benny shrugged.

The kid carried a pillowcase over his shoulder, filled with Kendra's stinky plant stuff in plastic tubs. It made him look smaller. Their stash for cash was practically dragging behind him. Rafe had given up offering to help the runt. Benny liked carrying it for Kendra.

"But my booty ain't hangin' out like yours." Rafe grinned and nudged Benny. "Unless you're trying to strut your stuff in front of the ladies. Now, that's different. If that's the look you're after, I got your back. Just say the word and I'll shut up about that belt, for real."

"Aw, man. Give it a rest." Little man scrunched his face, pretending to be mad. Rafe knew better.

As they walked to the health-food store, Rafe looked for a pay phone, someplace different that wasn't a beeline between the tunnels and their usual route for a "cash run." He never paid much attention to phones. He didn't have anyone who'd want to hear from him, but the phone number in his pocket—the one Lucas had brought with him—felt like a piece to a puzzle he needed to figure out. If it turned out to be nothing, no big deal.

Yeah, no big deal.

After they scored the cash for Kendra from the health-food guy, Rafe made sure he had coin to make the call and figured out a place to go. He'd used the phone before. It had a video arcade near it. That would keep little man busy while he dialed the number. When they got there, he handed the kid a few dollars.

"Here, take this. Knock yourself out, but stay where I can see you," he said. "And no hitting the john without me. You got that?"

Benny never asked why he always told him that about public toilets. Some things a kid didn't need to know. When little man got busy, Rafe took the number from his jeans. He tried not to think too much about what he was doing. He just did it. When the phone rang too long, he almost hung up, until a recorded message grabbed his attention like a stab in the gut.

"You've reached the Church of Spiritual Freedom, the office of Mia Darby. Please leave a message and—"

A woman's frantic voice interrupted the message.

"Rayne, is that you? Are you with Lucas?"

Rafe swallowed, hard. Darby, same last name. Lucas had a direct connect with the Believers. *Damn!* Rafe hung up the phone without saying a word. He didn't have to.

He'd heard enough.

His mind reeled with conspiracies. Kendra thought she'd linked to Lucas, but what if golden boy had earned a get-out-of-jail card in exchange for taking Kendra and her crew down? Maybe she'd pissed off the church enough for them to fight real dirty.

Rafe had to warn her—*if it wasn't too late.*

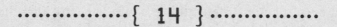

Downtown L.A.
Minutes Later

"Come on, Benny. We gotta book," Rafe said. The hair on his arms stood up like it was cold, but it wasn't.

"But I'm killin' it here." The kid didn't take his eyes off the video game. The display flashed a bomb explosion, and the sound of machine-gun fire got on Rafe's nerves.

"Forget it." Rafe shot a look over his shoulder. His gaze shifted fast, from the faces of strangers to dark corners where he couldn't see much. "We gotta ditch this place. Now!"

Benny stopped and did a double take. He scooped up his coins, stuffed them into a pocket and fell in step with him, trying to keep up.

"What's up?" the kid asked. He'd taken to looking over his shoulder, mirroring what Rafe did.

"I gotta talk to Kendra. That's all. Can't wait." Rafe ran a hand through Benny's hair. He didn't want to worry the kid. "Sorry to slam your mojo, little man."

Eventually Benny relaxed and jabbered about kid stuff and his best zombie kill shots, but Rafe had his mind on Lucas… and Kendra. *Always Kendra.* He didn't know what to make of Lucas having a direct connection to the church that had been hunting them. Screw coincidences! He didn't believe in that shit. Only suckers did.

He rubbed his arms. That weird chill wouldn't go away. He glanced over his shoulder again. Nothing.

That woman on the phone really spooked him. He still heard her voice in his head. It felt like Lucas had played them, and even though Rafe couldn't figure out why, that didn't mean it wasn't the truth. He felt sick. He liked the tunnels. Kendra had made it their home, the first real one he ever had. Walking away from what they had—'cause some loser kid with money screwed it all up for them—made him want to puke.

What would he tell Benny? If it was only him, he might risk staying with Kendra, even if it meant a fight. She had given him something to care about, but he had the kid to think about, too. *Damn!* How did things get so messed up? The tunnel entrance wasn't far. They'd be home soon, but instead of picking up his pace, Rafe slowed down.

Something isn't right.

The pit of his stomach tingled, in a bad way. He couldn't shake it. Rafe kept his feet moving. Even slowing down, he knew Benny had a hard time keeping up, but something felt… *wrong.* This time it wasn't about Lucas or Kendra or any of that.

Someone had their eyes on them. Rafe knew it for a fact.

Without warning, he ducked into an alley and pulled Benny with him. He dragged the kid to a metal Dumpster and they hid behind it.

"Hey." Benny almost fell. If Rafe didn't have him by the arm, he would have.

"Sorry, dude. Change of plans." Rafe grabbed Kendra's cash from his pocket and knelt down in front of Benny. His eyes darted back to the alley entrance, but no one came. He stuffed the money into the kid's pocket and grabbed him by his shoulders.

"No questions, okay? You gotta do what I tell you." He fixed his eyes on Benny. "Hide behind this Dumpster and count to a hundred. Don't come out for anyone until you're done. You hear me? You can count to a hundred, right?"

"Like, duh. Yeah." The kid smiled, but that didn't last long.

"Go straight home, the way I told you. No cheating on the rules, little man. We got rules for a reason."

He'd taught Benny how to be real careful coming back to the tunnels. Once he got in the dark, it would be hard for anyone to find him the way he crawled through the underground maze and squeezed through broken brick walls where he barely fit. Benny would be okay, but if someone had followed them, Rafe figured they hadn't come for Benny.

He had to lead them on a chase—one he hoped he'd win.

"What's happening?" the kid asked. "You're scarin' me."

"Not my intention, Benny. You'll be all right. I promise." He hugged the kid and said, "Just do what I say. I'll see you real soon. Somethin' I gotta do."

When Rafe stood, the kid asked, "What do you want me to tell Kendra?"

He took a deep breath and thought about it. "Tell her I got my lucky eight on. I'll be okay. We're family, right?"

The kid only smiled and started counting.

"Count in your head, little man. You're not getting a grade for doin' it right. Stay quiet."

Rafe would've laughed, but he couldn't.

Bristol Mountains

When Uncle Reginald said he had a plan to help, he hadn't been blowing smoke. Gabe stood next to Rayne and held her hand as he gazed around a room he didn't remember from his childhood at the estate.

"Cool," Rayne whispered and smiled up at him.

When they first arrived, Gabe had seen a dome at the end of one wing of the mansion. He didn't remember a structure like that from before. Parts of the domed room had a new-car smell that mixed with the musty odor that leached from the stone walls. The old with the new. Dim theater lights were positioned around a room with plush tiered seating. The seats looked as if they reclined. A big apparatus dominated the center of the main floor below. Probably a high-tech projector.

The place would make one helluva media room.

"What is this? Looks like a planetarium." Gabe's voice was muffled in the dark room. The acoustics were epic.

"I call it the Serenity room. Some people do yoga to find inner peace and center themselves." His uncle grinned. "I come here."

When the man smiled, his teeth glowed in purplish-white and his skin turned a dark blue. As he got closer to the machine in the center, a black light set his white shirt aglow, too. He nearly vanished, except for his teeth and shirt.

With a remote control, Uncle Reginald punched a button and the machine hummed like a *Star Wars* lightsaber and rotated. Lights spiraled around the darkened room, and images appeared and faded away above their heads. Planets and stars and breathtaking photography of Mother Nature's best on land and sea appeared before them.

"I gotta be here on movie night." Gabe couldn't take his eyes off the pictures shooting across the vaulted ceiling. "Amazing."

"Take a seat, Gabriel." His uncle waved them to sit anywhere. "Rayne, please join him."

Gabe chose a seat in the middle with Rayne taking the spot next to him. He shoved back into the chair until it reclined, and he smiled at Rayne. Seeing her in this light with the colors washing over her, he wanted to kiss her, but he had to settle for lacing his fingers in hers.

"Forgive the drama." Uncle Reginald's rich baritone voice came through a microphone, almost making it sound as if the man had gotten into Gabe's head. "With the acoustics I've built in this room, the microphone serves a purpose. I've found it can center your mind and relax you. Bear with me."

Gabe didn't say anything. He took a deep breath and focused on the mesmerizing light show.

"Anger and resentment toward your father have been your triggers. I saw it in you as a child," his uncle began. "From what you said, your anger is the source of your abilities. Is that a fair statement?"

It took Gabe a long moment before he answered, but he eventually said, "Yes."

"Real power does not come solely from anger. Your ability must be controlled and truly focused. It's like a muscle that needs exercise." His uncle smiled. "I believe that's why your mother chose a traveling circus."

"I thought she was—" Gabriel couldn't look his uncle in the eye "—ashamed of me. With a circus, she could pretend it was an act."

"Oh, no, dear boy. Is that what you thought?" Uncle Reginald grimaced. "Circus life wasn't easy for her, but she did it for you. She made working with you and your abilities into a big game so you'd accept who and what you are. The excessive travel was a way to hide among people she thought of as a second family."

Uncle Reginald poured a refill of coffee and left Gabriel to think.

"After Kathryn died, you disappeared. You've only half accepted who you are. You've been hiding it, haven't you?"

The man didn't expect an answer. "You must embrace your power. Own it."

"How do I do that?"

"I believe you need to find a place between your anger and the sense of peace you need. Rage can no longer serve you. It may even sabotage your abilities...or worse." Uncle Reginald let his words sink in. Only the hum of the equipment filled the room as the pictures and lights flashed.

Gabe felt a familiar struggle start inside him. He fought the agitation. Whenever his thoughts turned to his father, the anger began, but the beautiful, serene pictures and the slow, throbbing lights suppressed those feelings. His uncle's voice and the light show became a jumble of conflicting feelings.

"You must test yourself if you hope to gain a deeper understanding of your abilities and push your limits, Gabriel."

Gabe heard footsteps come toward him. He didn't look away from the spiraling lights over his head. He trusted his uncle.

"The next step is the challenge, dear boy." Without the microphone on, his uncle spoke closer to his ear. "Are you ready?" Gabe nodded and felt his uncle's hand on his forehead. Uncle Reginald's fingertips were warm and felt hotter the longer he touched Gabe, until a tingle started in his head and the room dimmed. He didn't feel the chair anymore. He didn't feel Rayne's hand. It was as if he were adrift in darkness, with only his uncle's voice to keep him there.

"You may not believe that you have true serenity in you, Gabriel, but it *is* there. Share it with me."

The dark swallowed him completely now. When he didn't sense his uncle with him anymore, Gabe gasped and his body stiffened as if he'd been pushed into the deep end of a cold pool. His breaths came in rapid pants until he slowed everything down. When that happened, a pinpoint of light turned into more. *Thousands*. They spiraled at him, like oncoming headlights, and when they came faster, things looked familiar, like puzzle pieces coming together

"Oh, my...God."

His words trailed off as glimpses into his memory swept to the surface of his awareness. He'd been transported somewhere else—to another time. He wasn't remembering stuff. He was there in the moment—*again*. The swell of emotions he felt then came back in a rush, too. More and more of the memories came back to him, times he'd forgotten or should've been too young to remember.

The first time he saw his mother's face, she held him in her arms at the hospital, with the beat of her heart still fresh in his ears. On a birthday, he saw her face lit by the candles on his cake. The glitter of the tiara she wore paled by comparison. The day his mother gave him Hellboy as a pup, he got a whiff of puppy breath and he gasped. Their circus act rehearsals, rugby matches, Christmas and Thanksgiving, he felt her love with the same intensity as when he was a young boy. The memories came faster and a surge of feelings magnified. They filled him until he thought he couldn't hold any more, but he didn't want them to stop—*until they did*.

The minute his uncle took his hand away, the rush of emotions came to a sudden end, leaving Gabe exhausted, as if he'd relived his whole life. With eyes wide, he jerked his head and stared at his uncle in shock.

"I didn't know I still had those memories." Gabe spoke through tears.

His most cherished memories still lingered. They were ebbing from his body and he ached to feel them go, but he had his mother with him. He'd smelled her hair and felt her touch— and knew she loved him...*still*. Even though her laughter faded back into his mind, he'd been there with her again, as surely as if she haunted him.

In that moment, Gabe had never felt so close to his uncle. He was the father he should have had.

"You've just forgotten," his uncle said. "You've blocked out the good in your life and buried it with the ugliness, but those lovely memories of your mother will always be a part of you. The good and the bad make up who you are and who you will become. When you can find that sweet spot—between rage and peace—that's when you'll accept everything that you are and reach your full potential. "

Gabe hugged his uncle and let the tears come in sobs. He didn't fight it, especially when Uncle Reginald did the same. Letting go had been a long time coming for both of them.

Downtown L.A.
Dusk

It took Rafe a long time to shake the feeling someone had eyes on him. He'd done his best maneuvers—ducking into crowded bars at happy hour to slip out the back, crawling out bathroom windows, even cutting through a ladies' underwear store—but he hadn't done enough to lose his tail until he hopped on a bus with commuters going home. Suits with places to go.

Without money, he got the boot from the driver, but not before he'd ridden blocks away. By the time he got off, he didn't feel the eyes anymore, but he had to hoof it back to the tunnels. It was almost dark by the time he made it. Although he was starving, he went looking for Benny before he drank water, before he did anything.

When he saw Kendra with Lucas in the commons, they sat at a table by her garden. It was Rafe's favorite time of day. Kendra always looked pretty under the fading light off the sun, but that didn't matter now. Rafe kept his distance and stuck to the shadows. He waited for her to look at him before he nudged his chin for her to come over. Kendra didn't hesitate. She came right away.

"What's up?" she said, keeping her voice low.

He wanted to tell her about Lucas, but Benny came first.

"Did Benny give you the money? Did he make it back okay?"

"What are you talking about? I haven't seen him," she said.

Rafe couldn't speak. He replayed his last moments with the kid and second-guessed his decision to leave him alone.

"Oh, shit." He couldn't catch his breath.

"Raphael, what happened?" When Kendra put a hand on his arm, he let her read his fear. Allowing her to connect to his pain was faster than talking.

I felt eyes on us. I thought they were after me.

He saw in Kendra's eyes that she understood his frantic thoughts. Her mind reached out to him, but he couldn't stop flashing on what happened.

I gave him the cash. Maybe I read it wrong. Maybe they went after him.

To stop him, Kendra pulled him close and hugged him. She whispered in his ear, "We'll find him. You were only trying to protect him." She squeezed him tighter, but he felt numb.

After she let him go, Rafe only nodded as his stomach tightened into a fist. He gritted his teeth as Kendra went back to the commons…and Lucas. As she told the others what to do, Rafe couldn't focus. He stared down at the black leather strap tied around his wrist, the one with the silver infinity on it. If anything happened to Benny, someone would pay—but the first name on the blame list would be his.

I never should've left you, Benny.

An Hour Later

Bad enough Rafe had lost Benny, but now he'd exposed all of them. Looking for the kid in the tunnels turned tricky. None of them could do it quietly, using their mind links. They had to call out his name. If the Believers or some pervert had followed the kid belowground, they all risked getting discovered. A chance they had to take. Kendra took one group and Lucas took another. They backtracked the main sections and covered every inch.

Rafe did his own search. He didn't feel like company, not after what he did. If the Believers found him, he didn't give a shit. *Bring it*. He deserved it.

He went over the route he told Benny to take and searched every step of it. No sign of the kid, and when he didn't get a psychic push from Kendra that she'd found him, the darker his thoughts got. Without seeing any trace of the kid, Rafe went crazy with worry. Benny wasn't like them. He had no chance at hearing their mental shout-outs.

Rafe rummaged through miles of tunnels in the dark, without using his ability. That made every minute agonizing. He hit every spot the kid liked to hang. When he finally reached the old train, Rafe heard soft sobs coming from inside the steel relic.

"Benny?"

Rafe's heart hammered as he bounded up the steps onto the old locomotive. He searched the engine first. When he didn't find Benny, he followed the sounds of the crying to another car. The runt had crawled into a storage compartment only he could fit in. It had muffled his voice, but Benny was too choked up to talk. Rafe opened the lid and pulled the kid down and held him in his arms.

Before he said anything to Benny, a familiar mist swept from the gloom. Aged hands and wise eyes took shape from a shadow that undulated like inky ooze—the dead guy in overalls. He had stood watch over Benny, even though the kid never knew it. As Rafe held little man in his arms, he mouthed the words *thank you,* and the dead guy actually smiled back. At least, Rafe thought it was a smile.

"I did everything you told me, Rafe. I couldn't get rid of them."

"What are you talking about?"

He put the kid down and knelt in front of him.

"I heard 'em. Some guys followed me. I couldn't lead 'em to where we are, so I hid."

"Did you see them? How many were there?"

"It was too dark. I only heard 'em." Benny's lips trembled and it broke Rafe's heart. "I hid and counted to a gazillion, but…"

"But what, little man?" Rafe couldn't catch his breath. "Did they…do anything to you?"

The kid cried for real now. Terrible thoughts raced through Rafe's head. Perverts in bathrooms when no one could hear a scream. Fathers with fists that hurt like steel. Nightmares that weren't nightmares came rushing to his eyes in the dark. Something had happened to Benny because of him.

Something bad.

"What happened? You can tell me."

He held the kid and covered his own misery with Benny's sobbing gasps.

"I pissed my new pants," the kid choked out. "I stayed put. I didn't want 'em to find me, not even when I had to pee."

When he heard that, Rafe shut his eyes tight, squeezing the tears from his eyes. He'd been so worried, he never smelled the pee. Now he did.

"You were real brave, Benny. You protected us, for real. I'm proud of you." He tried to keep his voice calm, but inside he wasn't.

"But my pants, they stink and everyone will know what I did."

"No one will know. It'll be our secret," he told the kid. "Besides, pants can be washed. I'll do it for you. They'll be good as new. You'll see."

Benny seemed okay with that. Rafe waited until he stopped crying. He wiped the kid's face and sent a mental message to Kendra.

Found him. He's okay.

Thank God, she replied. *Where are you?*

At the dead train, but we're okay. We got something to do first. See you at the commons. Let everyone know, okay? And thanks…

Even though Benny worried that his pee smell would get on him, Rafe held the kid and carried him all the way back. Benny got real quiet and put his arms around his neck. Rafe never had a little brother, but if he could order one, the kid would be Benny. *One hundred percent.*

He took Benny to his corner of the tunnels and gave him clean clothes to wear from his stash. After he fed the kid, he gave him his mattress to sleep on for the night. While he washed Benny's pants, Kendra found him.

"Missed you two at the commons. Is Benny okay?"

"Yeah, he was just scared." He stopped washing. "He said some guys followed him, but it didn't sound like the Believers. He hid and stayed put. Brave little runt."

He mentally blocked her from seeing what had really happened. She'd know he hid something, but he didn't care. Sometimes guys had secrets. He fished the money from his pockets.

"Here's the cash. Benny kept real good care of it. He didn't do anything wrong."

"I know he wouldn't, Raphael," she said. After he went back to washing Benny's pants, she touched his shoulder and forced him to look at her.

"Benny is one of us. If he's in trouble, we're all in it,"

Kendra said. "You didn't do anything wrong, Raphael. You protected your own. Sounds like Benny did the same. I'm proud of you. Both of you."

Even with his hands wet with suds, she hugged him. She didn't have to read his mind to know he could use one. With her holding him, it didn't take much for a rush of emotion to hit him hard. He'd almost lost Benny. He'd almost lost everything.

Now that he was alone with Kendra, he could've told her about Lucas, but almost losing Benny had been enough drama for one night. He kissed Kendra on the cheek and let her go. He had pants to wash and Benny needed looking after.

West Hollywood

Fiona lived in the "Bird Street" area of West Hollywood, exclusive acreage where the rich and famous held or rented prime real estate. Hollywood A-listers. With her income supplemented by the Church of Spiritual Freedom, she had been able to live in the lifestyle she deserved. After a long day at Haven Hills, she sat alone at her dining table, taking in the incredible, glitzy view of the city through ceiling-to-floor windows. She had brought home her pet project. Over a glass of red wine, she pored through the library book and the many copies of drawings that her new target had left her—clues to find him.

This mysterious new Crystal child had not intended to taunt her on purpose by leaving the book and his knapsack, but that was exactly what spurred her on. She pretended that he had challenged her to find him. Despite Alexander Reese expressly asking for her to focus on Lucas Darby only, she had gone against his wishes and pursued the new boy anyway—a surprise she'd present to Alexander when she had something worth telling him.

When she found what she'd been looking for, she smiled and raised her glass to toast her success.

"To us, Alexander."

It was in one of the drawings, of a boy and a girl sleeping together. She hadn't paid much attention to it, since she couldn't see their faces. Something drawn in the corner—a strange historic element—caught her eye, but little else. It wasn't until she found the exact drawing in the art book taken from the library that she saw what the boy had seen in the book.

"Where are you...exactly?" she whispered.

She read about the tunnels where the historic mural had been originally painted. Fiona got out a map and narrowed her search to the cross streets mentioned in the book. She had no idea that underground tunnels existed in downtown L.A. Next she got on her laptop and queried keywords that brought up more information.

She wanted the new boy. Perhaps he was with the Darby kid by now, but if she got a lead on Lucas and told Alexander first, ahead of O'Dell, she'd shine in the man's eyes either way. She glanced at her watch to check the time. It was late. Past ten, but she couldn't wait. She dialed the number to Alexander Reese's home, a place she'd only visited once. In her mind, she pictured how he might look at this hour. The wine helped her imagine.

When he answered, she said, "I had to call you. I've found something."

"It's late. Is it important?" he said.

Men. One minute they had a woman breathless. The next, they were suitable for strangling. Why would she call at this hour if it weren't important?

"Yes."

She told him what she had already rehearsed. If she admitted to broadening her search for the new boy, Alexander wouldn't listen to anything she said over the phone. She had to give him elements of the truth until she could read his reaction and body language when they met face-to-face.

"I commend your diligence. You're amazing, Fiona."

She finished her wine, fighting a smile, but what he told her next almost made her choke.

"But O'Dell has already tracked down the Darby boy. In the tunnels you found, too. I'll fill you in tomorrow morning. If all goes well, we should have Lucas Darby soon. You'll have a new test subject, worthy of your full attention. Your first Crystal child. One you discovered. Good night, Fiona."

After the line went dead, she could hardly breathe. Her body shook and she wanted to scream. She threw the wineglass against her dining room wall and watched the shards of glass fly. Alexander hadn't even kept her informed. O'Dell had an important operation going and she'd been cut from the loop.

Fiona's mind raced as she stared at the sketches. If O'Dell got the Darby boy, she still had another play. This new boy would be all hers.

Bristol Mountains
After Midnight

Rayne couldn't stop thinking about what had happened between Gabriel and his uncle that afternoon. They had made her a part of it, but she wasn't. Not really. Gabe barely talked after that. Uncle Reginald had kept up his end of the conversation at dinner, but she watched Gabe pull away even more. He had a lot on his mind, and after living a condensed version of his life, he looked worn-out.

Seeing him so alone reminded her of Lucas. Before he got sent to Haven Hills, he didn't talk much, either. It was as if he'd given up. All these things rushed back to her. She'd relived her past, too, and it didn't feel good.

Why hadn't she reached out to Lucas more? Why didn't she fight to get him released from that hospital? Guilt made it hard for her to breathe.

"Gawd." She wiped her face and pulled the covers over her head, but her mind wouldn't rest. Forget sleep. That wasn't going to happen, not when she couldn't get Gabriel and Lucas out of her head.

If being different like them was wrong, she didn't want to be on the side that thought they were right and in charge. Lucas had parents who loved him, at least. She couldn't begin to understand how it must feel for Gabriel to be treated like an outcast, especially when that terrible label of *freak* had first come from his father.

She felt more tears come. They drained down her cheek, and her sobs meant they weren't going away. When she thought about Gabriel and his uncle, seeing their love, she missed her mom and dad—and the childhood she'd left behind in a major crash and burn.

The crash of a jet.

Rayne couldn't take it anymore. She tossed off the blankets and sat up in bed. All she wanted to do was talk to Gabriel. Be with him. She jumped off the bed and pulled on her robe. She blocked out all the reasons that warned her not to go to his room in the middle of the night.

This time she'd do what Gabriel and Lucas would do— trust her feelings.

Minutes Later

Gabe had made a fire in the hearth of his bedroom. He'd never even tried to sleep. His bed was still made and the room was dark, to match his mood. Barefoot, he sat cross-legged in front of the only light in the room—the fire—still dressed in his jeans and his black Korn "Freak on a Leash" T-shirt that he'd forgotten had been in his room from before. He'd gotten it to piss off his dad, but he'd covered up the *freak* sentiments that morning with an oversize plaid shirt out of respect for his uncle.

Alone in his room now, he could embrace the freak he still thought he was.

He stared into the flames, imagining the scorching heat could burn away his doubts, but nothing helped. His uncle had touched something in him that Gabe didn't know still remained. It had been an amazing moment, to feel his mother with him again. Yet if what Uncle Reginald had said were true, that meant the trigger of his anger would only get him into more trouble. He'd reached the end of his capabilities. Anything more would tap him out and push him into a danger zone.

He'd have to give up what had gotten him this far to begin with—*and start over.*

He didn't feel strong enough to try something new, yet he had to. Rayne and her brother, Lucas, needed him, but he also had to get on with his life. He couldn't hide anymore. He had to deal with the pain of losing his mother and the relentless anger he felt toward his father to find a balance between love, hate and letting go that he could live with. In the dark of his room—alone—he felt the weight of those changes closing in on him. He didn't feel ready.

When he heard a soft knock on his bedroom door, he thought it would be his uncle checking on him. He took a deep breath and answered the door.

Rayne stood there, dressed in a silk nightgown and robe. Tears glistened in her eyes, and when she opened her mouth, she whispered something he never heard as he touched her face. Only the crackling fire behind him and the sound of his own heart stayed with him. Gabe cupped his hands to her cheeks and gently pulled her into his room and shut the door. He cradled her in his arms and kissed her. When her hands touched his belly under his T-shirt, Gabriel felt the tingle of firefly wings across his skin.

He wanted to remember this moment—with good reason. He'd fallen in love with Rayne Darby, something he should never tell her. He couldn't expect her to put up with his shit. Wanting her was selfish. He had too many secrets that he'd always have to hide from outsiders.

Rayne deserved better. She deserved a shot at normal.

{ 15 }

Bristol Mountains
After Midnight

The minute Gabriel opened the door, backlit only by the fire in his bedroom hearth, Rayne felt like an idiot for coming. She had nothing to offer this amazing boy except her understanding and sympathy. Her life with Lucas only mirrored a fraction of Gabriel's pain. After she'd met him at the Griffith Park Zoo, his already troubled life had been turned upside down. He'd lost his hiding place, thanks to her. Yet he still wanted to help.

"I'm...sorry. I shouldn't be here," she whispered, unable to take her eyes off him.

She should have left, but she couldn't move—especially not after he touched her cheek. Time stopped in that quiet moment as she stood at his door shivering and hardly able to think. Gabriel said nothing. He didn't have to. When he cupped her face in his hands and pulled her toward him, she breathed in the smell of his skin as he pressed his sweet lips to hers. The faint scent of smoke—*and boy*—teased her nose as she wrapped her arms around him and her fingers touched bare skin.

She closed her eyes to savor everything—the taste of his lips, the weight of his body pressed against her and the way he made her feel. Rayne wanted to stay with him forever. Heat rushed to her face as his hands touched her. When he kissed her neck, she couldn't catch her breath until—

Gabriel suddenly stopped. He pressed his forehead to hers and held her.

"Sorry," he panted.

"I'm not." She kissed his cheek and touched his face. "I couldn't stop thinking about this afternoon. I had to see if you were okay."

"I'm glad you did."

Gabriel led her by the hand toward the blazing fire in his hearth, only leaving her long enough to grab pillows off his bed. He tossed them at her feet, helped her to the carpet and joined her. The quiet of the night and the flickering shadows closed in on them.

"I couldn't sleep," she said.

"I know." He stared into her eyes, not hiding the underlying sadness that had always been with him since she'd first met him. His uncle had brought his grief to the surface to force him to deal with his past. Gabe lowered his chin and laced his fingers in hers.

"Sleep is a big hype." She shrugged. "Highly overrated."

Gabriel looked up and smiled. The amber of his eyes reflected the fire that painted its glow on his skin as if the light came from inside him. Gazing at him, Rayne wanted to always remember him like this. The feeling that her days with him were numbered hadn't left.

If anything, that feeling had gotten stronger.

"I miss my mother, especially here, but I needed to come." He breathed a sigh and pulled back a strand of her hair. The heat off the fire made her drowsy. His eyelids looked heavy, too.

"The act that you did with your mom looked really cool. I've never known anyone who traveled with a circus before."

"She had her reasons for taking me with her. I thought it would be weird, but…" He stared into the fire. "Those days turned out to be my favorite memories of her. We got real close."

"How did she…die? You never said."

Rayne regretted asking the question and couldn't take it back, but Gabriel didn't look surprised by it. He didn't say anything for a long time.

"A story for another time, perhaps." He pulled her into his arms and held her.

"Uncle Reginald gave me an amazing gift today," he said, his voice thick and low. His sleepy voice. "He made me realize that I've been too focused on her death and not on the way she lived. If you don't mind, I'd like to hold on to what he gave me for a while longer."

She understood him wanting to savor memories of his mother. She would have given anything to be with her parents once more, even if it would only be through a glimmer of the past. Yet from the moment she first met Gabriel and felt a reconnection to her parents and family, she realized he had given her a gift, too.

"Thanks for letting me come here with you." She felt the sting of tears, but she didn't want to cry.

"You're a good sister, Rayne. Lucas is lucky."

She put her arms around him but didn't say anything. For a second, it made her smile to think that Gabriel thought she made a good sister, but that was not how it felt to her. She'd learned so much about Lucas and her own past from Gabriel, she only hoped she'd get a chance to see her brother again to make things up to him.

"What your uncle said about embracing who you are and

balancing the good with the bad. If you could change and be ordinary…" *Like me,* she wanted to say. "Would you do it?"

Rayne wondered what Lucas would answer, and she thought about the good and the bad stuff in her own life. All of it had become a part of her—a piece she hid and didn't talk about with anyone. She didn't *own* it. She avoided it.

"Good question," he said.

Gabriel didn't answer for a long time. He only stared into the fire until he said, "Before today, I might have come up with a different answer. But to refuse what I am sounds insane. When I think of my mother, my power feels like a gift from her. How can I deny that? But ask me again in the morning. Who knows what my answer will be after biscuits and jam?"

Rayne wanted to smile, but she couldn't. She laid her head on Gabe's chest and nuzzled into his arms, listening until his breathing slowed and she knew he'd fallen asleep. She watched the fire until it died to embers and the room turned dark.

She heard every breath he took—and counted them—until she closed her eyes.

Darkness came first. A murky black beast he had to fight. Panting came next. That sound triggered everything that followed. It seized him until his throat burned. His heart pounded so hard his chest hurt. Eerie green lights floated in the dark. Streams of hot lasers, in molten red, shot across the gloom. He got up and ran and cried out a name—*Kendra*—until he fell and bashed his knee. He felt the warm stickiness of blood dripping down his leg and it hurt to move, but he had to.

He had to help the others—the children—even though he didn't know how. He sensed them. Felt their fear. Their terror magnified his.

Everywhere he turned, an army of shadows surrounded him and blocked his way. Their viciousness became a wall of hate.

Angry, scary voices came from men with green, glowing eyes. They shot red lasers from weapons and he saw lightning in the tunnels. Strange jabs of blue light flashed on frightened faces, and when loud explosions erupted, they left phantom images on his eyes and blinded him. He couldn't see. Couldn't hear.

Where are you? Help us! children cried and screamed. Pleading voices echoed in his head. He didn't know who they were. Too many. When hands grabbed him, he fought the shadows and shoved back hard.

"No! Leave them alone," he yelled. "They're only kids."

No one listened. He saw what they did and couldn't stop them. He could only watch in agony as monsters attacked children as they slept. He sensed these men were afraid of the kids. They attacked without mercy because of it.

"Kendra! You can't help them. Not now," he cried.

Hands pinned him down and he felt weight on his chest. He couldn't breathe. He heard a name and a distant voice that now sounded familiar.

"Let go," she begged. "You're hurting me."

When he opened his eyes, he stared into the face of a scared girl. *The wrong girl.* Not the one he expected to see. This one looked terrified. She had her knees on top of him and her hands grappled with his arms, but he'd wrestled free and had ahold of her wrist. His face flushed with heat, and rage flooded his body.

For an instant, he didn't know his own name. He'd been stripped of the saving darkness and pushed into the light. He had no idea where he was.

"Gabriel, you're okay. It's me. Rayne. You were having a nightmare."

He stopped fighting. He recognized her now.

When she let go of him, he pulled her to his chest and held on. Part of him was still in that dark reality. For the first time, he sensed his mother's presence. Only a glimpse, but she *had* been with him. When he looked around the room and re-membered where he was, his heart slowed and he fought for every breath. Rayne held him close until he calmed down. When she pulled away and let him sit up, his clothes felt damp and sticky, remnants of the dream.

"You looked lost. You were fumbling around for something. I figured it was your sketchbook, like the last time. I was so scared." Rayne looked miserable. Her lips trembled. "It was like you needed to draw to be released from the nightmare. Is that how it is for you? I didn't know. I feel so bad."

"You didn't lose my backpack. I did," he said. "None of this is your fault. We're in uncharted waters. I'm just glad you were here."

"Since you couldn't draw, tell me about your vision. Don't leave out anything."

Explaining what he saw, in visions he never knew he had, was hard to do with someone normal like Rayne. He only got glimpses and impressions that he had to interpret. He'd seen darkness and connected to the intense emotions of sev-eral souls. He'd hooked into the collective mind of the others and reflected back what they felt and saw. Gabe didn't know how to explain that to Rayne, but he did his best.

"You called out a name. Kendra. Do you know someone by that name?" she asked.

"No." He shook his head. "But I think…"

When he didn't finish, Rayne pushed for more.

"Think what? Just say it. No filter."

"I think I was inside her head. Lucas's, too. Maybe others'." Gabe narrowed his eyes. "I saw through their eyes, like I was watching a horrifying movie that I couldn't stop."

"What did you see?" Rayne's eyes welled with tears. "Did something happen…to Luke?"

He wanted to reassure her, to tell her that her brother was okay, but he couldn't. It wasn't what he saw but what he knew would come that made him the most afraid. For Rayne's sake, he stuck to what he had seen.

"I don't know. I got flashes that were all jammed together." He shut his eyes and forced the dark memories back. "I saw blinding explosions and strange lightning belowground. Men were attacking these kids in a tunnel. An army. They were hurting them and they didn't care."

"An army? Explosions? Were they police?"

"They didn't feel like police. These men were afraid. They attacked because of it. Police don't do that." He couldn't catch his breath. "It's like they hated these children."

Rayne clutched his arm.

"I asked you before, but I gotta know," she said. "Are your visions something in the future…something we can stop?"

He looked into her eyes and knew what she wanted him to say, but he wouldn't lie to her, not about this.

"I don't know." The tears that had blurred his eyes finally brimmed over and trickled down his cheeks. "I honestly can't tell you."

"Come on, Gabriel. This felt different, even for a bystander like me. You gotta tell me *something*. It's my brother."

"All I know for sure is that we should leave…*now*." He kissed her cheek. "I'll tell my uncle. He'll understand. You remember those cross streets where that tunnel mural is?"

She nodded and said, "Yeah. I can get us there."

Rayne left his room as he went to wash up and change. Gabe didn't let her see his worry. With Lucas in trouble, she didn't need the extra burden, but she had such faith in him. He saw in her eyes that she truly believed he could help—if only he believed it, too.

His anger had been an ally, but now that everything hinged

on him being at his best, he couldn't trust his instincts, and that killed him. It would be like a normal person being unable to rely on their own eyesight or hearing, but he knew his uncle had been right. To help Rayne and Lucas and the others, he'd have to attempt something he'd never done before when everything mattered.

If he failed, he wouldn't get a do-over.

But something far worse than his failing powers bothered him. When he looked in the bathroom mirror and saw the nightmare still haunted his face, he could finally put words to what he had sensed and couldn't tell her. The smothering darkness that had made it hard for him to breathe had carried the unmistakable stench of death. He didn't know if he could stop what he saw.

He only knew he had to try.

Downtown L.A.
4:30 a.m.

O'Dell jumped a curb and drove his SUV through weeds toward the rendezvous point Boelens had arranged. The location had been picked for staging the attack because it couldn't be seen from the road and it had steep embankments of thick vegetation for cover. It was also near an abandoned railroad-track tunnel, an underground entrance that would serve as the main assault point. O'Dell used his headlights for only a short while before he cut them and parked behind an Expedition he recognized. Boelens had his men at the tailgate of his vehicle, going over a map by flashlight.

With the help of the Tracker system, Boelens had played a hunch to snare Raphael Santana when he made another run to the health-food store and it paid off. The kid thought if he split from his little buddy he'd lose Boelens, but Boelens stuck to the smaller boy, an easier mark. After Boelens got what he needed—a likely assault target—he cut out before that nest of freaks figured out they'd been busted. He'd found where they lived.

Now it was time for O'Dell to reap the rewards of what he'd sowed.

After Boelens bribed a city official to get his hands on maps of the underground network, his man had enough to devise a strategy—one that he'd come up with after his last encounter with that head case, Kendra Walker. Boelens told him that he had a few payback surprises and couldn't wait to tell him about it.

O'Dell came dressed for the part. He wore full assault gear provided by the church that was stored in the operations bunker. With black BDUs, helmet, a holstered Glock 21 sidearm and night-vision goggles, he'd look like everyone else. When he walked up to Boelens, his man didn't bother with introductions. O'Dell had warned him not to use names.

"This is Cobra One. He's in charge of the op. I report to him." Boelens nudged his chin to O'Dell and said, "You ready for me to brief our men?"

"Yeah, carry on." O'Dell had been tempted to salute, but didn't.

"These are architectural schematics for the tunnels. We'll come in three ways and converge here to extract prisoners. Hit 'em hard with flashbangs and tear gas. We gotta keep these mind freaks disoriented until we can dart 'em with knockout juice. Don't let them get their hooks into you. They'll seriously fuck you up and scramble your *juevos*. If they get in too close, fry their asses with a Taser. Transport will be waiting at the extract point."

Boelens had learned from his last failed attempt to capture the Darby kid. His surprise retaliation utilized the tactics and weapons of a hostage-rescue unit, only there would be no rescue. Flashbangs were a first-assault incendiary device used to disorient hostiles. It blinded them, messed with their heads and took out their hearing for six seconds. Tear gas would be round two and Tasers would send a jolt of electricity to short-circuit their brains and body. His man had a solid plan for a good harvest operation.

"You have your team leaders and assignments. If we strike hard, they won't know what hit them." Boelens handed out photos of Lucas Darby and Kendra Walker to each team leader. "Remember these faces. They're our prime objectives for this mission. Must-haves, gentlemen. The boy's code name will be Skywalker. Hers will be Princess. Sing out when you have 'em put down."

"What about use of deadly force with the others, sir?" one of the men asked.

Boelens barely looked at O'Dell before he said, "If you feel you are in danger, take 'em out. End of story. But if you kill Skywalker and the Princess, you're a dead man walking. Got it?"

His man had given the order to kill without hesitating. His words reminded O'Dell that these men were paid mercenaries. The almighty dollar was their only moral code. Each man would carry an M4 assault rifle for protection, but they wouldn't hesitate to use them if things got ugly. When the briefing was done, Boelens pulled O'Dell aside.

"I brought shaped charges to blast through barriers these vermin could have in there. That's how that brat got away from me this afternoon. I don't want that happening again, but don't worry. The noise should be minimal underground."

"Shaped charges?"

"Yeah. C-4, man. Explosives are a real icebreaker. *Comprende?*"

"Understood."

Boelens stared at him with his usual stern expression until a smirk spread across his face. "You know, I've done black ops all over the world, but none for a church."

"Yeah. It's a calling. Go with God, my son."

Boelens turned to join his men, but when O'Dell didn't follow, he said, "We go in twenty. You comin'?"

"No." O'Dell took off his helmet. "Use your comm unit to brief me. I'll be in my vehicle."

Boelens narrowed his eyes. "Unbelievable," he muttered as he headed back to his men.

O'Dell pretended not to hear him.

Rafe woke up to screams in his head.

Go! Go! Go! They're everywhere!

Kendra! Where are you? Help us!

Rafe's body jerked straight up. It took a second to realize that he'd fallen asleep on the floor, and he fumbled for a flashlight that he kept by him at night. He flicked on the light and shone it into the darkness. The light found Benny. The kid was sound asleep on his mattress, where he'd left him. The tunnels were deathly still. Only Rafe's head buzzed with voices.

Evacuate! This isn't a drill. Get out now!

That voice he recognized. Kendra. She'd made them run drills for escape routes if they ever came under attack. Kendra had them split up on purpose. They slept in groups. That way they wouldn't be trapped in one location. They'd have different exits, too.

Rafe had hoped that the day would never come for real, but his luck was for shit. He shoved the flashlight into the waistband of his jeans and reached for something more useful. He grabbed a baseball bat that he kept with him, a reminder of his old man that had nothing to do with a ballpark.

"Benny?" He knelt by the kid and whispered, "Kendra's got another evacuation drill goin' on. Wake up, buddy."

The kid never complained. He rubbed his eyes and crawled into his arms, still dreaming. Rafe carried him and hit the tunnel outside his quarters. He used his senses to guide him—

self to the evacuation route in the dark. The flashlight would only make them a target.

When he got to the main passage, he stopped and clutched at Benny. Other kids were around and they saw the same thing he did. Two inky-black silhouettes stood in front of them and made a human barricade. They were big. A green glow came from their masked faces and red laser scopes shot across the darkness. Lasers pinned them where they stood. One red beam targeted Rafe's head. Another painted his heart. Too close to Benny.

"What's that?" the kid whimpered.

As the men stepped closer, Rafe backed up and whispered, "Plan B, little man. I gotta talk to these guys. I'll meet you outside. You got that?"

When the kid nodded, Rafe put him down and shielded him with his body. He sent a message to the others and tightened his grip on the bat.

Take Benny. Run when I make my move. I'll hold 'em off.

When he hit the flashlight, they did as he told them and scrambled into the dark. The stark light took out the night-vision gear these shitbirds had brought. As they shielded their eyes and cowered from the light, he ran straight for them with the bat.

Something punched his body and he smelled blood. When he thought of Kendra and Benny, he fought to stay on his feet. He didn't have her ability, but he knew how to swing a bat. His old man had taught him that.

Kendra had stayed with Lucas. Her first thought had been to take charge and protect the others, but a strong urge forced her to stay with him. She couldn't explain it, but she'd learned to trust her instincts when it came to Lucas. He had a quiet strength and she had felt his power grow. Now his brilliant blue aura with its crystal sparks burned with an intensity she'd never seen.

At first, she had told Lucas where they should go, sticking to the evacuation plan for their section of the tunnels. They headed for the garden to escape up the scaffolding and through the hole that led outside. When they got there, Kendra stopped in stunned silence.

Men in dark uniforms rappelled down on long ropes. In the bluish haze of the moon, they looked like deadly spiders with weird, glowing eyes. They had rifles and were geared for war. Lucas didn't hesitate. He changed their escape route to keep ahead of the men. While she gathered the youngest kids, Lucas fed her what he sensed. He stayed calm and never spoke. He'd learned to use his abilities naturally.

East tunnel is clear to the train. Head there now. The commons are out!

She sent telepathic messages to the others as Lucas moved, not knowing if anyone heard her. If these men knew about the garden, she had no doubt they'd attack at multiple points and trap them. They had to get ahead of the men, use exit strategies only they knew about, places where large men couldn't fit.

Her eyes burned and she couldn't breathe. What kind of cowards hunted kids with rifles and explosives and tear gas?

When they got to the dead train, Kendra's legs felt like they were on fire and she gasped for air. Backtracking over eleven miles of tunnels in the dark, while using her abilities to guide herself and the others, had drained her. But nothing was worse that the strain of her emotional reaction. Seeing her family being hunted by armed men left her spent and her head aching. Sweat drenched her body, and gas fumes and dirt stung her eyes.

Up ahead she saw more of her kids, but not nearly enough. She'd lost some. She felt it and that killed her. The Effin brothers and Benny had gotten through, but one of the twins had been hurt. He could barely walk. Kendra had never seen the twins so lost without each other. Their mental link had been damaged by the trauma of the injury. The boys were tightly connected. With one of them distracted by pain, the other had shut down. They operated in tandem and needed each other to be whole.

Kendra never knew. The twins were still only boys. Anytime they used their powers, to them it was a game—nothing more than a prank—but this was no game.

Follow me. Stick close.

Kendra grabbed for Benny, and Lucas helped the limping twin. She led them from the train and down another corridor. At the end of it was a crack in the brick wall, nothing more than a sliver of an opening. Only the littlest kids would be able to fit, but on the other side, they had a fighting chance of getting out and making it to the evacuation spot through a crawl space. The men hunting them couldn't follow the little ones.

That meant she and Lucas would have to find another way out. Before she had a chance to explain, Lucas touched her shoulder and looked into her eyes. Even in the shadows, she saw he understood.

I know. Just get them out, he told her.

He helped her hoist each kid into the crevice in the wall. When they'd tested the escape route before, the twins had been through the hole. They knew what to do and where to go. Some of the children barely made it and had to squeeze. Benny was the last to go. She kissed the boy on the cheek and said, "See you on the flip side, little man."

She wanted to ask Benny about Raphael, but didn't. She didn't want him to worry. The kid was already so scared, but she knew that Rafe wouldn't have let Benny go without him unless he didn't get a choice. Kendra felt hollow inside. She'd lost her connection to Raphael, another voice she couldn't hear anymore. Feeling Rafe gone, Kendra felt lost. She couldn't move. He'd been a part of her for so long that she didn't know where she ended and he began. It was as if her soul had been split in two. When her stomach tightened and her hands shook, she didn't know if she could stand any more.

But Lucas's voice—from inside her head—forced her into the moment.

Come on. We gotta go. They'll need us on the outside.

Lucas had sent her a message that kept her going. He was right. She had to stay focused and keep moving. She couldn't fail them. The children, her family, would need her. Raphael would have wanted that, too.

But when she heard another explosion—one that was too close—she and Lucas got knocked off their feet. He covered her with his body as shards of brick struck her arms and face. She felt the sting of cuts and smelled the coppery tang of blood.

What the hell was that?

Dust rained down on them and drifted in thick clouds. Kendra choked on it as she got to her feet and looked over her shoulder. The men were coming. Her kids were in trouble. She had to go back, but when more blasts erupted and a wall collapsed, Lucas grabbed her by the waist to stop her.

Let me go! I gotta help. She wanted to scream, but he held her tight.

"You can't help them. Not now," Lucas said aloud, using his voice so the others couldn't hear his thoughts. He sensed the same horror.

The children.

Eerie lights strafed the dark behind her. The Believers were close and they were far too many. Stunned, Kendra had never seen such violence. These men were like feral dogs on the scent of blood. And their prey? They hunted innocent, unarmed children who hadn't hurt or killed anyone.

No! Leave them alone. They're only kids!

Her pain slipped out, not meant for anyone else but Lucas. She didn't want her kids to feel her lose it, but she couldn't fight it anymore. She let Lucas feel her agony. She didn't feel Raphael anymore and everything she'd built had been wiped out in minutes as if none of it had mattered. These men had destroyed her dreams of becoming, of establishing a strong family of Indigos.

Kendra collapsed to her knees and emptied her stomach. These men had taken everything from her. Stripped of all hope, she had nothing left.

She'd failed them all.

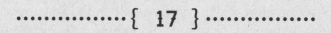

Near Downtown L.A.
5:00 a.m.

Traffic had been light and they'd made good time coming back to the city. With Gabriel riding behind her, Rayne pulled her motorcycle onto the shoulder of the highway near a car tunnel. She drove her bike off road until she reached a stand of trees where she could stash her bike. The mural she'd seen in a book at the museum library would be somewhere inside the lighted tunnel and belowground. She'd driven through the car tunnel many times—a section of freeway cut into a hillside—and never knew it had secret passages that led under downtown L.A.

She turned off her engine, took off her helmet and waited for Gabriel to say something. He only stared into the tunnel with his helmet in hand, narrowing his eyes as if he saw something she couldn't. She expected him to sense stuff, but the worried look on his face told a different story.

She didn't know how to help him.

"This is the location I read about," she said. "Any ideas where to look now?"

"Yeah, maybe."

Of course he does, she thought. *He has to.* He had Hellboy and the third eye, right? He probably had abilities beyond what she'd seen. She wanted all this to be true, but the look on his face worried her—for Lucas *and* for him.

When she got off her bike and fished out her flashlight, Gabriel said, "Oh, no. I'm going in alone. I'll have enough on my mind. I…" He didn't finish. He took a deep sigh and touched her cheek. "I'd worry about you. Please don't make me worry."

She knew he was right. The last thing she wanted to be was a burden to him. All the way to L.A., she had no trouble picturing Lucas and all the terrible things that could happen—or had happened to him already. The one thing she couldn't imagine was failing him again.

"I let my brother down. When Mia took him from the only home he ever had and gave him to strangers, I let that happen." She fought the guilt that always came when she thought about Lucas. "You say I'm a good sister, but that's not true. I just want the chance to become one. I hope that's still possible."

Gabriel looked into her eyes as if he were reading her thoughts. If anyone understood the importance of family, he did.

"This may not work," he said. "I may not be able to protect you…to protect anyone."

"No promises. No regrets." She nodded and reached for his hand. "I understand."

She could have argued that this had been her fight from the start. She'd only needed him to find Lucas. Rayne didn't need psychic powers to feel she was on the verge of doing just that, but Gabriel had a stake in this, too, now. Lucas and these kids were like Gabe. They'd linked their minds and shared things she would never understand or experience.

Despite the love she had for her brother, Rayne knew she'd never be a real part of his life or Gabriel's. Love had nothing to do with really understanding what it meant to walk in their shoes, but it had everything to do with accepting them as they were.

"Then let's go...kick some ass," he said. Hearing him say that with his British accent almost made her smile. *Almost.* Gabe didn't smile, either.

Rayne locked up her bike and grabbed her flashlight. She walked into the car tunnel with him holding her hand. The cement walls were solid. She couldn't see any entrance that would lead them down. She almost panicked until Gabe pointed ahead.

"I see it. Come on." He picked up the pace and ran with her.

Cut into a wall, not easily seen, was a section of the tunnel that had a metal ladder leading down. It was too dark to see much.

"I'll go first. If it's something, I'll call up to you," he said.

She nodded and knelt by the ladder, watching him climb down. She lost sight of him as the darkness swallowed him. All she heard was the sound of his hands on the ladder rungs and his footsteps crunching on dirt when he reached the bottom.

"Well?" Her voice echoed. "What's down there?"

When a car drove by, she hated being exposed with people watching. All she needed was a cop to cruise by.

"I think this is it. Come on down," he yelled from below. "Be careful."

After she stuffed the flashlight into the waistband of her jeans, she turned around and headed down the ladder. Tunnel lights faded and left her in pitch-black. She couldn't see how far to go and she climbed down far enough that the lights from above didn't help her. When she felt his hands on her hips, her jitters got replaced with a different kind of shiver.

She turned on her flashlight and caught a glimpse of him.

She didn't have to see him blush to know that he had. Despite what they were about to do, that made her smile.

"They have the rest locked down, but I think we can squeeze through, if you're game," he said.

She shined the light to where he pointed and saw what he meant. A metal gate had a chain lock on it, but the lower half looked bent, as if someone had squeezed in before.

"Yeah. Let's go."

She got through without any trouble, but Gabe had to push. He fussed and moaned until he got his way. It looked as if it hurt. Beyond the gate, more stairs led down and the narrower passageway eventually led to a corridor that split off.

"What now? Flip a coin?" she asked.

"Now I take over. I'll be your coin."

When he got quiet, she turned her light on him and watched him take a deep breath and shut his eyes. In seconds, she felt Hellboy brush against her leg. Only days ago, the dog's sudden presence would have scared her. Now she felt only relief that the ghost dog had come to his master.

"Hello, boy." She smiled and the dog wagged its tail.

"From here on, don't use the light unless you absolutely need to," Gabriel said. "If there's anyone else down here, we'll only make an excellent target, and the light will mess up our night vision."

"Okay."

On the surface, the morning air had been cool and breezy, but below it smelled stale and the heat was stifling. Sweat already trickled down her spine. With miles of underground passageway ahead of them, Rayne hoped Hellboy would make a difference to focus their search. Gabriel knelt by his dog and whispered to him. She never made out the words, but the phantom dog perked its ears and pointed its nose down one tunnel and did the same with the other.

Hellboy barked and took off running a split second before she heard a rumble deep in the tunnels. Gabriel didn't hesitate. He followed.

"What was that?" she yelled, chasing after him.

"It's my vision. It's happening."

Despite the sticky heat, a chill ran over Rayne's skin.

Lucas.

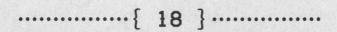 { 18 }

Downtown L.A.
Minutes Later

After Gabriel heard the blast, he flashed on his nightmare vision as he ran. The darkness and the sounds had started it. Now rage welled inside him like bile. He fought it, not even sure if he should. When he got close enough to hear boots on the ground and harsh voices echoing up ahead, he doubled over and gasped for air.

Too much pressure. He couldn't fail. Lives depended on him. Would he be too late and only turn into a powerless witness to something he was never meant to change? Or would everything hinge on what he'd choose? His ominous vision could trigger and unfold simply because he showed up, or he could make things worse.

Doubt made him stop. So much was riding on him.

"What's happening? Are you sick?" Rayne knelt by him and touched his arm. When he didn't answer her, she said, "Take deep breaths. Slow your heart."

He did as she asked and knelt by her. The cruel men who hunted children were distractions. Noise. He centered on the pulse of his heart and breathed deeply until Rayne's soft voice touched him. She reminded him of the beautiful images his uncle had shown him in his relaxation room and she whispered about them in his ear. When he was ready, his mother came to him and the warmth of her memory filled him.

"Your mother's with you, isn't she?" Rayne gasped. "I know because I feel mine, too. And my father. Oh, Gabriel, thank you."

Rayne stood back and Hellboy lifted a paw when Gabriel got to his feet and glared into the darkness. His rage was still with him, but it had been fortified by his mother's love. She had become his new foundation and the root of his power. When he held out his arms and clenched his fists, the muscles in his body radiated a growing heat.

He felt his power surge. It shook him the way it had at the museum library, a convulsion he could easily lose control of. It felt like his heart would rip from his chest. He groaned in pain when every cell in his body split apart but had no place to go. He held on, afraid to let go. Terrified he'd lose it again.

"I can't...do this."

"You can. Hang on, Gabe! Trust your instincts. This is who you are."

Rayne's voice shot through his pain. She made him try harder. She reminded him why he was here and what was at stake.

His body suddenly splintered and every fiber of his being swept through the dark tunnels, racing from him. When it happened, he cried out in sweet, beautiful agony. He'd become a million souls—past, present and future. He drew strength from the colony of minds and let the surge of their power magnify his own. He'd never felt anything like it, but it was the only thing that made sense. He had to do something he'd never done before—*trust*. When he felt others like him, trust didn't seem impossible anymore. He felt Lucas and Kendra most of all. They both shot rapid-fire images to him, faces of those who had hurt them and the others chasing them. That made Gabe stronger. He could direct and dispel his rage to the people who deserved it.

But most of all, Gabe had broken through a barrier that freed him, where the living and the dead converged. Their life forces bounded off him like light reflecting off glass. When they shot in all directions, he felt an awakening power coursing through his body and it didn't hurt anymore. He'd tapped into their abilities, magnifying their strengths as if they were his to control.

He had become a conduit for the Indigo collective.

"It's…beautiful!" he cried. "I feel…*everything*."

Kendra ran with Lucas as they felt their way through a section of the tunnels that turned into a narrow maze of switchbacks. She'd never been in them before. Only Rafe had. Thinking of Raphael almost made her stop and get sick again. She couldn't imagine her life without him, but when her mind severed from his, her world turned into a darker place.

You don't know what happened. Not really.

Lucas had read her thoughts. She'd been tired and hadn't blocked him. On top of everything else, she didn't have much strength for that. He hadn't invaded her privacy. Without mind blocks in place, her thoughts radiated out as if she'd sent him a message. She did her best to redirect her energies to repair her blocks. She wasn't strong like Lucas.

That was probably why he had seen into her past when he had his fever. With his body battling the effects of the concussion, he had tapped into the fraction of his brain that they would need to explore. That frightened her. It meant no one would have secrets from him. This new world she wanted to be a part of would demand rules and skills she didn't have.

Lucas was their future and others that would come after him. Not her.

"You feel that?" Lucas whispered. Hearing his real voice shocked her.

"No. What?"

Lucas stopped and turned, back the way they'd come. He got real quiet. Too quiet. It scared her.

"Someone's coming."

"From where?" Kendra felt useless to him now.

"From...everywhere."

She shut her eyes to concentrate her last strength on what Lucas sensed. When the hair on her arms stood at attention and goose bumps rippled over her skin, she gasped.

"Oh, my God. What is that?" Her eyes grew wide. She felt it, too. "*Who*...is that?"

Lucas didn't answer her.

He only said, "Come on. He'll need us."

Kendra couldn't sense everything Lucas could. She only felt the presence of someone very strong. Whoever it was had tapped into her mind, more easily than Lucas had during his fever. She had no idea who "he" was, but she had faith in Lucas—especially when she saw him smile.

With Hellboy whimpering at her feet, Rayne stumbled from Gabriel with tears streaming down her cheeks. He didn't have to tell her how beautiful he felt. He beamed in dazzling light. It came from inside him. It shot through his eyes and mouth as he cried out. The intense light consumed him like a white fireball. She saw his body in shadows inside the mass of energy, but she couldn't see his face.

When the ground trembled under her feet, she wanted to run, but something made her stay. She wouldn't abandon Gabriel. She felt a new surge of energy that resonated off him. Her insides tingled hotly as if she were cooking in a microwave. Gabriel had become something more than he ever had been before. She didn't know if he'd ever come back to her—in one piece.

Whatever had taken him over scared the hell out of her.

Wave upon wave of waking nightmares sprang from the shadows as if the darkness had given birth to them. Ghostly entities screamed through the dark passageways, heading toward the men who attacked the Indigo children. Growling pit bulls snarled and came from nowhere. They glowed in blue like Hellboy. Gabriel's legion of the dead had crossed over. Snakes slithered up through the floor like sprouting weeds, and when the walls rippled and moved, roaches erupted like a plague and dropped to the concrete. Their winged bodies glistened in Gabriel's light.

The creatures he'd conjured sought the dark, avoiding her and his light. When Gabriel moved down the passageway, his hellish horde followed. They would be unleashed on men who had earned the payback. Rayne clutched her arms tight to her body, too stunned to move. Gabriel headed for the men who hunted kids like him, armed with abilities beyond anything these cruel men would ever see. These men had explosives and weapons. She didn't know if Gabriel and his newfound abilities would be enough to make a difference. What if they were already too late?

Following his light and his macabre swarm of dead creatures, she felt numb until she heard a voice praying in the dark, not much more than a faint, trembling quiver. It took her a moment to realize that the voice had been hers.

Rayne prayed for Gabriel...*for all of them.*

Lucas held Kendra's hand as they crept closer. They stayed in the shadows and hugged a wall, inching their way toward the noise. When Kendra finally saw what Lucas had sensed, she gritted her teeth and fought the stark sickness in her soul.

Only yards away, she saw her kids. Uniformed men carried them on their shoulders and dropped them to the ground near a tunnel entrance. Their bodies glimmered under the moonlight. They looked dead.

She felt ripped up inside. Every sweet face brought back memories of how she'd found them. Their smiles. Their humor. The things that made them cry. Now she couldn't tell if they were alive or dead. She didn't know what the Believers had done to them.

They're alive. I can tell. Lucas sent her a message. She had dropped her mind blocks. Now wasn't the time for secrets. She had to trust him. She had no one else.

This isn't over. Lucas turned to look into her eyes. She saw his determination. He looked stronger than he ever had before. That should have made her feel better, but it didn't. Her children were unconscious. Even if they could overpower these armed men—just the two of them—where would they go? Where would they be safe from men like this? She had nothing to say to Lucas. She kissed him on the cheek as a tear slid down her face.

She loved him for wanting to try.

Have faith, Kendra Walker. You'll see, he told her.

When Lucas smiled, he almost convinced her. *Almost.*

"Any sign of Skywalker or the Princess?" Boelens asked over his comm unit. On the other end, he heard only an odd static. "Anyone hear me?"

In seconds, the crackle switched to dead silence. Boelens stopped and glared at the guy next to him, who only shrugged. Boelens looked at his watch and lit it up. His men knew what time they were leaving the extraction point. Even with the comm units out, they knew what to do. When he heard boots on the ground down one of the tunnels, he looked over his shoulder. Shadows approached. One of his team leaders and his men were carrying more bodies.

"Everything go okay?" he asked his man.

"We were chasing these kids and they slipped through a crack, like you said. We used your icebreaker."

"And? Cut to the chase," Boelens demanded.

"The explosion caused the tunnel to collapse. The old brick didn't hold up. We got bodies."

"You better not be delivering me bad news about Sky-walker and the Princess."

"No, sir. We had eyes on the ones who got hit. Those two weren't in the body count."

"Any of our men get whacked?" he asked.

His man only shook his head. Boelens didn't like losing money on two legs, but at least he wouldn't have to retrieve the bodies of his own men. That would take time.

"Collateral damage." Boelens didn't hesitate. "Cops may never find the bodies down here. If they do, by the time they figure out the walls had come down with a little help, we'll be long gone."

His men had taken the freaks by storm. They'd hit them hard and fast, like he'd planned. Now all that remained was collecting the ones they'd captured and delivering them to the bunker. A one-way trip for them. A payday for him.

But no matter how many head cases he turned in, the whole operation would be classified as a bust if he didn't score the Darby kid. That kid would be the only one who really mattered to Operations.

He was running out of time.

"You, give me a quick body count." He pointed to one of

his men. To another, he said, "See if you can reach the other teams. I gotta know if they found Skywalker."

"On it, sir."

"Let's load up these bodies. We got transport outside," he ordered.

Boelens gritted his teeth. If he didn't find Darby, he'd have nothing to brag about, but the scuff of a boot behind him changed all that. The guy he saw wasn't in uniform, but he looked familiar. So did the girl he brought with him.

"Looking for us?" Lucas Darby stood in front of him, looking like a present on Christmas morning. He'd brought the Princess with him. It didn't get any better than this.

Boelens smiled. He smelled a bonus after all.

Lucas tried not to look like a crazed lunatic as he stood in front of the man who had bashed his head in. The guy who didn't blink. Ever.

Kendra had grabbed at him when he stepped out. He knew she didn't agree with what he'd done, but gutsy until the bitter end, she followed his lead and stood at his side. Once the guy gave the order to haul out the kids, Lucas knew he'd run out of time. He had to stall, even though he didn't know why exactly.

If something didn't happen—if the powerful force he sensed in the tunnels didn't materialize soon—Kendra would have every right to call him an idiot. They'd both lose everything. All Lucas had was faith—in a stranger he had never seen.

"Come to join the party? Thanks for accepting my invitation." The man chuckled. "You two are the guests of honor."

"We can't let you take them." Lucas kept his voice calm and steady.

"Oh, really. Who's gonna stop me? You?" He grinned.

"Aren't you afraid of a repeat? The last time I saw you, my fist made an impression on your face."

"I don't believe in violence. At least, I didn't before I met you."

When he saw the amused look on G.I. Joe's face, Lucas felt like David before Goliath—without a slingshot.

"I guess we've got irreconcilable differences, then. Get in line after my three ex-wives. Not that I care, but if you don't believe in fighting for your freedom, what *do* you believe in? What's worth fighting for in your pissant world, kid?"

"I think I'm about to find out," Lucas said. "And I'll have you to thank for that."

The man in uniform narrowed his eyes, and the smile left his face.

"That's it. We're done here. Say good-night, kid."

Lucas stood firm, ready to face whatever came next. Blind faith took guts. He wasn't sure he had what it took, but he was about to find out. When G.I. Joe aimed a Taser at him, he clenched his jaw and waited for the pain, but a menacing rumble became his reprieve. They all turned to see a faint glow coming at them.

What came first shocked them.

"What the hell?" The man swapped out his Taser for a handgun, and his men took aim with their assault rifles.

A hot gust of wind, like an underground Santa Ana, whipped through the passageways and gained momentum. In southern California, the desert wind brought nothing good. Weird stuff happened, like on the nights of a full moon. Lucas grabbed Kendra's hand and braced for impact. The light grew brighter and blinded him. He shielded his eyes, and Kendra did the same. When the hot air buffeted his body, he wrapped her in his arms and shoved her toward a wall. He held her tight and covered her with his body, waiting for what he knew would come.

A shrill howl echoed through the tunnel and intensified as it hit. When he heard the distant bark of a dog, Lucas dared to look. Angry spirits spiraled through the dark, their ghostly faces locked in agony. Pure evil. At first, Lucas didn't know what they were. He only felt a fraction of the torment they would endure for eternity. They were spirits who had died a violent death and had deserved their fate, but Lucas sensed one other thing about these banshees from hell.

They had all died at the hands of these men.

Some men believed dying was the worst thing that could happen to them. Lucas believed taking another life was far worse. These men who chose to fight an enemy they'd already killed would have the unique perspective of understanding both sides of the argument.

Of those who took aim, their weapons were visibly shaking. Others dropped their rifles and ran, screaming. G.I. Joe, with his unblinking stare, barked his demands of the men who ran, oblivious to his share of the demons that had come for him.

"Stop! That's an order," the man yelled. "None of this is real. They're messing with your heads. Stop!"

Lucas didn't know anything about the powerful force that could conjure dead enemies, but he *did* appreciate a wicked sense of justice.

Seconds Later

"What the hell?"

O'Dell heard Boelens yelling on his comm unit. More voices and noise made his man nearly impossible to understand. His words came across as a garbled mess, nothing more than screams. Something had gone terribly wrong.

As he sat in his vehicle in the murky dark, with only moonlight coming through his windshield, his mind played tricks on him. The sounds of screams in his ear didn't help.

"What's happening? Talk to me," he yelled at Boelens. "Quit screamin' like a girl!"

He heard the panic in his voice and didn't like the way it sounded on him. When shadows around him messed with his head, he jerked to his left. He thought he saw someone and peered through the dark. With him being alone—listening to the cries of his men, which needled his nerves—it forced him to think of peculiar things. He thought about going inside. He was armed. Maybe he could help.

"Yeah, right," he muttered.

Hearing creepy stuff on his comm unit had jacked with his head, but when he felt something move under his sleeves, he jumped.

"Holy shit!"

He unbuttoned his cuffs, yanked back his sleeves, and stared in wide-eyed horror at what he saw. His snake tattoos glistened under the moon and something slithered out from his skin. Like a bad acid trip from hell, his tattoos had come alive. They spewed snake after snake that dropped to the floorboard of his SUV. They curled down his legs and pooled at his feet. He swatted and threw them, but they wouldn't stop.

"No, no!" He squirmed and kicked, but they kept coming. He reached for his door, but it had locked. He yanked at the handle, ripped at the lock, but couldn't budge it. In a panic, he reached across and tried the other doors, but none of them opened. When he cranked on the ignition to open the windows, his engine wouldn't kick over.

Now he had snakes to his waist. They wouldn't stop. They crawled over him, flicked their tongues and hissed. He felt the weight of them on his chest, between his legs and up his calves. In all sizes, they knotted their grotesque bodies around him, but when one large head came from the backseat and dropped next to him, O'Dell couldn't breathe.

A python. Inch by inch, its body glided from the back with no end in sight.

O'Dell had no choice. Trapped and locked in his SUV with snakes slithering over him, he couldn't think straight. He reached for his Glock and pulled it from his holster as the massive snake inched toward his chest. He knew how they killed. Pythons crushed their victims and ate them whole. He didn't want to end up as snake crap.

Reptiles were O'Dell's worst nightmare. He had tattooed snakes on his arms—the one thing he would always be deathly afraid of—as a challenge. A damned joke. He wasn't laughing now. As the python wrapped around his leg, he took aim and pulled the trigger.

The muzzle flash blinded him and his ears went numb with the blast, but when searing pain shot through his body— O'Dell screamed like a girl.

West Hollywood

When Fiona couldn't sleep, she gave up trying. Hours of staring at the dark ceiling of her bedroom, rehearsing a conversation she would never have with the man in charge, had finally run its course. Her anger had swelled to an unbearable boiling point. She'd been deliberately left out of a major covert operation by Alexander Reese, a man she thought counted her as his equal. O'Dell would get the privilege of abducting the Darby boy—*her* discovery.

It wasn't fair.

She turned on the light on her nightstand and reached for the file she had on the new boy—*the other one*—and glared at his photo. A good-looking boy she wanted to meet. One day, she would. Fiona had no doubt.

"Count on it," she whispered as she rubbed a foot against her calf when her skin tickled. Fiona stared at the enlarged surveillance photo, the best one they had of him. Scratching her leg again, she memorized every facet of his handsome face. Those eyes she would not forget.

When she heard a soft flicker of a wing, she glanced toward the lamp on her nightstand. She caught a shadow race across the light and she jerked straight up. Rolling her file, she sat up in bed and searched for the biggest bug she'd ever seen, ready to swat it.

She despised insects.

But this time, when she felt something on her ankles, she screamed and threw back her bedcovers. Roaches crawled all over her. They festered under her gown and crawled over her skin. They were everywhere. After she leaped from bed, she crunched them under her feet and slipped. They were in her hair. In unmentionable places. She couldn't stand it.

Fiona screamed, dragged fingers through her hair and scraped her skin bloody raw. When she looked back at her bed, the sheets moved and more scuttled from under her bedding. She couldn't take it anymore.

She stripped out of her nightgown and raced for the shower, but the vile creatures trailed after her. She couldn't escape them. When she flung open her shower door, they slithered up through the drain. She had no place to hide.

In utter desperation, she ran from her house—naked and screaming as the day she'd been born. Dogs barked. Security lights flicked on. One man taking out his garbage, dressed in his pajamas, stared as she ran screaming down the hill, racing toward him. He did nothing to help her. He only raised his cell phone and shot video of her degradation.

Fiona would trend and go viral on YouTube. Except for the great shape of her Pilates butt, it would not be her finest hour.

Downtown L.A.

Boelens felt his brain fraying at the edges. Fear took over and he couldn't stop it. A blinding light in the tunnel stabbed his eyes as vicious growls grew louder. He didn't know what was real or only a hallucination when he caught glimpses of pit bulls as they crossed the light. Their heads were bloodied and their teeth bared as if they'd already been in a fight. He prayed they weren't real, but he couldn't afford to be wrong.

He grabbed his assault rifle and took aim at the rabid dogs, but before he could get a round off, he heard his name. A raspy whisper brushed his ear. He swatted at it and jerked his head toward the sound. No one was there. When he heard his name again, he spun on his heels, ready to shoot.

What he saw stole his breath.

Faces of the dead stared back. They accused him with their sightless eyes. Their bodies were brutalized, wounds he'd inflicted. Head shots, gaping throats and mutilations he would never forget. These were men he had killed. He remembered every one—how they died, the sound of their last breaths, their eyes. He had never told anyone before, but these faces haunted his nights.

They were his penance for breathing.

No one knew about his recurring nightmares—his darkest fears—but Kendra Walker had wormed her way into his head once before. He'd been her victim and would never forget that violation. Having her in his head had made him stronger. It pissed him off. He didn't need permission to annihilate her ass. O'Dell only really wanted Skywalker. The Princess had gone too far this time. He didn't care what the church wanted when it came to that girl. She wasn't human.

"None of this is real," he said. "Only Skywalker and the Princess."

Boelens shifted his rifle and took aim at Kendra Walker. He knew he couldn't kill the dead, but he could get payback from the living.

19

Howling winds in the tunnel made it hard to concentrate as Boelens saw his mission come unraveled. His men had deserted him. The unconscious bodies of head cases ready to harvest lay at his feet. They each were worth a bounty to him, but some things, like payback, were more important to him than money. Although Boelens was still plagued by the nightmarish demons of the men he had killed, he didn't care. He had a feeling his torment would end with one kill shot, and he had Kendra Walker in his sights.

But something made Boelens stop. Movement in the corner of his eye.

"Drop your weapon…or I'll shoot." A small voice tried to sound fierce.

Boelens peered into the dark. A girl stepped into the moonlight. Her hair and clothes were whipped by the wind and her hands shook as she held a handgun pointed at him.

He smiled.

"You don't even have the safety off," he yelled, loud enough for her to hear him above the wind. "Put the gun down before you hurt someone."

The girl blinked and swallowed, hard.

"Rayne, what are you doing here?" the Darby kid called out to the girl. "I told you not to look for me."

In an instant, Boelens knew who she was.

"I couldn't do that, Luke." The girl gripped the weapon and kept her eyes on Boelens.

"Who is she?" Kendra asked.

"She's my sister and she's not like me. Please don't hurt her." The kid pleaded with him for his sister's life. *Real touching.*

In a sudden rush, the fierce, hot winds died and an eerie stillness left his ears ringing. Boelens turned to see his demons vanish one by one, before his eyes. *What the hell?* From a distance, he heard footsteps in the dark. As they echoed and got louder, he gripped his rifle and pointed it into the shadows.

A tall boy dressed in jeans, hiking boots and a black Dead Gone Wrong T-shirt emerged from the dark. With long dark hair, he could have passed for a rock star on the streets of L.A., except he had the face of a choirboy. His eyes were intense. He used them like weapons.

"Hello," the boy said.

The kid glanced at the Walker girl and the Darby kid. They had a moment—a geek stare fest—before he shifted his focus back to him and smiled.

"Out for a stroll, are we?" Boelens laughed. The guy had balls, he'd give him that. "You're gonna wish you never took this shortcut."

"On the contrary, I'm exactly where I want to be. Can you say the same?"

The kid had the accent of a Brit, but that wasn't what got his attention. The control in the kid's voice surprised him. Boelens narrowed his eyes.

"So are you a freak like them?" he asked.

"A freak? No. Haven't you heard? We're the new normal. You're the one in the minority here. Does that bother you? It should." The boy didn't expect an answer. Instead, he shifted his attention to the girl. "Rayne, please do me a favor and put down the gun. We won't need it."

"But…" she stammered, and fixed her gaze on him. "A little insurance?"

"I thought you trusted me."

The girl swallowed hard before she did what he told her. She bent down and set the gun on the ground and stepped toward rocker boy. *Cocky bastard.* Boelens grinned. Things were getting interesting. He felt like a lucky man.

"As long as you're being so obliging, why don't you come with us?" Boelens asked. "I have people who would love to get their hands on you. There's room in the truck. What do you say? We can make it a party."

"The Church of Spiritual Freedom would be quite happy to see me, I assure you." When rocker boy said that, the Darby kid and Kendra did a double take and exchanged looks. Boelens had been shocked to hear the name of the church, too.

"But I have no intention of going with you…or letting you take these kids. So you see, unless we can negotiate something, you will not leave here a happy man."

"That supposed to scare me?"

"It should, but that would depend on how smart you are, wouldn't it?"

Boelens gritted his teeth and clutched his M4. It wouldn't take much for him to pull the trigger.

"You won't need that rifle," the boy said. "Please put it down."

Boelens snorted a laugh, but when his hands started to burn like acid, he looked down to see his M4 glowed molten red.

"Shit!" He tossed it and glared at the kid. "I don't need a weapon to take you out."

The rocker didn't flinch. "I don't need one, either."

That made Boelens stop.

"Your men are nowhere in sight," the kid said. "You're without your rifle and you're not leaving here with our family, but you don't have to go away empty-handed."

The Darby kid and the Walker girl stood at his side. The sister, too. Boelens faced a wall of attitude.

"I'm listening."

"What if I had something that you'd pay dearly for, in exchange for our freedom? You'd simply walk away and leave us alone. A temporary truce."

"Is that all?"

"Well, actually, no. Thank you for asking. I also need you to deliver a message, but we can talk about that later. I'm quite sure you won't mind."

Boelens shook his head.

"What do you have that I could possibly want, smart-ass?"

"I sense something in you." The kid stepped closer, not taking his eyes off him. "No amount of bonus money can buy you peace of mind. Would you agree?"

"What are you talking about?"

"I was asked by a very sweet and smart girl if I could change my life, would I do it. I pose that question to you. What would you give for a good night's sleep?"

Boelens glared at the kid who talked in riddles, until he figured out what he meant.

"You. You were the one," he spat. "How did you do it? I never told anyone about my nightmares. You're one cruel bastard."

"Come on." The kid grinned. "I only gave you a taste. I've seen plenty of Wes Craven movies, and *Saw 3D* is classic. I could conjure far worse, believe me." Before Boelens opened his mouth, the rocker said, "I could wipe the slate clean, literally. You wouldn't remember the horrors you committed for

God and country and the almighty dollar. I could give you a fresh start. What would that mean to you?"

Boelens didn't say yes, but he didn't exactly say no, either.

"The next guy you kill will be on you, though." The kid shrugged. "I don't warranty my work."

Boelens had found another kid he could truly hate. "Guess I'd be a fool to turn your offer down."

"Now, *that* we can agree on."

"But that's exactly what I'm doing. No deal." He expected the kid to be surprised by his sudden turnabout, but that didn't happen.

"I'm sorry. Did I give you the impression that I asked your permission?" The kid grinned. "My bad."

When the mind freaks came toward him, Boelens reached for his knife but found he couldn't move. He couldn't even blink.

It shocked Rayne to see what Gabriel did to a man who would have scared the hell out of her if she had to face him alone. But to watch as Lucas helped without any of them talking about it, that freaked her out. It was like they knew what the other was thinking. It reminded her that she wasn't like them and never would be.

She could imagine a future of human beings like Gabriel and Lucas. That seemed very cool, but what if others would come behind them with not-so-good intentions, yet with the same powers? She had to admit that scared her even more.

After Gabriel had worked his mojo on the guy with the rifle—and given him a message to deliver—Kendra went with Gabe to make sure the man left without taking the truck and the keys. That left her alone with Lucas.

Given her supervised hospital visits, she couldn't remember the last time she'd had him to herself without the meds that fogged his brain.

"I can't believe you came for me," he said.

When Rayne heard him say that, a knot wedged in her throat. He looked tired, but he had a fire in his eyes that she'd never seen. She liked it. She wanted to explain, to apologize, to pour everything out of her heart in that moment. She finally had her brother in front of her, but Luke never let her speak. Rushing to her, he grabbed her in his arms and pulled her off the ground. He spun her until she got dizzy. She shut her eyes and held him tight, blocking out all the times she'd visited him in the hospital and he didn't recognize her—when drugs had robbed her of her baby brother.

Rayne couldn't help it. She cried. He did, too. She felt his quiet sobs and knew they came from a lifetime of regrets and grief that they shared.

"I love you, Luke."

"Never doubted it."

Their future had plenty of uncertainty. Whatever they'd had, it was gone, but they would have a precious do-over. They had each other.

It would be a start.

An Hour Later—Dawn

In the aftermath of the attack, the sun came up as usual and bathed its early-morning light on Kendra's garden. She took no joy in that. It only reminded her that life went on, despite her world—*their world*—being torn apart.

Those who had survived gathered in the commons, watching her as she sat in silence. No one spoke. They waited. Every sniffle, every sob stabbed her heart. Whenever a noise came from the tunnels, every kid turned to see who would be there. She did, too, but as time went on, she felt hope drain from her soul.

She felt the hole where Raphael had been. The damage to the hive—and everything she had tried to build with him—made her soul ache and compounded her misery. She couldn't fathom a future without him. Seeing the survivors had been her only comfort.

Those who'd been drugged were slowly waking up. Lucas's sister Rayne took care of them. She asked for something to do. She needed to keep busy. Lucas and Gabriel had volunteered to search for the missing. They'd only come back once. Lucas had found an infinity bracelet in the rubble of the explosion and brought it back to give to Kendra.

Raphael.

His name was the last message she sent to all of them. Luke knelt in front of her and kissed her cheek. She clutched the bracelet in her hand and rocked.

"You should know, we may never find him. That explosion took out too much," Lucas whispered and ran a hand through her hair, but she couldn't look him in the eye. All she saw was Raphael.

"We're still searching for survivors. The twins are making their way here, a few others." Gabriel stood near her destroyed garden and spoke to everyone. "Where the explosion collapsed the tunnel, we're looking where we can, but the damage is too extensive and...we're not safe here. If some of the missing were taken during the attack, we may never know what happened to them."

Kendra felt the futility of what they were trying to do—the harsh reality of it—especially with a clock ticking. The Believers would be like vultures. They wouldn't leave them alone, not when they had an advantage. Any truce had come because of Gabriel. She didn't know how long that would last.

She looked down at the black leather bracelet she held tight in her hand. She understood that the safety of the living had to come first, but her gut twisted at the thought of leaving their dead and missing behind. That felt wrong. Another bitter injustice heaped on the growing pile of her failures. Now Raphael had become one more.

In that moment of realization, she almost lost it, but when a sudden hush settled over the commons, Kendra turned to see what everyone looked at and it broke her last will. She stood on shaky legs with her lips quivering.

With his eyes locked on Kendra, Raphael walked into the commons in stone-cold silence, his face etched with an agony she suddenly felt, too. Each step looked as if it pained him. A dark stain of blood glistened on his jeans. She couldn't tell if the blood was his, but something far worse gripped her by the throat. If she had any shred of hope left in her for their future, it died.

Raphael carried the dead body of Benny.

20

As the children in the commons cleared Raphael's way to Kendra, one by one they touched the dead boy's head. Rafe carried Benny in his arms as if he were only sleeping. He looked as if he'd collapse. When he stopped in front of her, Kendra cupped a trembling hand on Benny's cheek.

His skin was cold.

She wanted to take the blood away, to breathe life into his little lungs and to hear his heart beat softly again, but that would never happen. She thought of his short, tormented life, made worse by those who should have loved him—and now this.

When she saw Rafe still wore his bracelet, she tightened her grip on the one in her hand—the gift he'd given to Benny. Raphael saw what she held in her hand. He stared down at her with his jaw clenched tight. Rage and pain tortured his face.

She had no words to console him.

"We c-can't…l-leave him here." Raphael choked on every word. "This isn't our h-home anymore." He shook his head and stared down at Benny's face. "I don't know how to bury him."

Raphael collapsed to his knees, clutching at Benny. His tears came in sobs as Kendra held him, with little man's body between them. Rafe had been hurt, both inside and out. His connection to the hive must have been severed when he got injured. That was why she lost him and thought he'd been killed. When she'd first seen Raphael walking into the commons—alive—Kendra felt a rush of joy that he hadn't died. After she realized who Rafe carried in his arms, she knew he would have gladly taken the boy's place.

Death had claimed more than one small boy.

"I did this. I left him. I should have been more careful." Raphael let everything out. "They followed Benny back here. He was so scared."

"No, you tried to warn me about staying off their radar. I didn't listen."

Kendra heard footsteps behind her. Until she heard his voice, she didn't know who it was.

"What happened to this boy...to the home you built here, it's on them. Grieve for Benny, but don't blame yourselves for his loss." Gabriel Stewart didn't hide his feelings over what had happened.

"I have a place we can bury him, where we can honor his life." When he talked of Benny, Gabriel only spoke loud enough for them to hear. "My mother is buried there."

"Where is it?" Kendra asked.

"Not far. I'll take you. Anyone who wants to come is welcomed."

"Will we be safe there, at least for a night?" she asked. "We have wounded. Raphael is hurt, too. He's so pale. I think he's lost a lot of blood." She turned to Rafe, but he looked dazed. If he was wounded, he didn't care anymore. She had to care for both of them. "We need medical attention, and the children need to eat. They need..."

She stopped when Gabriel knelt beside her and Raphael. He put his hands on their shoulders.

"I know you don't know me, but I want to help. You don't

have to do this alone." He looked down at Benny and touched his head. "You need time to heal…your bodies and your souls. Please let me help."

With tears in his eyes, Raphael nodded and Kendra followed his lead, but she couldn't think straight. She heard the words come out of her mouth about Rafe and the wounded and food for the kids as if someone else spoke them. She sounded stronger than she felt.

Who was she fooling? She was a kid with nothing and now she had even less.

Burbank Command Center
Hours Later

O'Dell had spent the morning in a hospital E.R., explaining how he'd shot himself in the foot. It got reported to the cops. The church would not be happy. No matter how many times he'd replayed that moment of sheer panic in his head, he still felt like an ass. The snakes had vanished in the blink of an eye. *Gone!* He'd imagined the whole thing, but he had no idea how. Blinded by muzzle flash, he screamed at the burn of the gunshot and the pain that jolted through his body.

He bled like a stuck javelina.

He didn't wait for Boelens to report in. He took off before he bled to death. Now, hours later, he had messages on his encrypted cell phone. The operation that had started out as a piece of cake had turned into an unexplainable mess—an embarrassment that could cost him more than his job. Boelens was on his way in to Operations. He'd be there any minute. Until then, O'Dell avoided the phone his new boss had given him. The man had been calling every five minutes.

What the hell would he say?

When Boelens reported in, he was no help.

"What happened to you?" The man stared down at O'Dell's

bandaged foot elevated on a chair and the crutches that leaned on his desk.

"You don't remember?" he asked. When Boelens shook his head, he said, "Intense frontline action. I took a bullet for one of your guys, but I'll live."

Boelens narrowed his eyes.

O'Dell pushed him on what happened. He got nowhere. That was good news and bad news. Bad that he'd never know how things got screwed up. Good that he could blame everything on a guy who didn't remember, one of the privileges of being in charge.

After O'Dell grilled his man, Boelens didn't add anything worth knowing, except for one thing he insisted on. He had a message to deliver to the head guy. Boelens wouldn't back off about it, either. The only reason O'Dell decided to make the call was that he had every intention of throwing Boelens under the bus.

As Boelens sat in front of his desk, O'Dell pulled out the encrypted phone, his secret hotline to the big guy. His call got answered on the first ring.

"Where have you been? Why haven't you returned my phone calls?" Listening to the strange mechanical voice on the other end of the line gave O'Dell the willies.

"I got shot. Took one for the team, but I'm okay. Thanks for asking."

"I didn't."

O'Dell ignored him.

"My man Boelens says he has a message. Says it's for you… from those kids."

Silence. It took the man so long to reply that O'Dell thought he'd been disconnected.

"Get Boelens on the phone," the man said.

"Not that kind of message. He needs to hand it to you personally, he says."

O'Dell heard a heavy sigh on the line and cringed as he waited to hear what the man would say.

"I'll send a car, but you're coming, too."

The call went dead. The man didn't give him an option. He'd ordered him to come. O'Dell hoped he wouldn't be taking a one-way trip.

Two Hours Later

From the observation window, Alexander Reese watched as three of his men ushered O'Dell and Boelens into the stark room below. They wore black hoods, a preventive measure to keep their location secret. Alexander didn't need to see O'Dell's face to know which one he was. He limped in on crutches.

This time he hadn't bothered to drug them. He didn't have the time. Once he made the arrangements, he contacted Fiona. After his bodyguards left the two men alone, she was the only one with him behind the two-way mirror when he put on his headset and spoke into the mic.

"Pull off those hoods and tell me what happened."

Fiona stepped closer to the glass and kept her eyes on the men as they sat in two metal chairs. Both men fidgeted in their seats and couldn't keep their hands still as they stammered nothing of importance.

Fiona couldn't hide the faint smile on her face, something Alexander had expected. He wished she knew how to gloat without taking pleasure in the failure of his mission. When the two men had nothing new to say, Alexander stopped them.

"This does not please me, gentlemen." He clenched his jaw, trying not to look at Fiona. "What is this personal message you were to deliver, Mr. Boelens? You've kept me in suspense long enough."

"I got it right here." The man pulled a folded piece of paper from his pocket.

"Is there anything you can add to what I'll see?"

"I didn't look at it. Figured you wouldn't want me to. It's personal, you know?"

"Then leave it and go. I'll be in touch," he said. "Hoods on, gentlemen."

He waited until O'Dell and Boelens were taken out before he sent Fiona to retrieve the message. When she returned, he got a closer look. *Odd.* One side of the paper had a detailed map on it, a schematic of an architectural structure that appeared to be in downtown L.A. It didn't take him long to realize that what had been drawn on the back had been the real message. He recognized the work, but what startled him was the face staring back.

His face.

His shocked expression made Fiona curious. When she looked over his shoulder, she gasped.

"Who did…?" She didn't finish. She'd seen the artist's work before, too. "How could he know about…*you?* We've been so careful."

Fiona had been stunned, but as she got a closer look at the details in the sketch, she finally saw the worst of it. She held up the drawing to compare the background and took a closer look at him.

"How did he know the exact location you'd be…and what you'd be wearing?" she asked.

Alexander Reese gritted his teeth as he grabbed the drawing and stared at it again. He had no intention of answering her.

Bristol Mountain
Three Days Later

As Gabe expected, Uncle Reginald opened his home to the Indigos. His uncle had actually been touched that Gabe asked for his help. Even though many were offered their own rooms, the kids chose to sleep together. They were used to it. They shared beds and crashed on floors, anything to avoid being alone. Nights were especially hard. Gabe walked the halls and heard soft sobs in the middle of the night or heard the others comforting a kid that had a nightmare. They took care of their own.

Too bad they had to.

His uncle called in favors to get medical attention for the wounded and to see that Benny would get a proper burial. He made the arrangements with great care for privacy. If anyone understood the need for secrecy when it came to Indigo children, Uncle Reginald did. Protecting them came naturally to him. It was his nature.

Frederick did his part to make their unexpected guests feel at home. Beyond Gabe and his uncle, the only one who could actually see the dead butler, without him "popping" in, was Raphael. Frederick made it his personal mission to remind Rafe how special he was—*every day, in every way.* He took care of the boy and watched over him, even in his fitful, tormented sleep.

With looks that could kill when he was awake, Rafe refused to acknowledge the ghost butler, but Gabe had his money on Frederick.

After Dark

Rafe hadn't spoken to anyone since he'd carried Benny into the commons and said what he needed to Kendra. He did what they told him, but he really wasn't there. Blood loss made him weak, but losing Benny killed any feeling he had left. Even when Kendra changed his bandage on the bullet wound in his side—after one sorry bastard trumped his baseball bat with a bullet—he had nothing else to say. A thunderstorm had moved in and stayed. The storm's rumble and unrelenting rain magnified his grief and made him feel more alone than ever, even though Kendra was with him.

Sprawled on an unmade bed, wearing only jeans, he let her work on him. She thought she could hurt him, but that wasn't possible now. He felt dead. Kendra told him stuff about the others that he never really heard, until she said...

"We're burying Benny tomorrow." She gave him the time, but it never stuck.

He shifted his eyes toward her. He wanted to tell her how he felt, that he should have been the dead one, not Benny, but nothing came. The final act of burying Benny in the ground didn't feel real. When he had the ability to see the dead, why couldn't he feel Benny anymore? Why couldn't little man haunt *him,* even for a while? Maybe he didn't want to know the answer.

Eventually Kendra left him alone in a room big enough for all of them to sleep in. He never even realized she was gone. All he could think about was Benny. He didn't know how he would say goodbye to him tomorrow. People would expect him to say something. He had no idea what that would be. Words meant nothing now.

"Forgive the intrusion." A man's quiet voice came from nowhere. Almost a whisper.

When Rafe turned, he saw Frederick. He glared at the ghost but didn't say anything. Seeing the spirit only reminded him of how much he wanted Benny to haunt him...forever.

"It's okay. You don't have to say a word. I only came to let you know where Benny is. Before they seal the coffin, I thought you might..."

Rafe struggled to sit up. He had only one word for Frederick, a word that surprised even him.

"Yes."

Rayne felt restless, especially when the punishing storm had ramped up its assault on the estate. The sound of rain and thunder made her nervous, but that wasn't all that made her anxious. After she helped feed the kids and saw the youngest were in bed, she realized she hadn't seen Gabriel in hours. He hadn't eaten with them.

She searched the dark corridors of the estate and looked in his room but didn't find him until she saw light coming from the Serenity room. When she pushed the massive door open, the room glimmered in fierce beauty. The sound of thunderous crashes vibrated the amphitheater as blinding and violent bolts of lightning catapulted across the dome. The projection mirrored the raging storm outside to touch an audience of one.

Gabriel sat alone. He didn't move. He stared up at the ceiling that bathed him in vivid colors. When she sat next to him and slipped her hand into his, he shifted his beautiful eyes to her. In that moment, she forgot to breathe.

"Rain reminds me of my mother."

Through the rumble of the storm, his voice captivated her as if it was the only sound in the room.

"She loved it, in all its forms. The magnificence of a dark storm, a gentle spring rain. It never scared her. My mother respected its power to cleanse and renew." He squeezed her hand. "She shared the love of rain with me and taught me to dance in it."

He smiled without any real joy. Something darker had a grip on him.

"My mother died in her car. It had been raining." He heaved a sigh. "She'd run some errands and was coming to pick me up at a motel we were staying in. We were taking a break from the circus, visiting the Grand Canyon, actually. But it wasn't the bad weather that killed her. It was my father."

"How? What happened?" She clutched and kissed the back of his hand.

"He'd found out where we were and had sent men to take me. She knew what that would mean, that she'd never see me again. She couldn't let that happen." A tear ran down Gabriel's cheek. He didn't wipe it away. "She called me from her car. I barely had time to pack our stuff and hide. She'd been right. They came, but we had a plan to meet up later. That never happened. I had to hear about her death and see it on TV."

"That's awful. I'm so sorry." Rayne knew what it felt like to lose everything. "How was your father connected to the accident?"

"It wasn't an accident. State troopers said she'd been run off the road. Her vehicle had paint from another car on her rear bumper. They shoved her off a cliff and didn't stop. As far as I'm concerned, she was murdered, Rayne. The investigation is still open with no suspects. My father had a convenient alibi, but that doesn't mean he didn't hire it done."

Whatever rift had started with a father who didn't understand his son now carried the bitterness of a lifetime of hate and suspicion. Gabriel stared into the flashing images over his head and breathed deeply until he could speak again.

"So rain carries memories of my mother. The way she lived, the way she died. I came here to feel her again."

Benny's death had touched Gabriel the way it had her, reminding them both of what they had lost, and grief took shape in countless ways. But Gabriel looked as if he had more on his mind than reopening old wounds. When he touched her cheek and kissed her under the virtual storm, she knew he would tell her.

"Lucas and Kendra have asked for a meeting with me before Benny's funeral tomorrow. The others will be there, too."

"What do they want? Did they say?"

"They have questions. Hell, so do I. It's the answers I'm lacking."

He shrugged and stared up at the clearing sky of a world washed clean. The fake storm had subsided. Gabriel had brought on the storm in the Serenity room to bring him closer to his mother. He had come for her guidance, any way he could get it.

"You'll figure it out." Rayne smiled, for real. "But it's time to come clean, Gabriel. Whatever happens going forward, it doesn't have to fall on your shoulders alone. Give them a choice and let *them* decide. Whatever comes next, you'll do it together."

Rayne already knew what she would do. She'd crossed Gabriel's path because of Lucas. She'd stay and fight for the same reason. No one had the right to hunt these kids and treat them like animals.

Gabriel took a deep breath and grinned. He pulled her into his lap and held her in his arms, cradling her as if she were fragile. She breathed in the smell of his skin and stroked her fingers through his long hair.

"You're brilliant," he whispered.

His voice sent tingles across her skin, as it always did. When he raised her chin to kiss her, she felt and heard the distant rumble of a storm passing.

In truth, the storm was coming.

Frederick drifted through the shadowy corridors of the mansion and didn't look back as Rafe followed him. He didn't make his body solid, like some ghosts did. Frederick swirled like a faint mirage, nothing more than solemn vapor. He led

Rafe to a room downstairs on the main floor, near the front entrance. When the butler got to the closed door to a room that looked no bigger than a closet, he turned and swept his hand toward the knob.

"Take as long as you need, dear boy." Frederick didn't wait for his answer. He vanished in the blink of an eye.

Rafe knew what he'd find on the other side of the door. Before he reached for the doorknob, he shut his eyes and took a deep breath. He felt a chill through his T-shirt and jeans, a cold that hadn't only been from the storm outside. When he opened his eyes, he flung the door open. Nothing had prepared him for what he saw.

A small coffin the color of glistening copper had its lid open with Benny inside. His body lay in folds of white and he'd been dressed in a suit. *A real suit.* Dozens of candles had been lit and cast a pale glow on his little face. He almost looked alive, as if he were sleeping.

With just him and Benny in the room, Rafe let his tears fall. He couldn't stop.

"Hey, little man."

He bent down and kissed the boy on the cheek. Whatever doubts he had about what he would say to the only little brother he would ever have, he'd been wrong. It had always been easy to talk to Benny.

The Next Day—Afternoon

The day of Benny's funeral, the mansion became a quiet place. Each kid grieved for him in their own way. Gabe didn't feel a part of them, even though they didn't block him. He was an outsider who had explaining to do. Since the attack in the tunnels, Lucas and Kendra had time to think about what they'd seen him do.

They'd asked for a meeting before the funeral. He stood

before them in the great room, under the poster of his mother. He would need her strength. Lucas and Kendra asked about how he'd found them. Whatever he told them now, they would test him until they trusted him. That wouldn't be easy for a guy with secrets.

For the first time, he'd be accountable to someone else.

"We saw what you did," Lucas said. "None of us are as strong as you. How did you do all that?"

"I didn't. *We* did it." His answer was simple. Too simple.

"What are you talking about?" Kendra stood in front of him with her arms crossed. "What you did, I've never seen anything like that."

Gabe sighed. He wasn't sure he could explain if he didn't understand it himself, but he had to give it a shot.

"I borrowed from all of you. Your strengths became mine, only magnified. It was…amazing." He saw by the looks on their faces that he needed to say more. "Together we're stronger than we are alone. It's the best I can figure. I don't know if this ability is mine or we can all do it, but a wise man once told me that our abilities are like muscles. We need to exercise and train them."

He pointed to Kendra and said, "You have the amazing ability to track others like us. I can't be sure, but I think that's why my visions became more intense. The twins can tap into a person's worst fear or make them crave pizza. Totally awesome, guys." The twins grinned at him. "And like me, Raphael has an epic connection to the dead."

Gabe almost lost it when Frederick waved to Raphael. The kid only rolled his eyes.

"And you, Lucas. I felt your connection most of all. It felt like whatever I imagined, I could amp it up because of you."

The kids were paying attention now. They looked at one

another and their chatter filled his head until Kendra tested him again.

"You knew the church name. How? What's your connection?" she asked.

He wasn't used to answering to anyone else on stuff he considered personal. He'd have to get used to it. Like Rayne had said in the Serenity room last night, none of this had to fall on him alone, but not flying solo complicated things, too.

"They've been looking for me. That night in the tunnels was the first time I'd surfaced in a while. They'll be after me again." He looked at Rayne when he said, "I don't regret what I did. We need to take the fight to them. The church secretly hunts us and gets away with it because we can't report what they do. They bribe people in power. We won't know who to trust."

"He's right," Kendra said. "Reporting them to the cops will only make things worse for us. That would put us in a spotlight we don't need or want, but we can't let them hunt us without fighting back. We're outnumbered and we're losing too many of our own."

"But they have weapons and men willing to use them," Lucas argued.

"We have the weapons we need...in us. We can train here, but no one will be forced to. That will be up to each of you. You decide," Gabriel said, sounding more confident than he felt. Rayne had been right. Whatever they did going forward, they had to make that decision together.

"They have their army," he told them. "We'll have ours... and we can recruit more."

That set the room on fire with the chatter inside his head. The debate raged. There were countless voices with questions and fears. He felt an adrenaline rush being joined to the collective in such a profound way. He'd never experienced it before, but Rayne looked completely lost. To her, the room was dead silent. She looked at him as if he'd told a joke that fell flat.

He loved that she looked sympathetic. He smiled at her and shrugged.

"If the church is secret about what they're doing, how is it that you know so much about them?" Lucas asked.

Gabe had expected his link to the church to be questioned, but not what happened next.

"You're questioning *his* connection to the church? What about yours?" Raphael spoke up for the first time. "Your sister works for those bastards. Why haven't you told anyone about that, golden boy?"

All eyes fixed on Lucas.

"Is that true?" Kendra asked him.

Before Lucas said anything, Rayne defended her brother.

"Mia is our older sister. She works for the church, yes, but she had Lucas committed to a mental hospital and drugged. He escaped to get away from them. Any one of you would've done the same. There's no conspiracy here."

"All I know is that we were doing fine until they came after him," Rafe argued. "Now Benny's dead and we got no place to live."

"I don't mean to intrude." Uncle Reginald spoke up. "But you can live here. Whether you choose to train or not, you have a home."

Raphael stared at Gabe's uncle as if he'd spoken in a foreign language. Trust wasn't easy for him. Gabe knew how that felt. When Rafe took a deep breath, he let it go, but Gabe knew he wasn't done.

He felt the kid's rage and understood it.

"When Rayne told me about her sister, I freaked, too," Gabe admitted. "It's normal for us to have that reaction to any-one linked to that so-called church, but not everyone knows about how they hunt us. One man, Alexander Reese, is in charge of their North American operations. He's here in L.A. These men work for him. I'm sure of it."

"How is it that you have a name?" Kendra asked.

"It pays to know your enemy. For those willing to fight, you'll know him, too," he said. The room got quiet again. When the mind buzz died, a grandfather clock in the great room chimed the top of the hour. Everyone knew what that meant.

It was time to say goodbye to Benny.

"It's time. Please follow me," Uncle Reginald said, and he led the way.

Rayne didn't know what heaven would be like, but the beautiful images flashing on the dome of the Serenity room were as close as she could imagine. Uncle Reginald had dazzling lights and stunning photographs in a slow spin over a small coffin.

He put on a show for Benny and he was the first to speak.

"No foot is too small that it doesn't leave an indelible mark on this world. I did not have the pleasure of knowing Benny, but I wish that I had. I see how he is loved by each of you. Your love for him fills this room. I feel it. Benny will be missed."

Uncle Reginald spoke from his heart. His rich baritone voice made for a solemn start to Benny's funeral. Others stood and said what they wanted. Some had sweet, funny stories; others shared things that brought tears.

When it came time for Raphael Santana to speak, the room got still as he walked toward Benny's coffin. He put his hand on the lid and shut his eyes, saying goodbye in his own way. When he pulled a small leather bracelet from his pocket and laid it on the casket, Rayne knew every heart in the room reached out to him, but she wasn't sure how much he felt. Lucas had told her that he'd shut down to everyone. He'd severed his link to the hive and no one knew how long he'd punish himself.

Raphael was a beautiful boy with a fire in him that made her sad. He was the oldest, but there was a part of him that felt like a broken child.

"I didn't have a little brother," he said when he turned around. "I wouldn't have wished my father on any kid, but God hit one out of the park when he made Benny." A tear drained down his cheek. "I don't know why some people get to live and others don't. What happened to Benny wasn't right. I can't stand here and talk nice about him, 'cause I...I just want to hit something. I want someone to pay for what they did. Maybe someday I'll be able to think about Benny and remember only the good stuff, but not today."

When he left the room, the sound of his boots echoed in the chamber. The only person who went after him was Kendra.

She had to run to catch up to Raphael. Even weak and wounded, he moved fast to outrun the demons they shared. She could only imagine a fraction of the agony he felt. After Kendra lost sight of him, she found his jean jacket tossed on a hallway floor and she knew which way he went. She found him in a small courtyard that reminded her of her garden. The sounds of trickling water from a fountain brought back memories of the life and home they'd both lost—dreams and hopes gone in one night.

Raphael wore his pain in every muscle of his body. He'd blocked her from his mind and heart. Now he had his back to her, too.

Please...don't shut me out. I need you.

She willed him to hear her, but he never turned.

"You were good to him," she said. Kendra touched his arm,

but he didn't acknowledge her. "You gave him something he never had. Benny knew he was loved."

Kendra understood Raphael's misery more than he would ever know. It killed her that he wouldn't let her in. She couldn't feel him. She had no idea what he was thinking. This boy who wanted a family so much he'd built one, she understood that need—and he knew her, too. She didn't have to link to his mind to see that she had lost him.

She couldn't handle that, especially not now.

"Don't make me go through this without you."

He barely glanced over his shoulder.

"You've got Lucas. The others. You don't need me."

"You're wrong." She felt the sting of tears. "God, you are *so* wrong."

She had to look into his eyes to show him what was in her heart. She reached for his hand, and when he turned, Kendra wrapped her arms around him. At first, Raphael didn't react. He didn't hold her, but she didn't care. She held him tight until something happened.

When Raphael caressed her, he felt good against her, and she drew from the strength he always had for her, but when he lowered his lips to kiss her, she felt her body stiffen against him. Yet she didn't stop him. A part of her let go. A part of her wanted this to happen. She kissed him back and her body wanted more.

"Oh, God, I can't do this. I shouldn't." Breathless, she stopped and gazed into his eyes. "I'm sorry."

She ran before he could say anything. She flushed with the heat of embarrassment. Kendra didn't know what had happened.

Dusk

After the funeral and burial, Gabriel disappeared. Rayne went to his bedroom, searched the house and the patios, and even went to the domed Serenity room, thinking he might want the peace and quiet he'd found there, but Gabe was nowhere to be found. It wasn't until the sun's dying light bled through the windows of her bedroom that she went looking for him again.

This time she had help.

When she saw the evening sky filled with fireflies around the grounds of the mansion—and the children laughing and playing under their fairy magic—she found Gabriel not far away. He sat on a large boulder that overlooked a lush valley below the Bristol Mountains. He wasn't alone. Hellboy was with him. When she joined him, the ghost dog wagged his tail and vanished.

"I think Benny would have liked this," Gabriel said, but didn't smile.

Rayne nuzzled into his arms and breathed him in. With the last warmth of the sun losing to the night's chill, she welcomed the heat and the comfort she always felt in his arms. When he lifted her chin and kissed her lips, nothing could have been more perfect.

Gabriel had given her another sweet gift that she always wanted to remember.

"I want to thank you for finding Lucas, but I don't know how to do that. Nothing feels...right." She pulled from his arms to look him in the eye. "How do you thank a guy for risking everything...for a stranger?"

"I'm the one who owes *you*." He curled a lip into a shy smile. "Uncle Reginald said you're making arrangements for another guest to stay here. Should I be jealous of this guy? What kind of name is Floyd anyway? Very retro."

"He's very...quiet. I think you two will have a lot in common."

Their talk came easily. They touched and kissed, and for

the first time, Rayne felt that Gabriel had no more secrets. She didn't feel the walls he always had between them. She felt like a girl talking with a cute boy, but that wasn't all that Gabriel was.

"That vision you had, where you saw those men attack the kids in the tunnel."

"Yeah."

"We got there in time, sort of. I mean, it took us a couple of hours to drive to L.A., but we got there in time for you to see it happening. You know what that means, right?"

He shook his head.

"It means that you can see the future. You had the dream and it happened."

"Yeah, but I couldn't save Benny. I couldn't stop any of it."

Hearing him say that made her ache inside.

"Maybe next time you will." The way she said it, even *she* didn't believe it.

What Gabriel had done was nothing short of amazing. With all his gifts, she wanted him to feel good about what she'd seen him do, but if he had visions of the future—of terrible things he couldn't stop—that would be torture.

He didn't deserve that, but he had no choice—just as he had no option in the future that lay ahead of him.

"Did you mean what you said…about taking the fight to them?" Rayne asked as she watched the smaller kids play with the fairy light Gabriel had conjured for them. "I can see why, but most of them are…just kids."

"No, they *were* kids. The Believers have their army. We need ours." Painted in the soft pastel of a fading evening's sunset, Gabriel had a haunted look on his face. "Uncle Reginald is worried. So am I, but we can train them. We have to."

He'd come a long way from a boy with secrets who only

wanted to be alone. Whatever decision he'd made about his future, she'd seen the same determined look in Lucas's eyes.

"We have a fight ahead of us," he said. "We don't have a choice. Kendra is right. Getting the police involved will only make things worse and the church won't leave us alone."

"But this could be only a small group of crazies. You said Alexander Reese is here in L.A. and is responsible for all their operations in North America. Are you sure he knows what's going on here? Maybe…"

Gabriel didn't let her finish. He shook his head and said, "He knows, Rayne. He's behind it." He sighed. "Alexander Reese will learn from what we did. He underestimated us this time, but he won't make that mistake again. We have to be ready."

"You never answered the question Lucas had. If the church is so secret about hunting these kids, how is it that you know so much about the guy in charge?"

He looked as if she'd punched him. When he fixed his mesmerizing eyes on her, Gabriel touched her cheek and said, "Because Alexander Reese is my father."

★ ★ ★ ★ ★

Excerpt from Book 2 of

········{THE HUNTED}········

series

CRYSTAL
STORM

Los Angeles, California
12:45 a.m.

Gabriel felt his way through the darkness as easily as if it were
daylight. Inside the formidable walls that surrounded the se-
cluded estate, he kept watch of the men who patrolled the
grounds. Dressed in black uniforms and armed, they guarded
the posh residence in pairs.

He sensed every turn they made and anticipated their moves
even before they made them. In evasive and fluid maneuvers
that looked more like perfectly timed choreography, he ducked
behind shrubs and crept through the deep shadows cast by the
trees, almost daring the men to catch him.

The moon shed little light. That didn't matter to a gutsy
eighteen-year-old boy with a reckless spirit and an unrelenting
taste for revenge. Like a child playing a dangerous game, he
navigated the dark using his powerful gifts of second sight. The
darkness would be a handicap only for the men who guarded
the estate—protecting the man Gabriel had come to face.

As he got close to the house, Gabriel melded into the shadows and vanished. His physical body dissolved into dust that drifted and swirled in the evening breeze, but when a floorboard creaked on the grand staircase that led to the master suite, the boy crept in silence toward the bedroom where his father slept.

He opened the master suite door without a sound and listened before he moved again. Everything had come to this moment. The years of running, of hating, of grieving had gathered force to drive him here. He stood over the bed of his sleeping father and glared at the man who had ruined his life and destroyed his mother.

Hatred stirred in the center of Gabriel's brain, and the power radiated through his body and heated his belly. It forced its way out into shooting spears of light that spiraled around him. The burst of energy concentrated its power and thrashed around him like a mounting storm—a Crystal storm.

Through the fierce light, he saw a man awake in terror and scream. When Gabriel fixed his glowing eyes on his father, he knew the man saw him for the very first time—and his last.

Alexander Reese finally understood what his son had truly become.

"No!" he yelled and leaped off his pillow.

Alexander Reese gasped for air like a drowning man and stared into the darkness of his bedroom. With his body drenched in sweat, he searched the room, looking for anything that moved. At first his eyes played tricks on him. Shadows shifted and even noises that should have been familiar made him strain to listen harder. He had to blink to make sure he was awake.

"Gabriel," he whispered. A tear trickled down his cheek.

That nightmare felt as real as if it had happened. A part of him wanted his runaway son to be there for purely selfish reasons. Except for a blurry surveillance photo, he hadn't seen the boy since his mother had taken him with her in the middle of the night too many years ago. Beyond wanting to see the young man he'd become, Reese never wanted to lay eyes on the boy again—for Gabriel's sake.

Even though he still felt the haunting presence of his son in his memory, he sensed that he was alone. Only his shame lingered, over what had happened to Gabriel and his mother, Kathryn. A twist in his gut always came when he thought of his sworn responsibility to the church. He'd made a choice that had destroyed his family. He had no one else to blame, even though he believed he'd done the right thing.

Yet something more disturbed him.

Given the security at his estate, Reese knew breaching the defense measures of his home and grounds would be hard for anyone to crack. He found it odd that in his hellish nightmare he believed that Gabriel had done it.

"Damn."

With a shudder, he sank back onto his dank sheets and stared at the ceiling with the sound of his breathing and the thud of his heart filling his head. Ever since he'd found out that Gabriel had come back to L.A., nightmares were his constant companion.

In truth, he feared his son. Not merely for what he had become, but Reese feared what he'd be forced to do in the name of duty. After he took a deep breath, he almost dismissed the lasting remnants of his bad dream, but something made him sit up and search the darkness again.

"What the hell?"

His nightmare could have merely been triggered by the chronic guilt he felt over Gabriel and Kathryn—except for one hard-to-ignore, undeniable fact. Something very real had been left behind.

The smell of Kathryn's perfume.

Bristol Mountains—East of L.A.
1:30 a.m.

Raphael Santana paced the grassy hillside behind the Stewart Estate dressed only in jeans and boots, too restless to kneel by the grave he visited every night. A cool mountain breeze swept through his dark hair. It should have chilled the bare skin of his chest, but the fire in his belly kept him stoked with heat.

When his boot struck a rock, he picked it up and tossed it in his hands as he stared into the gloom. His heart searched this world and beyond for the spirit of a small boy who had left an ache in his soul, a gaping wound no one else could ever fill. With the moon hoarding its light—nothing but a razor slash across a pitch-black sky—the dark became a part of him. After living in the tunnels beneath the streets of downtown L.A., Rafe craved the hush of shadows.

For him there was darkness even in daylight now.

"Haunt me, Benny. Torture me. I deserve it."

He flung the rock into the dark and heard it hit trees. The move made his side hurt, where he'd been shot in the same fight where Benny had been killed.

"You should be the one standing here, not me."

Rafe collapsed to his knees at the grave with his throat wedged tight. He winced when he hit the ground and clutched his side. The others had left trinkets for Benny—a worn teddy bear, flowers and a toy that spun in the wind. Every time he came to the grave, he had to face what had happened to Benny. He wanted to remember the kid smiling and funny, but guilt wouldn't let that happen.

"I miss you, little man."

He ran his fingers over the name etched on the headstone—*Benny Santana*. He had given Benny his own last name and had it carved into stone forever. The kid didn't deserve to be buried with the family name he got stuck with, so Rafe claimed Benny as the little brother he wished he had.

"I don't know what to do." Tears cooled his cheeks. "I don't know who I am anymore."

Rafe glared over his shoulder and stared up at the mansion that had become his new home by default after the Believers had destroyed the tunnels. Kendra Walker and the others, like him, had come to live here, too, but that didn't make things better for him. The place looked like a fancy castle built on the peak of a mountain. He'd grown up on the streets of L.A., carrying everything he owned on his back.

"I don't fit," he whispered. "Not here. Not anywhere."

Rafe got to his feet and took off his black leather "forever" bracelet—the one that used to mean something—and left it on Benny's headstone. He stared down at the grave marker and wiped his eyes with the back of his hand. They'd buried Benny in the ground, but Rafe didn't feel him here. He could think of only one place that the kid's spirit might linger—the place where he died, the only real home that either of them had known.

If he had a shot at "seeing" Benny again, he had to risk going back to L.A.—and steal Rayne's Harley to do it.

Downtown L.A.
4:30 a.m.

In the early-morning hours, Rafe sped down the interstates on Rayne's Harley with his body pummeled by the wind and his blood fueled with a rush of adrenaline. He'd hot-wired her ride, stolen cash from Kendra, ripped off a bottle of liquor from Gabriel's uncle, and when he didn't take a helmet, he wondered if he didn't have a death wish. All he had on were the clothes on his back—jeans, boots, a T-shirt and a worn jacket.

Everything he had done felt like a one-way trip. He hadn't

given any thought to what he'd do next. He kicked the bike into high gear with the wind lashing his hair. *Speed*. He couldn't get enough.

When he got to one of the tunnel entrances—the location where the Believers had staged their attack—he downshifted and hit the throttle to rev the Harley. If the bastards had staked out the place out to see if anyone would come back, he had made an unmistakable announcement of his return.

Rafe killed the engine and hid the bike in the bushes, near a thick stand of trees. He headed into the darkness of the tunnels without an ounce of fear as he cracked the seal on the bottle of liquor and downed a long pull. It burned his throat, only the start of the abuse he deserved. He felt the alcohol burn into his body and kindle a fire in his chest. His old man only drank the cheap stuff. He had no idea what he'd ripped off from the estate. Probably some fancy shit. As long as it got the job done, the kind didn't matter.

Drunk or sober, he knew the danger of returning to the very place where the Believers had hunted his kind and destroyed everything. He didn't care. If they came after him again and wanted a fight, he'd give them one, but as he wandered into the tunnels alone, he felt numb. He didn't recognize the place. The Believers had come in afterward and burned everything. Kendra's garden—the beautiful oasis she had created that had fed and healed them—had been uprooted, doused with gasoline and torched.

Their home had been wiped out as if they'd never existed.

He sucked down more liquor and wiped his mouth with his jacket sleeve as he stumbled over the old railroad track that led to the cyclops, the old locomotive that had been abandoned in the tunnels. The metal beast loomed in the darkness as he rounded a corner, half-buried in old brick rubble caused by the explosion that had killed Benny. Its bared teeth of steel hovered over the rail and its blinded eye—a broken headlight—still breathed a fierce life into the old engine that was covered in dust and debris.

Benny had loved the steel beast. Rafe stood in front of the dead train, and looked up at its busted eye as he drank—remembering one of the last times he saw the boy.

"Yo, Benny. It's me. I got something for ya."

"For me?" A little head had popped out from the engine compartment. *"What is it?"*

"I got you something to bring you luck. Your own piece of magic."

Not nearly drunk enough to forget, Rafe shut his eyes tight and willed the kid to come to him. Little man had played on every inch of the old rusted train. It made Rafe sad to think that Benny's fingerprints were still on every gauge and lever, the only mark of him left behind.

"No one's ever gotten me anything before," the kid had said in a shaky voice. With little fingers, he'd stroked the leather brace-let with Kendra's infinity charm on it.

Rafe pictured Benny sitting on the train's step with that crooked grin on his face and his eyes welling with tears. The kid had broken his heart that day, but he didn't know how much worse he could feel until he held Benny's dead body in his arms days later. Rafe stared at the spot he'd tied the brace-let to the kid's wrist and his eyes stung with tears.

"Screw infinity!" he yelled to no one. "What happened to forever, Kendra?"

He didn't feel Benny, not like he sensed the dead. *Who am I kidding?* He wasn't worth sticking around for. When he took another gulp, he felt dizzy and sick. Nothing killed the hurt. He grabbed the bottle and smashed it against the train. A shard of glass cut his cheek but he didn't care.

He'd come to the tunnels—a place where he could be closer to Benny—but that place didn't exist anymore. Rafe stumbled back the way he'd come, not knowing where he would go. He only knew it wasn't here.

When he hit the night air, he wanted to puke. Bile churned in his stomach, mixed with the burn of alcohol. He wouldn't outrun his booze slug to the brain. Heading for the Harley, he half decided to sleep it off, but when an arm grabbed his neck from behind, he couldn't breathe. His side wound felt as if it were on fire, like it had ripped open again. He kicked and fought to break free, but every move felt like a crushing weight against his chest. Rafe couldn't see faces in the dark. Men grappled with his arms and legs until he couldn't move. He sucked air into his burning lungs in fitful gasps. When he saw stars, he felt his body give out.

"Boss man said you'd be the weak link, kid."

Rafe felt the sharp sting of a needle stab his neck. It spread a burn under his skin, and his arms went limp.

"Guess he got *that* right."

The gruff voice was the last thing Rafe heard before he drifted into a deeper darkness than he'd ever seen. Only one thing gave him comfort.

He felt Benny with him.

ACKNOWLEDGMENTS

Real life and headlines often inspire my books and this time is no exception. Conspiracy theorists have linked the CIA, the UN and the Pentagon to the phenomenon known as "Indigo or Crystal Children," a concept heavily queried on the internet with thousands of websites and resources to research the topic. Query *Crystal child* online and you will get millions upon millions of hits. Indigo kids have been featured on mainstream TV and in dozens of newspapers and movies.

For the purposes of fiction, I took liberties in my portrayal of this phenomenon, but Indigo kids are generally described as highly intelligent, gifted teen psychics with a bright "indigo" aura and a mission to save the world. They have high IQs, have been known to see angels and commune with the dead. Because they are frequently misunderstood, they are diagnosed by therapists and doctors as having attention deficit or behavioral disorders and are often medicated.

Are Indigo children real or are they manipulated by adults to believe their sensitivities are special? Are they dysfunctional misfits or saviors who must be respected as the next evolution of mankind? You decide, but I find the notion of an evolution for mankind very intriguing.

The best part of writing a book comes from those who help or add to the inspiration. They can make things gel for an author. A fellow YA author inspired my villain, O'Dell. To thank him, I gave him what he'd always wanted—a bunker. I gave O'Dell a nasty sidekick, Boelens. Since this is fiction, I made Boelens quite dastardly, when in reality he is one of my favorite people on the planet.

In the first chapter, I mention a pop-punk band, Archimedes Watch Out, a group from Lubbock, Texas. Friend them on Twitter or find them on MySpace. They are seriously awesome and quite real, unless they are onstage, when they turn into Rock Gods. Whenever AWO comes to my city, they have a place to stay and play, even at two in the morning. *Love you guys!*

Thanks always to my family—my mom and dad, sisters and brothers, and dear friends. To my best friend and love of my life, my husband, John, I couldn't do this without you. For Kathryn, this time I gave you a tiara. When mentioning thanks to my family, I include my amazing agent with a big heart, Meredith Bernstein. I also include my talented editor, Mary-Theresa Hussey at Harlequin. Matrice, you have a gift for collaborating that I dearly love. Thanks for your magic touch. And my gratitude to Natashya Wilson, her amazing team at Harlequin Teen and the best PR person ever, Lisa Wray. You guys *ROCK!*

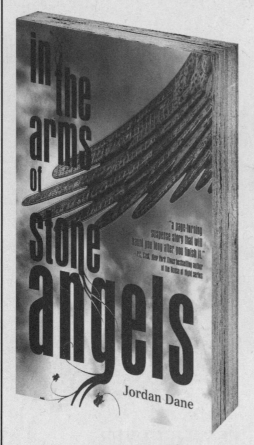

HTITAOSATR

The Clann

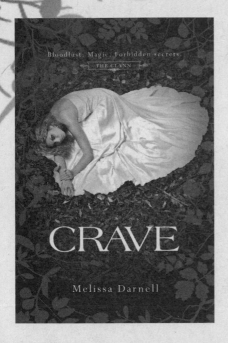

The powerful magic users of the Clann have always feared and mistrusted vampires. But when Clann golden boy Tristan Coleman falls for Savannah Colbert—the banished half Clann, half vampire girl who is just coming into her powers—a fuse is lit that may explode into war. Forbidden love, dangerous secrets and bloodlust combine in a deadly hurricane that some will not survive.

AVAILABLE WHEREVER BOOKS ARE SOLD!

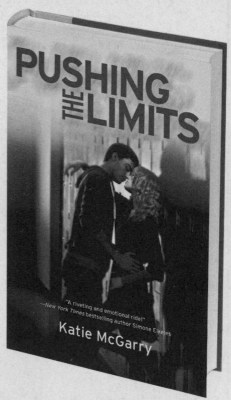

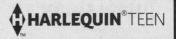